"You just don't get it, do you?"

Leanna rose, sidestepped around Jackson and crossed the room before turning back.

"Get what?" he pleaded. "You wanted your ex-husband gone. Now he is."

Leanna knew at that moment that he'd never understand, but she did owe him an explanation.

"I want control of my destiny, Jackson, not to have it arranged for me. My former husband did that. He made decisions, ran up debts and kept me in the dark. I won't be a victim again."

"Lee, I wish the world were full of only nice people who never did anything mean-spirited, who never hurt anyone else. But it isn't, so I will do whatever I can, whatever I must, to protect the people I love."

There was the word again. Yet he was twisting this around, making her the ungrateful recipient of his largesse.

"You've been very generous to me and my daughter, and for that I'll always be grateful."

"What are you saying?" Panic raised his voice.

"That there's no future for us, Jackson."

"Lee…"

"Please go."

D1042856

Dear Reader,

I reckon we all have our own colorful images of "the South." For some it may be Tara, from *Gone with the Wind*, and sun-drenched fields of cotton. For others it might be sultry afternoons, Dixieland jazz and streetcars named Desire. Or perhaps it's the strong-willed descendants of Scarlett O'Hara, those ever-so-genteel steel magnolias. And let's not forget Rhett Butler.

All those images are valid but each is incomplete.

I had the pleasure of spending time in Louisiana recently. It's a state that is truly dominated by the Mississippi River, a state rich in history and heritage, of diverse cultures and warm hospitality. Naturally, it started the "what-if" game.

Strong wills aren't confined to Southerners, of course. Yankees, or as they say south of the Mason-Dixon Line, damnyankees—one word—can be pretty tough, too. So what happens when a single-minded woman from up North meets an equally determined gentleman from an old Southern family? Well, I guess you get the picture.

This is the third and last book in the RAISING CANE trilogy, set on a sugar plantation just outside Baton Rouge, Louisiana. I hope I've captured some of your images of this beautiful part of the country and the indomitable people who live there.

I enjoy hearing from readers. You can write me at P.O. Box 61511, San Angelo, Texas 76904, or you can visit my Web site: www.kncasper.com.

Sincerely,

K.N. *Casper*

Jackson's Girls
K.N. Casper

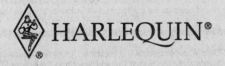

HARLEQUIN®

TORONTO • NEW YORK • LONDON
AMSTERDAM • PARIS • SYDNEY • HAMBURG
STOCKHOLM • ATHENS • TOKYO • MILAN • MADRID
PRAGUE • WARSAW • BUDAPEST • AUCKLAND

ISBN 0-373-71134-4

JACKSON'S GIRLS

Visit us at www.eHarlequin.com

Printed in U.S.A.

In researching for this trilogy we discovered that everything we've ever heard about Southern hospitality is completely true. Our heartfelt thanks go to Kenneth and Mary Jane Kahao, longtime sugar growers in the Baton Rouge area, for squiring us around. Because of them we were able to tour cane fields during cutting season and get an in-depth look at a working sugar mill.

Nor would our books be rich with the history of the sugar industry if not for the generosity of Caroline Kennedy, director, and Jim Barnett, curatorial assistant, of the West Baton Rouge Museum (Caroline was quick to inform us she wasn't *that* Caroline Kennedy).

Our apologies for any errors or bits of poetic license we may have taken in order to weave the fictional fabric of our linked stories. They are totally the three authors' doing.

I must also thank my partners in this exciting endeavor, Roz Fox and Eve Gaddy. We exchanged hundreds of e-mails and spent hours on the phone discussing and coordinating details. Denny Fox and Mary Casper were invaluable in reading our manuscripts and helping us keep the story threads from unraveling.

Last but far from least, we owe special tribute to our editors, Paula Eykelhof, Laura Shin and Beverley Sotolov, for the confidence they placed in us when they asked us to take on this project. Without their inspiration and patience, it would never have happened. Ladies, you do us proud.

This book is also dedicated to the memory of Rosalie Shambra Whiteman, the heart of RWA Outreach.

CAST OF CHARACTERS

Gilbert Alain: Owner of apartment complex where Leanna Cargill lived

Remy Boucherand: Police detective investigating suspicious events at Bellefontaine

Andy Breton: Gas company inspector

Harold Broderick: Convicted saboteur who tried to destroy Bellefontaine

Leanna Cargill: Insurance investigator for the Sugar Coalition

Richard Cargill: Leanna's ex-husband, father of Elise

Tanya Carson: Megan's nanny

Delphine: Newly hired nanny for Megan and Elise

Nick Devlin: Riverboat casino owner and builder; married to Casey

Murray Dewalt: Roland's son and longtime friend of Casey and Jackson

Roland Dewalt: Long-standing neighbor of the Fontaines

Elise: Five-year-old daughter of Leanna Cargill

Cassandra (Casey) Fontaine: Bellefontaine plantation manager and daughter of Duke

Duke and Angelique Fontaine: Owners of Bellefontaine, recently deceased

Esme Fontaine: Duke's opinionated sister

Jackson Fontaine: Bellefontaine business manager and son of Duke and Angelique

Megan Fontaine: Jackson's four-year-old daughter

Noelani Hana: Illegitimate daughter of Duke Fontaine and Anela Hana; married to Adam Ross

Janis: Jackson's former girlfriend, mother of his daughter

Paige Paturin: Jackson's former fiancée

Mrs. Peltière: Elise's baby-sitter

Shelburne Prescott: Fontaine family lawyer

Betty Rabaud: Fontaine family cook

Chuck Riley: Copilot who flew with Duke Fontaine

Denise Rochelle: Current Fontaine employee, romantically interested in Adam Ross

Adam Ross: Nick's friend and historic home renovator

Judge Harlan Sarratt: Local judge, friend of Fontaine family

Ripley Spruance: President of the Sugar Coalition

CHAPTER ONE

THE BLACK RIBBON OF HIGHWAY twisted and rolled. The ground grumbled. Instinctively, Jackson Fontaine tightened his grip on the leather-wrapped steering wheel, slammed on the brakes and skidded the Jaguar to a dusty stop at the side of the road.

"What the—" An earthquake? In Louisiana?

Only then, through the windshield, did he see the orange ball of fire mushrooming into the sky on a gray and white column.

His breathing stopped. There was only one thing beyond the expanse of cane fields ahead of him. The sugar refinery... His sugar refinery.

Heart-hammering adrenaline kicked in a second later. He reached for the cell phone on the seat beside him and stabbed in 911.

"There's been an explosion at the old Dewalt...at the Fontaine refinery."

"I heard it," the female voice at the other end stated calmly. "Where are you? Can you tell me the extent of the damage and if there are any injuries?"

Jackson slipped the transmission into gear and cut back onto the hardtop. "Don't know. I'm on Refinery Lane about two miles west, headed in that direction." He rammed the pedal to the floor. The wheels dug in and the car shot forward, its engine screaming.

A mile down the road, he heard fire engines wailing somewhere off in the distance. Lord, he hoped no one had been injured or killed. He checked the digital clock on the polished-wood dashboard. 8:40 a.m. No longer in operation, the place should be deserted at this hour—unless Murray Dewalt decided to show up. He hadn't said anything about coming by today, but that didn't mean he wouldn't. Jackson's jaw tightened. If his friend had been killed or injured, he'd never forgive himself.

He tapped the brakes, executed a controlled skid onto the narrow, gravel access road to the refinery, rocketed as far as the fence guarding the front of the compound and swerved to a tail-tilting halt on the grassy shoulder. No vehicles in sight, and the gate was still locked. That didn't mean a thing. The sides and rear of the complex were open to several un-improved byroads. This barrier was nothing more than a cosmetic facade, designed to discourage the curious.

Like the woman yesterday.

She'd been skulking around the warehouse behind the main building. When he'd called out to find out what she wanted, she'd bolted. He'd considered giving chase, but his car was parked at the opposite end of the compound. By the time he reached it, she'd be long gone. Did she have something to do with this explosion?

After fishing a key from his pants pocket, he opened the hefty padlock and spread the doors of the gate wide. Fire engines would approach from this direction.

The cloying stench of burning sugar, charring wood and hot metal put an acrid taste in his mouth, but his watering eyes were already assessing the situation as he ran toward the smoke-enshrouded plant. The refinery proper seemed untouched. A quick scan of the small high windows suggested there was no fire inside. He hoped it was true. Hoped, too, the place was as deserted as it appeared.

He dashed around the side of the massive structure to the source of the smoke. The galvanized tin roof of the attached single-story warehouse had been blown clean away. Twisted pieces of jagged metal hung in trees on the edge of the compound. Light-brown, raw sugar covered everything: trees, bushes, the refinery itself and the ground, while smoke billowed from the gaping shell of the structure. Amazingly, the warehouse walls appeared perfectly intact. The sliding doors weren't even buckled. Through the single window of the now-topless building, Jackson saw orange flames shooting sideways from the main building into the storehouse. A gas line. Had it ruptured in the explosion? Or was it the cause?

The nerve-shattering blast of an air horn announced the arrival of the first fire engine. A crew member jumped down and ran toward him. The rest of the team set about unrolling hoses with swift efficiency.

"You all right?"

"Fine," Jackson shouted over the noise of the roaring fire, grumbling engines and blaring radios. "I just got here."

"Anyone inside?"

"Not that I know of. Gate was still locked when I drove up. Haven't seen any vehicles around." What if someone came here on foot? He didn't voice the question, but it worried him.

A tanker truck pulled up.

"I have the key to the main building, if that'll help." He handed it over. "Maybe you can get to the gas cutoff from there."

"Thanks." The man grabbed it. "Stay here." Which Jackson interpreted as "Stay the hell out of the way." He had no intention of interfering. Some jobs were best left to professionals. But standing still was torture.

Dear God, he'd almost brought Megan along this morning. His daughter had been living with him now for almost six months, but the four-year old still hadn't completely adjusted to her new surroundings. She'd stopped asking about her mommy, but he knew she still missed Janis. He would do anything for his little girl, but bringing back her mother was beyond his power.

"Children are resilient," Aunt Esme told him. "She'll come around."

She was right, of course, but patience didn't come easily to him, not when it had to do with Megan's welfare or happiness.

Last evening when he was reading her a bedtime story, she'd asked where he went every day. Janis had always been home and until recently, so had he.

"I go to work, sweetheart. Don't worry—it's not far away," he'd assured her.

"But you work in the room downstairs." He used to keep his office door closed when he was there; he left it open now so Megs could pop in whenever she wanted.

"I have two places to work in," he'd explained, "just like you play here and at preschool."

"Oh." That seemed to make sense. "You came

to see my preschool. Can I see the other place where you work?''

Her sweet innocence brought a lump to his throat. "You bet you can."

He'd given her a big kiss and pledged to take her to the refinery real soon, but she had preschool till noon, and he didn't want to disrupt her schedule. Having a routine was important to her sense of security.

Suppose he'd left the house twenty minutes earlier with her... They would have been here, maybe inside, when the place exploded. Megan could have been killed or injured.

An icicle of dread slithered down his spine. In his twenty-eight years, he'd done things he wasn't particularly proud of, made his share of foolish mistakes, but Megan wasn't one of them. Megs was the brightest thing in his life. The thought of losing her terrified him.

Amid the orderly chaos of firefighters unloading equipment, the crackling pops of burning timbers and the noxious smell of molten sugar, the team captain made a call on his phone.

Scant minutes later, the roar of the fire and the blowtorch jet of blue-and-yellow flame abruptly ceased. The gas had been cut off. The relative silence that ensued was stunning and disorienting, the sense of relief exhilarating.

The inside of the warehouse, however, was still burning. Jackson watched in fascination as firefighters attached hoses to the tank truck and a fire hydrant twenty yards away. Within seconds, huge streams of water arched into the air, dumping tons of water onto the blaze. Jackson's heart sank. The sugar the fire hadn't destroyed would be lost now in the deluge.

Within an hour the conflagration was virtually extinguished, though wisps of smoke still drifted up from the ashes. A few firefighters in bulky yellow protective coats and thick boots continued to rummage through the debris, searching for sleeping hot spots, while others doused the charred wooden framework and saturated already blackened grass and weeds.

The chief removed the visored helmet from his balding head as still others in his crew began packing their gear neatly into its assigned places.

"Looks like you had a gas leak."

The implication was that it was an accident, but Jackson didn't believe it.

"The gas was turned on only a few days ago," he said.

He'd been testing the turbines that powered the complex and the centrifuges that spun the last impurities out of the raw sugar. With Murray Dewalt's help, he'd hoped to come up with a game plan to make the operation profitable. There weren't many options. Jackson's father, Duke, had been a savvy businessman, and this relic was his baby, but occasionally he overreached. From all indications this was definitely one of those times.

"Well, you're lucky," the fireman assured him. "The damage appears to have been confined to the utility room and warehouse. If the explosion had gone in the opposite direction, into the refinery itself, you would have lost a lot more than the sweet stuff. This whole place would probably be nothing more than a memory."

Jackson plunged his hands into his pockets. The utility area was where he'd had his office. Fortunately, he'd kept very few records there. The important ones were at home.

"The gas company inspected everything before they turned the gas on," he pointed out.

The chief nodded. "I'll check to see who performed the safety inspection. Whoever it was should have used sniffers at every juncture."

"Andy Breton," Jackson told him. "I walked around with her myself. She was meticulous." He surveyed the roofless shell of the warehouse. As far as he could see, nothing was salvageable. "Is it okay to go into the refinery?"

"Stay out." It was a command. "An inspector will be here to investigate first thing tomorrow morning, after everything has had a chance to cool off. There doesn't appear to be any major structural damage, but no sense taking chances. Besides, it's pretty messy underfoot."

Jackson nodded, thanked him and shook his hand.

Roland Dewalt moved up beside Jackson as the fire captain was leaving with the last of his team. Murray's father had driven up a few minutes earlier, using one of the back roads.

"Where's Murray?" Jackson asked.

"Left for New Orleans this morning around seven," he said absently as he surveyed the destruction.

In his younger days Roland had been a dashing and handsome man, but he hadn't aged well. At sixty-five, his massive shoulders were rounded, his belly gone to pot and his once-dark hair little more than a few threads stretched across a shiny pate.

"Had some sort of computer software to deliver to someone," he continued. "I never have understood that stuff. I saw the smoke cloud from my house. Figured it had to be this place. What the hell happened?"

"Gas leak, apparently."

Roland shook his head. "Nobody hurt, I assume. I didn't see any ambulances."

"Thank God."

They stood in silence for a minute, studying the devastation.

"Doesn't look like the operations area was hurt any," Roland noted.

"The fire wall restricted it to the warehouse."

"Hmm. Yes, I remember Murray installed it a month or so before I finally shut the place down. Building it seemed like such a waste at the time," Roland commented. "Now I'm glad he did."

"That makes two of us."

Roland didn't mention he'd been forced to cease operations because the refinery was hopelessly out-of-date and losing money, or that two years earlier Murray had recommended closing it. The old man had refused to listen. Father and son had grown progressively apart in the past few years as Roland became increasingly more stubborn and secretive.

"Not to worry," he said casually. "The coalition will reimburse you for the sugar." The Sugar Coalition brokered virtually all the sugar production in the state, from planting to mass marketing. "And your regular insurance will cover the property damage."

Another insurance claim. The family had already had two big ones this year—for the fire that almost destroyed Bellefontaine, the family's antebellum home, and the cane harvester that had been stolen a month later. Those settlements alone had cost the insurance company over half a million dollars. Pretty soon, Fontaine holdings would be too hot to handle. He twisted his mouth at the unintended pun.

"If you want to kick around ideas," Roland said with his arms folded over his ponderous belly, "I'll be glad to contribute my two cents. I ran this place for twenty-five years, so I know more about it than anyone."

"Thanks. I appreciate that." Jackson had no intention of taking him up on the offer.

"Frankly, your best option may be to simply tear the whole damn thing down and start from scratch."

Jackson wondered if total destruction had been the intent of whoever engineered this latest disaster, or if the raw sugar alone had been the target. Whatever the plan, the big question was who was behind it and why?

The senior Dewalt climbed into his fifteen-year-old black Mercedes-Benz and gave a friendly wave as he drove away.

Jackson would have liked to poke around inside the refinery, to see what damage might have been done, but decided to obey the chief's order and stay out. He didn't want to disturb anything before the authorities had a chance to investigate. Besides, he had other things to do, like visit his lawyer. As far as he could determine, the only ones making a profit from all the misfortunes that had befallen the Fontaine family in the past six months was the legal firm of Prescott, Walters and Simms.

He walked out the gate and was turning to lock it

when he spotted a dull-gray Toyota sedan parked on the dirt service road that ran along the west side of the compound. The same car he'd seen yesterday.

Someone was sitting in it, but because of the way the vehicle was hidden in the copse of pines that hugged the fence, he couldn't make out who it was. He was willing to bet, though, that it was the brown-haired woman who'd been sneaking around the afternoon before.

Pretending he hadn't noticed her, Jackson snapped the padlock, jiggled it to verify it was secure, then climbed into his car. Instead of driving all the way to the main road, however, he stopped at midpoint, past a stand of Afghan pines, shut off the engine and backtracked on foot. Before he reached the gate, he detoured to the side road and advanced toward the shabby automobile in what he hoped was its blind spot. As he got closer, he could see her head was down. Could she be dead?

The thought unnerved him. So much had been going on lately he didn't know what to expect. Then she moved, and he realized she'd been eating. Quietly, he crept up on her side of the vehicle, still undetected, reached out his hand and yanked the door open.

"Who the hell are you? And what are you doing here?"

LEANNA'S HEART LEAPED as panic flashed her. Before she had a chance to answer, he reached inside, came within an inch of her face and fisted the ignition keys.

He glared at her as he pulled back, then withdrew a cell phone from his pants pocket. "Whoever you are—'' he started hitting numbers ''—you're trespassing on private property.''

At last she found her voice. ''I have a perfectly legitimate right to be here, Mr. Fontaine.''

Her assertive tone seemed to take him by surprise. ''Fine. Then you won't mind explaining it to the police,'' he declared.

''Go right ahead and call,'' she shot back. ''Save me the trouble. But don't you want to know who I am and what I'm doing here before you make a fool of yourself?''

His brows rose. He clicked off the cell phone. ''What the hell are you talking about?''

She took a fortifying breath. ''My name is Leanna Cargill.'' She shoved aside the remnants of the baloney-and-cheese sandwich she'd packed that morning and retrieved the handbag on the seat beside her. ''I have identification.... I'm an insurance investigator for the Sugar Coalition.''

His eyes went wide. ''You're what?''

She almost smiled. ''I'm an insurance investigator for the Sugar Coalition,'' she repeated more slowly, as if he were slightly dim-witted.

''Really? And what might an insurance investigator for the Sugar Coalition be doing on my property?''

She had his full attention now. ''First of all, I'm not on your property. This is a public road. Second, I'm checking out an anonymous tip that raw sugar is being stored at this site illegally. From the evidence—'' she looked around at the tan crystals that glinted off everything in sight ''—I'd say the report was correct.''

He opened his cell phone again and started clicking numbers. To her quizzical expression, he explained, "I'm calling Ripley Spruance. You know who he is, don't you?"

Leanna rolled her eyes and clucked her tongue. "Is that supposed to be a trick question, Mr. Fontaine? He's the president of the Sugar Coalition."

"Go to the head of the class." He frowned. "Hello, Rip? Jackson...yeah, a mess, but everything's under control. Does the name Leanna Cargill mean anything to you?"

She sat on the edge of the car seat, facing him, her emotions on a roller-coaster. He'd scared the daylights out of her when he'd yanked the car door open. Which reminded her, she ought to keep it locked, but with the air-conditioning not working in the summer and the heat running full blast in winter, she had to keep the windows open, so what was the point? She'd worry about that later.

In other circumstances the sight of Jackson Fontaine standing over her might have been a real heart stopper of another sort. He wasn't exceptionally tall, probably not quite six feet, but he was lean and muscular and had that air of dominant-male confidence that could make a woman's heart trip when she gazed into his dark-blue eyes. A nice voice, too. Those long fluid Southern vowels carried so well on his smooth baritone.

"So you did hire her?" he said into the tiny instrument, and cast her a disgruntled glance.

She'd done her homework when she got this assignment. Having worked for an insurance company up North for several years, she was good at digging up facts, checking public records. Here in Baton Rouge, she'd talked to Ripley Spruance and conferred by phone with people in the sugar industry, mostly in Sugarland, Texas, where the biggest refinery was and the destination of most of the raw sugar produced in this part of Louisiana.

She'd also learned that the Fontaines were one of the most powerful families in this region, that they owned their own mill for transforming cane into raw sugar and that they'd recently acquired an obsolete refinery. This sugar refinery.

"I completely understand, Rip," Jackson said into the phone. "No hard feelings, although in the future you might try asking me your questions directly. If you don't trust me to tell you the truth, at least hire someone competent enough to investigate discreetly."

Leanna felt her cheeks warm.

"Hey, no harm, no foul, Rip. See you at the meeting next week." Jackson clicked off, returned the cell phone to his pocket and crossed his arms over his chest. He peered at her for several seconds, then seemed to come to a decision.

"I'll make a deal with you, Ms. Cargill," he finally said. "Since you were trespassing yesterday on my private property—"

"Trespassing? I told you who I am, and you've verified it. I have a legitimate right to be here."

"Not without my permission. You can explain why you didn't request it to the judge. I'm sure he'll understand."

"To a judge? This is outrageous. That could take hours—"

"Maybe days." He smiled viciously. "I know all the judges around here. Most of them are pretty reasonable, actually. I hope you don't believe all those terrible stories about Southern judges being hostile to Yankees.''

She did a slow burn and was about to lash out, when she decided a change in tactics might serve her better.

''Be reasonable, Mr. Fontaine. We both know a charge of criminal trespass won't hold up. I'm a single mother. Think of my daughter. If you persist in this frivolous charge—''

''Child Protective Services will take good care of her while you're waiting to see the judge or sitting in jail pending a hearing.''

Her mouth fell open, appalled at what he was suggesting. ''You can't be serious. You would do that to my daughter to get back at me?''

''You would let that happen to your daughter?'' he shot back.

They stared at each other. She didn't doubt that he knew all the judges. The Fontaines had a reputation for wheeling and dealing. She also didn't doubt that she'd be exonerated. This threat of harassment was a bluff, but could she afford to take a chance?

She closed her eyes for several seconds and compressed her lips. Trying to hold her temper, she glared at him. ''What do you want from me, Mr. Fontaine?''

''Your cooperation. I want to know who turned me in.''

She sagged against the back of the seat. ''I told you it was an anonymous tip.''

''Find out.''

She shook her head, desperate to make him understand. ''The home office won't tell me, even if they know, and I honestly don't think they do.''

"How can I be sure you aren't the person who set the charge that almost destroyed my refinery?"

"Me?" Shock had her dropping her jaw for the second time. She closed it, then stated firmly, "I investigate fires, Mr. Fontaine. I don't set them. I'm not a pyromaniac."

"Hmm. You showed up yesterday, were slinking around, then ran when I called out to you. The place blew up this morning, and here you are again. Looks pretty fishy to me."

"If I were responsible for this mess, why would I be here now?"

He cocked an eyebrow. "I understand many criminals, especially pyromaniacs, like to revisit the scene of the crime."

"Give me a break." The idea that she was responsible for what had just happened was utterly ridiculous. He must see that. "I've already explained who I am, Mr. Fontaine. An investigator for the Sugar Coalition. You've verified that I'm telling the truth."

Jackson hooked his thumbs in his pockets and regarded her. "Here's the deal. You want to know if I'm storing raw sugar in my warehouse. I'll fess up. I'll even show you."

She looked at him skeptically, as if waiting for the other shoe to fall.

"And I'll give you whatever information about it you need."

One of the things she'd learned as an investigator was to be a patient listener. Silence was intimidating, especially to people who had something to hide. Wait long enough and many of them felt compelled to make excuses, often for things that had nothing to do with the issue at hand. Swallowing her natural urge to prompt him, she held her tongue.

"In return I want your word that you'll help in my investigations." His brows drew together as if he were suddenly aware that somehow the tables had been turned, and he was now the supplicant. She had the distinct impression it was a position he was neither accustomed to nor comfortable with, and that emboldened her.

"What investigations would they be, Mr. Fontaine?"

"Someone is out to destroy Bellefontaine and my family. I want you to help me find out who it is."

"I'm not a private investigator. I work for the coalition."

"A position you may not have much longer. You're already on record as having blown your cover on this case."

She stiffened her spine. "Do you always get your way by threatening people?"

He slouched on one hip and dragged a hand down his face. All the bravado seemed to drain from him.

"This has been a rotten day, Ms. Cargill, one of many lately, and there doesn't seem to be an end in sight. No, I'm not in the habit of threatening people, and I don't hold children hostage. I owe you an apology. I'm sorry I used your daughter to scare you. I would never do anything to harm a child. Never. I'm a single parent myself, and believe me, nothing is more important to me than my little girl." He inhaled deeply. "The truth is I need your help. I'm willing to share my secrets with you, if you'll assure me you'll keep them confidential."

She blew out a breath, caught off guard by his

sudden contrition. He seemed so sincere, but she had to ask herself if it was just another way of manipulating her. "Mr. Fontaine—"

"Jackson. Since we're going to be allies, you might as well call me by my first name."

"Mr. Fontaine," she repeated, "if what you're going to tell me falls under the heading of criminal activity, keep it to yourself. I will not be an accessory—"

"You're judging me without knowing the facts." Anger suddenly inflamed his words. "How about giving me a chance to explain before convicting me."

She shook her head. "I repeat, if what you're about to tell me or show me is against the law, I cannot withhold it from the authorities."

He studied her a long minute, then he stepped back and beckoned her out of the car. "Come with me."

Her case of nerves immediately resurfaced. "Wh…where are we going?"

"You want to see what's in the warehouse, don't you? Isn't that why you were sneaking around here yesterday?"

Still she hesitated.

His annoyance gave way to humor. "Here," he said, holding out his cell phone. "You carry this. You can punch in 911 and keep your finger on the red button. If at any time you feel in danger, all you have to do is hit Send." At her confusion, he added, "Lee, I'm not going to attack you."

His instinctive use of her nickname took her by surprise. In an odd sort of way, it seemed to bond them. He really did sound sincere. She took the instrument but didn't actually program the call.

They walked across the gooey, sugarcoated path to the center of the compound. She gaped at the destruction but said nothing. He led her to the warehouse, took a key out of his pocket and inserted it into the sooty padlock. Remarkably, it clicked open smoothly.

"Ready?" he asked, his hand on the big handle of the sliding door.

She nodded.

The metal screeched as he tugged the door open.

"Oh," she said, amazed and maybe a little frightened.

CHAPTER TWO

"YOU ACCUSED ME of storing raw sugar illegally. You got it half right, Ms. Cargill. I am...was stockpiling sugar. What you see is all that's left of two-and-a-half million pounds of unrefined sugar. But it's all perfectly legal."

They stood side by side and stared at the gigantic mottled-brown glaciers, the aftermath of fire and water.

Her attention finally shifted, and she looked up at him. "Can you prove that?"

"You don't believe me." Under the circumstances, he probably wouldn't, either.

"Follow me back to Bellefontaine." He closed and relocked the door. "We can talk more comfortably there, and I'll furnish you the proof you need."

She hesitated, and why not? A few minutes ago he'd accused her of sabotage. He'd seriously doubted she fitted the profile of a hired hit-woman, but getting her reaction had been interesting and had confirmed what he'd already suspected—that she was in no way involved in this mess. That made her useful, and at this point he was desperate for help, voluntary or coerced, to protect his family.

"If you would like to let someone know where you'll be," he offered, "go ahead."

Only then did she seem to remember she was holding his cell phone. She poked in a series of digits. "Mr. Spruance, this is Leanna Cargill…yes, I'm fine. I'll be at Mr. Fontaine's house for a while. Yes, as soon as I know anything."

Jackson smiled at her. "Ready?"

She nodded without conviction and started back to her dilapidated Toyota. He watched her walk across the gravel parking area. There was a determination in her carriage, but she was leery, too, on guard. An intriguing combination, he decided—confidence and vulnerability.

A puff of blue smoke belched from the tailpipe of her jalopy when she cranked the engine to a start. Jackson wondered if the clunker would even make it to the estate as he climbed behind the wheel of his Jag. It hummed as he crunched down the coarse lane to the paved road. A glance in the rearview mirror confirmed she was following.

Since this would be her first visit to the old manse, he decided on the scenic route. Bypassing the side road he normally took, which led directly to the six-car garage behind the house, he continued on and turned at the main entrance. The great iron gate used to stand open all the time. Now he had to swipe a card across an electronic reader and wait for the gate to swing wide.

At the far end of the long magnolia-bordered divided driveway loomed the mansion with its massive pillars. The lawn in the median was dotted with four splashing fountains. Each was unique, each contributed by a different generation. In the rose garden behind the west side of the house was the newest addition, the one his parents had built twenty years earlier. Jackson and his sisters would design their generation's contribution to Bellefontaine, this world of beautiful fountains. They planned to erect it on the east side of the manor where the original kitchen had stood. Sometimes he feared theirs might be the last fountain before this plantation went the way of so many others—the land subdivided and used for other purposes, the house demolished or turned into a museum.

Not if he had anything to do with it, he vowed. He didn't consider himself a sentimental man, but he did believe in heritage. He wasn't proud of everything in the Fontaine annals, either, but it was still his family's history.

Another check in the rearview mirror confirmed Leanna was still right behind him. He wished they were together in his car so he could explain the significance of the fountains and tell some of the anecdotes that went with them. Later, he decided. On foot. He rounded the first, biggest and most elaborate of the fountains, the one in the circle in front of the mansion, and came to a stop. Leanna had already turned off her engine by the time he strolled back to her car, or it had quit, which seemed equally likely. He reached for the door handle.

She didn't jump with fright this time when he opened her door, just looked up a bit self-consciously, smiled and accepted his hand.

"This place is lovely," she commented, and gently extricated her fingers from his. "Like something out of a movie."

He chuckled. "Movies are something like this, only not as real."

She surveyed the Corinthian columns and banistered balcony of the second floor.

"The house was built in 1835 by André Guillaume François, duc de Fontaine."

"It's magnificent."

"Come inside." He cupped her elbow and escorted her up the five wide stone steps to the main entrance. "I usually use the back door, but my aunt would have a fit if I brought a newcomer in that way. Aunt Esme is very particular about decorum."

Having grown up here, he tended to take the place for granted. With Leanna at his side, he tried to see it as she did. The pillars, French windows and wall-mounted gas lamps—all invited a certain formality.

Jackson turned the shiny brass handle of the front door, swung it inward, backed out and, with a sweeping gesture, beckoned her to step inside.

The wide breezeway was dominated by an elegant, curving staircase and smelled faintly of lemon oil. Double doors led to rooms on the right and left. His father's sister descended the stairs and stepped forward. Slender and wearing a striped gray blouse and burgundy leggings, she smiled in greeting to their guest. Toodles, her miniature Schnauzer, was cradled in her left arm.

"Aunt Esme," Jackson began, "may I present Leanna Cargill. This is my aunt, Esme Fontaine."

"Welcome to Bellefontaine." She extended her right hand, palm down. At sixty-two, she sometimes acted a generation older. It was part of her charm, a source of mild amusement and occasional embarrassment.

If Leanna found her etiquette strange, she showed no sign of it. "You have a beautiful home, Ms. Fontaine."

Jackson doubted she noticed the momentary quirk

of his aunt's neatly plucked eyebrow at the sound of her clipped Northern accent. Still, good manners always won Esme's approval.

"Would you like a grand tour?" he asked.

"I'd love one," Leanna said, then added, "but this is your home. I wouldn't want to pry."

"That's why I won't show you the skeletons in the closets," he replied. "We save those for the second visit. They go back more than a hundred and fifty years, to the days of slavery, stone cane crushers and open cauldrons, not to mention the odd lunatic relation locked in the attic."

"Jackson, really," Esme intoned with a grimace, and addressed Leanna. "My nephew's sense of humor is occasionally—" she eyed him with mock sternness "—*outré*. I can assure you we've never confined mad family members to the attic."

"Actually, we kept them chained in the backyard." He chuckled at his aunt's tight-lipped disapproval, then kissed her fondly on the forehead.

"I hope you enjoy your visit, Ms. Cargill," Esme said. "Just don't believe everything he tells you."

"Please call me Leanna or Lee."

"You shouldn't have any trouble with that name," Jackson said to his aunt. "Where are Megan and Tanya?"

"In the kitchen, eating lunch." Esme turned and retreated the way she'd come.

"Let's see what the girls are doing." Jackson escorted her past the staircase.

The kitchen they entered was large, with a high ceiling and polished wood floor. Sunlight streamed in through two widely spaced windows. There was an archaic formalism about it, yet it still felt comfortable and efficient. At a scrubbed oak-topped table near the far window, a blond woman sat with her back to the door. Facing her was a girl with curly dark hair and gray eyes.

"Well, what are we having for lunch?" Jackson asked brightly.

The young woman turned. "Hello, Jack—" she saw Leanna, and the sparkle in her eyes dimmed "—uh, Mr. Fontaine."

He nodded absently, his attention drawn to the girl. "What's that you're eating, sweetheart?" He knelt by her side and kissed her on the cheek.

"Peanut butter and jelly," the girl responded. Her fingers were smudged purple.

"Looks delicious. Can I have a taste?"

She offered the half-eaten wedge in her hand. He nibbled a corner of the bread and chewed exaggeratedly. The girl giggled, and Jackson's face softened as he gently tucked a loose strand of hair behind her ear. "Lee, this is my daughter. Megan, honey, say hello to Ms. Cargill."

"Hello," the girl mumbled, glancing up shyly.

"Hi, Megan." Leanna moved to the other side of the table. "I have a little girl, too. Her name is Elise. How old are you?"

"I'm four," she said, holding up her free hand, all five fingers splayed.

Leanna raised her hand in the same fashion and pointedly tucked in her thumb to make it four. Megan looked at her own hand and mimicked the motion. "Elise is five," Leanna continued, this time extending the thumb, "so she's just a little older than you."

"Is she pretty? My daddy says I'm the prettiest girl in the whole wide world." Megan seemed proud of the fact, but there was wariness in the statement, as if she wasn't completely sure he was telling the truth.

Leanna recognized a test when she heard one, not just for her but for Jackson. She glanced up at him. His eyebrows were raised; his expression, merry and curious about how she was going to handle this. She fished for a way out.

"He's absolutely right. I've never seen a prettier four-year-old."

Megan cocked her head. "Where is she?"

"In her kindergarten class right now. Perhaps one day you'll get to meet her." Time to divert attention. "PBJ, huh? What kind of jelly?"

"Grape." The girl took a bite.

"That's Elise's favorite."

"It was that or baloney and cheese." The young woman's flaxen hair was pulled back in twin ponytails.

Jackson shot Leanna an amused grin. "Lee, this is Tanya Carson, Megan's nanny."

"Nice to meet you." Tanya started to put out her hand, but there was jelly on it, as well. She withdrew it sheepishly. "Sorry, I'm a mess, too."

"Would you like something to eat?" Jackson offered Leanna. "Perhaps another baloney and cheese. You didn't get to finish your last one. Or a PBJ for dessert?"

She couldn't help but chuckle. "Thanks. Maybe another time."

"Finish up, sweetie," Tanya prompted her charge. "Then it's nap time."

"I don't want to take a nap," the girl whined.

"Tell you what, sugarplum," her father replied

gently, "you finish your sandwich and wash your hands, and I'll come back in a few minutes and tuck you in with a story. Okay?"

Frowning dramatically, the little girl seemed to sense this wasn't a battle she could win. "Will you read me Br'er Rabbit?"

"You bet." He bent down and kissed her again, this time on her forehead. "I'm going to show Ms. Cargill around, then I'll be right back."

A nod was her only reply.

"Megan is delightful," Leanna commented, after they left the room.

"She's only been living here a few months, and she's still shy." He led her upstairs to the front of the hall and opened the wide, glass-paneled door onto the balcony. They stepped outside. It was breezier here, the late-autumn air a bit more biting.

Leanna wanted to ask him more about his daughter, where her mother was, if he had sole custody, and was about to broach those subjects, when Jackson pointed past the fountains.

"You used to be able to see the river from the front *galerie* downstairs, until they built up the levee," he said. "Now you have to come up here to see it."

Through the shiny green alley formed by ancient magnolias, Leanna glimpsed the broad, muddy Mississippi as it flowed relentlessly south, a burnished expanse of sienna silt, on its way to the sea. Old Man River.

"It's very restful here," she noted.

He smiled, as if she'd said exactly the right thing. "I like to come out early in the morning, sit with a cup of coffee and just watch the river go by."

She hadn't expected the nostalgic image. Jackson Fontaine didn't strike her as a dreamer, not at first glance, anyway. Yet, in the brief encounter she'd had with him, she'd come to realize he wasn't a simple man.

He spun around. "Hey. I'm supposed to be showing you around the place. Aunt Esme will have my hide if I don't perform my duty."

Leanna laughed softly. "I gather your aunt is a strong-willed woman."

He escorted her back inside and made sure the door was tightly closed. "She's a Fontaine. It's in the blood. We're all tough as nails with steel spikes for backbones."

"Ouch." Leanna laughed again. "Never married?"

"Nope. I'll tell you about it sometime. When she can't eavesdrop," he muttered in her ear.

The caress of his breath against her cheek was like a low-voltage shock—not enough to make her jump, but definitely enough to make her aware.

"Therein lies a tale," he added.

Secrets somehow fit this house, this setting. She found herself intrigued.

"We started giving house tours several years ago. My mother was a member of the local historical society. We've had an open house every Christmas for as long as I can remember, and the tours became so popular that Maman decided to continue them throughout the year."

Referring to his mother in French came as a surprise, though Leanna realized, it shouldn't. Jackson Fontaine was Creole, pure French stock going back to the original settlers in the region. The language—

or a New World version of it—was still widely spoken in Louisiana's southern parishes—which is what they called counties in the Bayou State.

"Aunt Esme plays hostess," he added, "a role she glories in."

He squired her through several guest rooms, pointing out the pineapple carvings, which symbolized welcome, before they returned to the entranceway downstairs, where his aunt was waiting for her.

"I'm going to tuck Megan in," he said. "Why don't you show Lee around down here, Auntie E. I'll join you in the drawing room presently."

Leanna raised an eyebrow. She couldn't remember ever hearing anyone say *presently* or refer to a drawing room except in books and plays.

Over the next few minutes, she found herself lulled by the mellifluous cadence of Esme's Southern drawl, and captivated by her grace and refinement. Her air of genteel sophistication perfectly matched the charm and dignity of the old mansion. As for the decor... Leanna's father had been an amateur antique restorer. That didn't make her an expert, but she knew enough about old furniture to recognize their periods and styles. Her hostess filled her in on details and dates about nearly every piece.

"Sorry to keep you waiting," Jackson said, when he joined them in the drawing room twenty minutes later. "I had to read her two stories before she would settle down."

"I'll excuse myself, then," Esme said, getting up from a brocaded fiddleback chair and lowering her dog, Toodles, to the floor. "It's been very pleasant meeting you, *ma chère*. You're welcome anytime."

Leanna thanked her for her hospitality. Esme left

the room and mounted the stairs, her pet once more in her arm.

"It's her nap time, too," Jackson confided sotto voce. "But don't tell her I said that."

"Certainly not," Leanna rejoined archly. "It wouldn't be ladylike."

He snickered. "You've got her pegged."

Leanna softened. "I like her."

"So do I. Let's go into the office. That's where I keep my records."

He led her to the rear of the house, to a room that was obviously a masculine work center. An ornately carved desk dominated the area between French windows. Behind it, a computer sat on a credenza, sandwiched between ledgers, manuals and folders. Newspapers, magazines and periodicals crowded other surfaces, yet even at first glance, Leanna sensed order in the clutter.

"You accused me of illegally hoarding raw sugar," he said, his tone less friendly than it had been only a minute earlier. "So let me set—"

"I didn't accuse you of anything, Jackson. I merely informed you of an allegation I'm investigating."

"So let me set the record straight," he went on. Assuming his usual seat behind the desk, he swung around to the computer, turned it on and waited for it to boot up. "Here's the provenance for the twelve-hundred-and-fifty tons of raw sugar you saw in the warehouse—or what's left of it."

They had been reviewing data for nearly two hours when there came a tap on the door. Jackson dumped the file folders he'd pulled from the cabinet onto the desk.

"Jackson, y'all have been cooped up in here for so long I thought you might like a refreshment." Esme wheeled in a tea cart with a pitcher of tea, a bowl of sugar, another of lemon and a third of mint, a silver ice bucket and two heavy crystal glasses. The tongs and spoons, Leanna noticed, were sterling.

"Perfect timing," Jackson told her. "We're ready for a break." He turned to Leanna. "Don't you think?"

"Complètement. Merci bien, Mademoiselle Fontaine."

The well-pronounced, fluid French brought a subtle smile to the corners of the older woman's mouth. "Jackson, perhaps Miss Lee would like to stay for supper."

He tossed Leanna an amused grin and took the tongue out of his cheek long enough to ask, "How about it?"

She found herself flustered. "Oh…uh…that's very kind of you, but I really can't. I have to pick up my daughter from school."

"Daughter?" Esme paused, her carefully plucked brown eyebrows raised. "I didn't know you were married." The older woman glanced at Leanna's left hand. There was no wedding band. She'd taken it off long ago.

"I'm not," she confessed.

Esme clucked her tongue. "Oh."

"I'm divorced," Leanna explained evenly.

"Her daughter, Elise," Jackson said, coming to the rescue with a conspiratorial wink toward Leanna behind his aunt's back, "is just a year older than Megan."

Esme recovered quickly. "She's welcome to join

us, too, of course. In fact,'' she added thoughtfully, ''I'm sure Megan will enjoy having someone near her own age to associate with.''

''That would be a terrible inconvenience for you. Perhaps another—''

''Au contraire.'' The perfect hostess waved the notion aside. ''It's no inconvenience at all. Jackson, I'm sure you can use your considerable charms to persuade your friend.'' She gave him an encouraging smile. ''Now, if you'll excuse me, I'll tell Betty we'll have two more for supper.'' Esme glided out of the room, quietly closing the door behind her.

Leanna turned to Jackson. ''Your aunt's invitation is very generous, but I really can't accept.''

''Why not?''

She was hard-pressed to come up with a good excuse, other than that it was an imposition, which they had both already adamantly denied.

''It's settled, then,'' he declared, before she had a chance to argue the point. ''What time does Elise get out of kindergarten?''

Leanna looked at her watch, to find the cheap thing she'd picked up on sale at a supermarket had stopped a couple of hours earlier. She sighed. You get what you pay for. If she was lucky, she only needed a new battery. Keeping appointments without a timepiece was tough.

''At three o'clock. Then I take her to a baby-sitter until I quit work for the day. That's usually around six,'' she added, unsure why. Except that she felt guilty about leaving her baby with a stranger. Mrs. Peltière was a pleasant woman who seemed to take genuine interest in her charges, but she wasn't family.

"That gives us half an hour." He poured tea into the two glasses that already contained ice. "Let's drink up, then we'll go get her. Do you have to call the sitter and cancel? Will she be upset at the short notice?"

Leanna chuckled. "She'll probably be relieved. She has five other kids to handle." Of course, Leanna would still have to pay her the minimum one-hour fee.

Ten minutes later, they were in Jackson's Jaguar. Leanna felt like a princess, cocooned in the front seat of the luxury sedan. The fine leather upholstery and rich interior were also mildly intimidating. She'd never ridden in a car that cost more than any house she'd ever lived in. It thrilled and unnerved her at the same time—or maybe it was the man sitting beside her. She'd met him only a few hours ago, under less-than-auspicious circumstances, yet she felt safe with him.

"Elise is at Dubois Elementary," she told him, as they drove down the green-arbored lane.

"Are you satisfied yet that I'm not a swindler?" he asked with a sidelong glance.

"I told you I wasn't the one making the charge." Being accused of double-dealing obviously stuck in his craw.

"Still, under the circumstances, you must have gone into this matter with the assumption that I was guilty until I proved myself innocent." He said it without resentment. "Have I met the test?"

Actually, he'd been more forthcoming about the family's holdings than she'd expected. Unless there was another set of books hidden away somewhere, the raw sugar stored in the warehouse was perfectly legal, but...

"You have to understand," he explained, "my father enjoyed nothing better than playing both ends against the middle, and he was good at it. He took the usual coalition loan for planting on our land, but Duke also leased other acreage that he put under cultivation using private money. That's what we have...had stockpiled in the warehouse."

"To dump on the world market if the price goes up."

"*When* the price goes up," he corrected. "Price fluctuations are inevitable. It's simply a matter of timing."

"And when you get your own refinery up and running, you'll have additional leverage."

He shrugged, displaying no offense at the implied rebuke. "It's called good business."

Some would call it *sharp* business, she mused. There was, however, nothing illegal about what he'd done. Sugar growers obtained loans every year from the coalition to plant their crops. Along with the low-interest rate came insurance that protected them against loss in case of weather or other natural disaster. The twist was that they had to sell the entire mortgaged crop to the coalition at established prices. They made decent profits, but while the contract limited their liability, it also prevented them from hedging against rising demand. Planting with personal capital outside the coalition meant a grower could play the market. Old-fashioned capitalism. Gamble for big profits. The downside was that they risked losing everything. Which was what had happened when the gas explosion and fire reduced the Fontaine cache to burned goo.

"Who knew you were stockpiling?" she asked.

"Duke and Maman, and my sister Casey, of course, not that she's ever been interested in the marketing aspect of the business. Growing is her thing. Then there's my other sister, Noelani. But I'm certain she wouldn't divulge the information. She's very sensitive about keeping confidences, and she's devoted to Bellefontaine's success."

"How about your aunt?"

"It's remotely possible Duke mentioned it to her, I suppose, though I doubt it. Can you imagine Esme blabbing?"

Leanna had to smile. "How about your mother? Could she have confided it to anyone?"

"Believe me, Maman excelled at keeping secrets. She knew my father had an illegitimate daughter in Hawaii and never said a word about it to anyone, not even Esme, her closest friend. I'm sorry she did. Your parents' funeral isn't a fitting occasion to learn you have a half sister. It was rough going for all of us at first, but she's part of the family now. I'm damn proud of her."

Logic said the words were nice; instinct told her he meant them. "What about the workers who did the harvesting, milling and storing?"

Jackson turned onto Dubois Street. Other vehicles were parked in front of the sprawling brown-brick building. He pulled in behind a double-parked silver Buick with a crumpled fender.

"They had no way of knowing they were dealing in private production." He put on the emergency brake. "Since few people gamble on sugar futures, they would naturally assume it was all part of the coalition crop.''

Leanna got out of the vehicle, closed the door and stood beside it. ''So anyone seeing it stored past the time it would be sent to the refinery would be inclined to figure it was being illegally held back,'' she concluded, when he came around the front of the car to stand next to her.

He nodded. ''You have no way of finding out who dropped the dime on me?''

She shook her head, her eyes fixed on the front entrance of the school. A bell sounded. A minute later, kids burst through the doorway. ''There she is.'' Leanna began waving.

The girl who ran over had honey-blond hair that was long and straight. The resemblance between mother and daughter was unmistakable. The same oval face, wide-set violet-blue eyes and a dimple in her chin.

''Mommy, I got a star. See?'' She presented a piece of pale-green construction paper with a house, trees, a dog and a man and woman holding the hands of a little girl between them. The message didn't take much imagination to decipher.

Leanna examined the drawing and gave it the appropriate praise, then directed the girl's attention to Jackson and introduced them.

''I'm very pleased to meet you,'' Elise said with adult seriousness.

''We're going to Mr. Fontaine's house for dinner.'' Leanna motioned her into the back seat of the car and quickly buckled her in. ''His daughter is just a little younger than you.''

''Does she go to school, too?''

"She's in preschool," Jackson explained, as he checked his side mirror and carefully edged out into the stream of slow-moving traffic.

"Mommy, this car smells funny."

Leanna swallowed a chuckle. She was tempted to call it the smell of money. "That's because the seats are leather, honey. Nice, huh?"

"Does Mr. Fontaine and his family live in an apartment like us?"

"They have a big house in a beautiful park," Leanna replied. "Wait till you see it."

Elise continued to chatter as they made their way to Bellefontaine. Jackson realized she was a very bright child, well spoken, gregarious and full of energy. A contrast to Megan, who was reserved and shy. He wondered how the two girls would get along.

CHAPTER THREE

WITHIN A MINUTE, Elise had talked Megan into showing her her room. They scampered up the stairs, practically on all fours.

Jackson turned to Leanna with a wide smile on his face. "I wish you'd shown up months ago. I don't think I've ever seen Megs move so fast."

A clash and clatter reverberated from the head of the stairs a minute later.

"Whatever are they up to?" Esme asked.

"I'll go and check," Leanna replied apologetically. "Sometimes Elise gets a bit carried away."

"I simply want to make sure they're safe," Esme stated, apparently aware she'd sounded judgmental.

Jackson cocked his head. "I don't hear any crying, so they must be okay. Tanya's with them. If there's a problem, she can handle it. Let's go back to work. Cocktails will be served in less than an hour."

Leanna raised an eyebrow. "Cocktails?"

"In the drawing room." Jackson escorted her to the office. "Aunt Esme enjoys a mint julep before dinner."

Leanna's brows went even higher. "For real?"

He suppressed a laugh at the note of incredulity. "In warmer weather, we even have them under the magnolia trees in the back garden."

She snickered. "Oh, dear, and I left my hoop skirt at home."

He clucked, his face a mirthful grin. "I don't suppose you brought your fan, either."

She shook her head disconsolately.

"Aunt Esme can loan you both." He winked and they laughed.

They took seats, he behind his desk, she at its side.

"How familiar are you with sugar processing?" he asked.

"I don't claim to be an expert," Leanna admitted. "I've read up on the subject and toured the West Baton Rouge Museum right after getting here. It was fascinating. Like most people, I didn't realize the process was so complex or so scientific."

"How did you think sugar was made?"

She gave him a light shrug. "To be honest, I never gave it much thought. I figured cane was pressed for its juice, the juice boiled till it crystallized, then ground into granular form."

"That's basically true. It certainly was a couple of hundred years ago when cane was first cultivated. We're a little more sophisticated now. The word *pure* on packages of refined sugar means just that. It's sugar. Nothing more, nothing less. Not many products that can boast that."

"The cane itself is different, too, isn't it?"

He nodded. "If you want to learn about advances in cane, talk to Casey. She's been working with Louisiana State University for years to develop new varieties that produce higher yields and are more pest resistant—a win-win situation."

"I see I have a lot to learn."

Without thinking he placed his hand on the back of hers. "And I'm prepared to teach you."

"That's very kind, Jackson," she said, as if neither of them was aware of the brief physical contact, "but I can hardly accept tutoring from the man I'm investigating."

"You're right." He didn't seem in the least discouraged. "But I'm not offering to advise you on my case. Call it background research, if you like. We can tour cane fields, sugar mills and other refineries. You can verify anything and everything I tell you with outside sources."

She mulled over the idea. At the very least, having him help her gain access to such places would be an advantage; and having him available to go to for answers to her dumb questions would be nice. "What about your own work? I can't impose on your time that way."

"I may have to adjust my schedule a little, but I've got a cell phone. People can get hold of me whenever they wish," he assured her. "We'll take my car."

Was it wise to ally herself with the man who'd just lost a warehouse full of raw sugar? Could, would, he be objective? Or was this a scheme to divert her to the conclusions he wanted her to reach? Was she compromising her job and her reputation by associating too closely with Jackson Fontaine?

On the other hand, he'd substantiated that the sugar hadn't been coalition financed or insured, and he wasn't making a claim for reimbursement. So where was the conflict of interest?

What concerned her more than the question of ethics was the idea of spending time with him. After

leaving Richard Cargill, she honestly wasn't interested in men. Being a single mother with responsi-
bilities was enough. Now Jackson Fontaine was
awakening an awareness of what she was missing—
someone…a friend…to share adult time with.

She was about to decline his generous offer, when
the sound of voices in the hallway distracted her.

"Come on." Jackson bounced from his chair.
"Let's meet the rest of the family."

He leaned over her shoulder to shut down the computer. She had to resist the reflex to pull away from
him. She didn't want to give him the impression he
frightened her. He was, after all, simply turning off
the computer. Besides, fear wasn't what his closeness
inspired.

"There'll be time for this later." He took her hand
and led her out into the hall.

Standing inside the back door was a striking couple. Jackson introduced his sister Casey and her husband, Nick Devlin. Casey was taller than Leanna,
had long wavy brown hair tied back with a ribbon at
her nape, and enchanting green eyes.

"It's starting to get cold out," she said, as she
shucked a light windbreaker and hung it on a coat
tree.

"You might have worn a dress, since we're having
guests," Esme said, as she approached from the front
of the house.

Actually, Casey was wearing a very attractive—
and Leanna suspected, very expensive—khaki pant-
suit.

"Wouldn't want to put on airs," she said dryly.
"Whatever would our guest think?" She pecked her
aunt on the cheek.

The older woman frowned. Apparently, it was an old issue. Esme herself had exchanged her leggings and blouse for a mauve shirtwaist number that managed to hug the line between formal and informal. The kind of understated elegance, Leanna recognized, that came from exclusive boutiques.

A couple of inches over six feet, Nick had jet-black hair, gorgeous blue eyes and a smile that could easily turn a woman's head.

"Shall we retire to the drawing room?" Esme said, as if it were déclassé to stand around the back hall gabbing.

"Lee, what would you like?" Jackson asked, after they'd entered a room that could have been taken directly from *Southern Breeze* magazine. "Aunt Esme usually has a julep. Casey likes beer."

Esme pursed her lips in abject disapproval.

"So does Nick," Jackson continued. "But I also have white and red wine, if you'd prefer, and of course juice and soft drinks."

"Have you ever had a julep," Casey asked in a drawl that resembled her aunt's but lacked the practiced charm.

"I'm not much of a drinker," Leanna explained.

These days she couldn't afford to be, even if she wanted. There had been a few occasions when a glass of wine would have gone well with a bubble bath, but iced tea and hot showers had had to suffice.

"Jackson—" Casey turned to her brother "—you drink juleps. Why don't you fix Lee one. If she doesn't like it, you can finish it." To Leanna, she said, "They can pack a wallop if you're not used to them."

Leanna watched him prepare two of the drinks,

mulling fresh mint into fine sugar, adding bourbon, a splash of soda and plenty of shaved ice.

Esme all but smacked her lips as he performed the ritual. ''It's my mother's recipe, but nobody makes them better than Jackson. Even his father admitted that.'' It was her first reference to her late brother. Leanna observed no overt reaction from the others, though a momentary lull settled in the room.

Jackson handed Esme hers, then passed the other crystal old-fashioned glass to Leanna.

She inhaled the minty aroma. ''Smells wonderful.'' She took a sip and coughed. Her eyes watered. ''I should have believed you when you said it was strong.''

Casey and Nick chuckled as Leanna handed the julep back to Jackson.

''Perhaps you'd care for a sherry, my dear,'' Esme said from the brocade fiddleback.

Jackson cocked an eyebrow at Leanna.

''I think I better stick to orange juice,'' she replied, ''if you have any.''

''Coming up.'' He withdrew a small bottle from the under-the-counter refrigerator. The sound of more people could be heard emanating from the back of the house. ''Must be Noelani and Adam.''

Leanna wasn't prepared for the two people who entered the room. The woman was tall and slender, with dark-brown almond eyes and a flawless, olive complexion. Her hair, curly rather than sleek, was long and shiny black but with fascinating reddish highlights. No question about it; the woman was a knockout in her casual burgundy slacks and pale-blue silk blouse. Leanna noticed a blood-red ruby ring on her right hand, as well as the diamond wedding set on her left.

Her husband, Adam, could have been a model for a Ralph Lauren advertisement. Tall, lean-muscled and suntanned, he had medium-brown hair and pale-blue eyes. His hand, when he took Leanna's, was work roughened, but the gentleness in his touch contradicted the coarseness.

"Your usuals?" Jackson asked when the introductions were complete. Receiving nods, he handed Adam a bottle of beer and a glass, and prepared another julep for Noelani.

They were about to settle into chairs and couches, when the clatter of feet on the stairs caught their attention. Tanya and her two charges stood in the doorway a moment later.

Leanna introduced her daughter.

"Class tonight?" Jackson asked Tanya.

"Yes, sir." She kept her eyes focused on her employer. "Finals coming up, then one more semester and I'm finished."

"Tanya is getting her degree in music," Jackson explained to Leanna. "Drive carefully," he told the nanny.

Giving him one more, almost wistful, glance, the young woman retreated into the hallway and exited through the rear.

"She's madly in love with you, Jackson," Casey told her brother, and sipped her beer from the bottle.

"Don't be ridiculous."

Leanna laughed. The infatuation in Tanya's eyes was unmistakable. Some men capitalized on their looks; others weren't even conscious of them. Jackson seemed to belong to the latter group—unlike

Richard. Either way, it was definitely a point in his favor.

Everyone found a place to sit; Leanna chose a love seat so Elise could join her. She, too, had an orange drink. Megan sat on the couch with her father, and Toodles jumped into Esme's lap.

From the magazine article she'd read, Leanna recognized Adam Ross as the guy who'd made the repairs on Bellefontaine following the kitchen fire several months earlier. Jackson explained that Adam was now restoring Magnolia Manor, a nearby plantation house that had once belonged to his family.

"How's the project going?" Jackson asked his brother-in-law.

"We've torn out the floor in the central breeze-way," Adam replied. "I found enough original planking under the staircase to confirm that the pine was installed later, probably as an economy move. It'll cost a fortune, but I'm going to go back to cypress, which is true to the period."

"Cypress was used extensively in quality construction in the mid-nineteenth century," Casey explained to Leanna, "because it was very hard and naturally impervious to rot and termites, both of which are major threats to wooden structures in the area."

"Why did the floors have to be replaced then?" Leanna asked.

Noelani laughed. "Apparently, the sons of wealthy planters were often spoiled brats who were subject to very little discipline. The mid-nineteenth century equivalent of drag racing apparently was riding horses through the breezeways that ran from the front to the back of houses."

"Good heavens."

"You seem to have immersed yourself in Adam's project," Casey observed.

Noelani laced her fingers with his and gazed up at him with the kind of admiration reserved for young lovers. "It's fascinating."

"Shod hooves tend to do a number on wooden floors," her husband commented. "When it came time to repair or replace them, less expensive yellow pine was frequently substituted."

"What brings you to Bellefontaine, Ms. Cargill?" Nick asked.

"Please call me Lee. I'm an insurance investigator for the Sugar Coalition."

Nick cocked his head.

"She's examining my books." Jackson winked at her.

She wanted to ignore his teasing tone, but it was impossible not to smile.

"My daddy likes little books," Elise announced proudly.

Eyebrows rose. Leanna would have urged her daughter to be quiet, if she could have done so discreetly, but everyone was staring at them.

"Little books?" Jackson asked.

The five-year-old giggled. "He calls them book-ies."

Dead silence. Leanna closed her eyes and nearly groaned.

"Does he read to you often?" Noelani asked, as though the term had no nefarious connotation.

"Sometimes." The girl grew suddenly sad. "But he's not here. Mommy left him, so I don't see him anymore."

Leanna felt the heat rising to her cheeks and imagined them turning beet-red.

"I bet your mommy reads books to you," Casey ventured, catching Leanna's eye.

"I can read some of them all by myself."

A woman wearing a tie-dyed dress appeared at the door. Wooden beads dangled from her scrawny neck, and an unlit cigarette was tucked between her ear and pulled-back graying hair. "The food's on the table," she declared. "Come get it if you want it hot. I'm gone."

Esme rolled her eyes and shuddered in a ladylike fashion. "Thank you, Betty," she said sarcastically to the empty space where the woman had stood. She rose from her chair, deposited her empty glass on the bar and led the way across the hall.

Leanna was entranced by the dining room. Large and high-ceilinged, it featured a gilt chandelier with teardrop crystals. The oblong, round-cornered table was set for nine, though it easily could have seated twice that number.

"Daddy, can Elise sit next to me?" Megan asked. Leanna noted she asked rather than told her father what she wanted, as some children might.

He rested his hand on her shoulder. "You bet, sweetheart."

"But I want to sit next to you, too."

"How's this? You take your usual place by me, Elise can sit beside you and her mother on the other side of her."

Megan bobbed her head happily. "Okay."

Jackson took the chair at its head with Esme, presumably in her usual place, on his right. Casey sat beside Leanna opposite Nick, Noelani and Adam.

In spite of the insouciant attitude of the cook, the food was handsomely presented, smelled heavenly and, Leanna soon learned, tasted even better.

Conversation flowed easily. She learned that Noelani was from Hawaii, where she'd also grown up in the sugar industry.

"Not much left of it," Noelani said a little sadly. "Even pineapples, once the most prominent agricultural product of the islands, is declining. Tourism is by far the most profitable enterprise these days."

"Are you homesick for the islands?" Leanna asked.

The exotically beautiful woman swept her shiny hair back as she paused to consider her answer. "In some ways. But I really don't have roots there anymore. This is my home now." She rested her hand on Adam's arm. "I'm very happy here."

"Where are you from, my dear?" Esme asked Leanna.

"Ithaca, New York. It's upstate."

"What was your maiden name?"

"Jerome," she responded, surprised by a question that wasn't normally asked.

Esme pursed her lips. "Jerome," she repeated, giving it a French pronunciation. "There is a large Jerome clan in Iberville Parish. Many of them, if I'm not mistaken, went north after the war." Leanna had no doubt she was referring to the Civil War.

"So maybe you're not really a Yankee after all," Casey suggested, and brushed her shoulder against Leanna's.

"It's damnyankee, Sis," Jackson corrected her. "One word, indivisible."

"Jackson, really," Esme said, though there was a twinkle in her eyes.

"How about you?" Noelani asked. "Do you miss New York?"

Leanna thought a moment. "We've only been here a month. Everything still feels sort of temporary. I won't miss the icy winters. I can tell you that."

When the others started to clear the table after dinner, Leanna offered to help.

"Maybe next time," Casey told her. "Tonight, you're a guest." She smiled. "If I know my brother, you'll have other opportunities."

Jackson invited Leanna out into the garden. The sun had already set, but small lanterns dotted the brick path among well-tended flower beds.

"Elise is a great kid, Lee. She answered everyone's questions politely, and her table manners met with even Aunt Esme's approval. You can be very proud of her."

A warm glow spread through Leanna. "She's the most precious thing in the world to me."

He motioned her toward a stone bench that faced a square garden plot. "She seems to miss her daddy," he said. "How often does she get to see him?"

Leanna hadn't discussed her personal life with anyone since her arrival in Baton Rouge, nor had she any reason to talk about it with this man.

"Back home, he had visitation rights on weekends, but he rarely showed up more than twice a month. When he did, it would take me three days to get Elise back into her routine after he left."

Jackson sat, not at the other end of the cool slab of granite but in the middle. Closer. "Why's that?"

She chuckled without mirth. "Dinner would be ice cream and cookies. He bought things I couldn't afford to give her, took her places I didn't have the time or money for. It should have been a win-win situation for Elise and me, but he did it primarily to undermine me."

Jackson frowned. "Sounds irresponsible."

"That's Richard."

"How did you meet?"

"We were at Cornell University together. He was majoring in hotel administration—I was taking comparative literature. Not a very practical field of study," she admitted. "People don't talk much about books anymore, certainly not French classics."

Jackson could easily imagine her curled up on a window seat on a rainy afternoon with a volume of Proust or Balzac in her hand. "But it interested you."

"Looking back now, I should have made it a minor and concentrated on something practical."

"Like hotel management?"

She laughed. "Richard's the extrovert, not me."

Hearing the lightness in her tone, seeing the easy grace of her movements, stirred something inside him.

"Everybody likes Richard," she said. "He's always the life of the party. A great cook. A charming host. Actually, he's perfectly suited to the hospitality industry."

He sounded like a boor, like a loud overbearing traveling salesman. What kind of man could walk away from a marriage to this woman? Even worse, what kind of man could neglect his child? "But not to marriage and fatherhood."

"He has his weaknesses," she muttered.

Jackson didn't hear accusation in her words. More like pity, an acknowledgment that his flaws were tragic and unavoidable. Did she still love him? Did she blame herself for his failures? "Care to elaborate?"

She hesitated, then said, "He has trouble managing money, and he likes to gamble."

Two major weaknesses, the kind that reinforce each other. "Were you aware of this before you married him?"

"I knew he was a spendthrift." The moon behind her added glitter to her shiny brown hair. "At the time I thought of it as generosity, since he was always giving me expensive things."

If I were engaged or married to a woman like you, I'd want to shower you with expensive things, too. He'd been in love once. Paige Paturin had been a beautiful debutante, a polished socialite. They made a perfect couple. Everybody said so.

"The gambling addiction didn't become apparent until later." Leanna sighed. "The fact is, I was too young, too immature—"

"And too much in love." Blindly in love, just as he'd been.

"I thought so at the time."

"Is that why you divorced him—because you discovered you didn't love him?"

"Not really. I would have stayed with him, for Elise's sake, if I'd thought we had a chance of making a decent home for her. But things never got better, only worse. Creditors kept hounding us. At first he insisted he didn't have a problem. Then he said he had it under control. I tried to talk him into counseling, but he refused. Finally, I had no choice but to file for divorce.''

''How did he take it?''

She snorted. ''Personally. Vindictively. New York is a community-property state. Richard hired himself a real shyster of a lawyer who convinced the court I was as much responsible for the condition of our finances as he was. The judge awarded me half his debts. Richard then declared bankruptcy. I refused.''

''Why?''

''Because in a way, I was responsible.'' She folded her hands in her lap. ''I should have taken a more aggressive role, should have rejected the expensive jewelry, the fine clothes, the fancy dinners he showered on me. Besides, it isn't fair that the people who sold him those things in good faith should end up the losers.''

Jackson wondered how many of his friends would have acted as she had under the circumstances. Not many. ''That's pretty altruistic.''

She snorted. ''I'm really not being noble. I'm just accepting the consequences of my actions—and inaction. I don't deny it's been a struggle sometimes, but I manage.''

Until his father's death, when the lawyers and bankers told him the bottomless pot was nearly empty, he'd never worried about money, much less where food, clothes, car insurance or rent payments were coming from. Discovering the family was nearly bankrupt had sent a shock wave through his system. His ace in the hole had been the tons of raw sugar his father had stored at the refinery. Now that was gone. If he didn't find a way to reverse their fortunes, Bellefontaine and the Fontaine legacy were faced with total bankruptcy.

"Can I make a suggestion?"

Leanna looked at him quizzically. "What's that?"

"We have two *garçonnières,* guest houses. You can move into one of them. It won't cost you anything, and Elise can stay with Megan after preschool. They get along well, and Megs would love the company. I'm afraid she's lonely here with just adults around."

Leanna bit her lower lip and raised her hand to touch his face. "That's very kind of you, Jackson. Thank you, but I can't accept."

He wasn't really surprised. The offer had been impulsive, one he couldn't explain. But he was amazed at how disappointed he felt.

"Maybe someday I'll have to accept charity." She smiled sadly at him. "I hope that day never comes. If it does, I'll do what I must for my daughter. Until then—"

"I didn't mean to offend you," he told her.

She shook her head and broadened her smile. "You haven't. And I sincerely thank you for the kindness of your offer." She stood up. "Now, I'd better get Elise home. It's already past her bedtime, and tomorrow is a school day."

THAT NIGHT, after her daughter was asleep, Leanna turned on her computer with the intention of catching up on work. Her concentration, however, was stuck on Jackson Fontaine, on the time she'd spent with him, the honesty with which he'd answered her questions, the generosity of his offering her his guest house free of charge.

Ruthlessly forcing him to the back of her mind, she focused on the business at hand. He'd recounted the litany of misfortunes that had befallen the family in the past six months—the fire at Bellefontaine that could have killed his daughter and aunt, as well as the nanny, and nearly destroyed the antebellum house. A few weeks later, their sugar harvester was stolen. Shortly thereafter, his sister and half sister were physically attacked. Fortunately, nobody was seriously injured, and the police were able to apprehend the culprits—two disgruntled employees. By then, the family had received word that Duke and Angelique Fontaine had been killed in their private plane in Italy. Jackson had thought, hoped and prayed that the crisis was over. Then, this morning, the explosion at the refinery.

Obviously, the Fontaines had enemies. That wasn't astonishing. Powerful families often did, and from what Leanna had heard, Duke Fontaine, Jackson's father, was a wheeler-dealer of the first magnitude, which meant he must have stepped on a lot of toes. Trying to burn down a treasured landmark, endangering people's lives and stealing hundreds of thousands of dollars' worth of equipment, however, suggested more than ruffled feathers.

There existed another possibility. From all indications, the untimely deaths of the senior Fontaines had thrown the family into a financial as well as an emotional crisis. Buying the obsolete sugar refinery had apparently strained cash reserves. One old and well-established method of recouping losses was through insurance fraud. The idea bothered her, not only because of the seriousness of the offense, but because of the man himself. She didn't like people who used other people. He'd apologized for his threat against Elise in their first encounter, and after seeing the way he loved his own daughter, Leanna still believed him, but it also demonstrated that he was a manipulator. A very charming one, to be sure, but wasn't charm a prominent characteristic of the best con men?

The next morning, she called Ripley Spruance.

"Jackson Fontaine was storing sugar in the warehouse," she reported. "Two and a half million pounds of it, but it wasn't coalition insured, so he's off the hook as far as you're concerned. Since my company also insures his facilities, I still have to investigate the explosion and fire."

"He couldn't have been involved in that," the president of the Sugar Coalition assured her. "What would be the point?"

She didn't know. The building wasn't worth nearly as much as the sugar stored in it, and he'd have to eat that loss. "I'd like to establish a few dates, if you don't mind," she told him.

"Shoot."

Her theory that Jackson might be trying to trade assets for cash had a couple of big holes in it. The house fire and the theft of the harvester had happened before Duke and Angelique had been killed. Jackson hadn't come into control of the family fortune yet.

"Were there any prior indications that the Fontaines might be strapped for cash?"

"Not a whisper," Spruance said decisively. "Even now, people figure that if he'd lived, Duke would have maneuvered around the money crunch. Jackson's a chip off the old block, though. He'll figure a way to work things out to the Fontaine advantage.''

When Leanna hung up, she was no closer to an answer than she had been.

CHAPTER FOUR

"NO DOUBT ABOUT IT." Hank Jensen closed his aluminum notepad. "This was sabotage."

Not exactly what Jackson wanted to hear, but the fire inspector's verdict didn't surprise him. Hank and his two assistants had already sifted through the debris and charred remains of what had been Jackson's refinery office by the time he arrived that morning. Leanna showed up a few minutes later.

Watching her climb out of her clunker of a car—she was wearing jeans and a bulky gray sweatshirt to ward off the damp morning chill, her brown hair held away from her face with barrettes—he decided he liked looking at her, enjoyed the way she made him feel. As she closed the distance between them, plastic mug of coffee in one hand, notebook and pen in the other, he was also reminded that she was an insurance investigator, which put her in opposition to him. He had a claim—correction, *another* policy claim—not for the sugar he'd lost but for the building, and her job was to save her employer the expense of paying it. She smiled a greeting, and he remembered his blackmailing her into helping him. She'd promised to do so. He hoped she would.

"How can you be sure?" Murray Dewalt asked. He'd pulled through the open gate only seconds before Leanna, driving his father's black Mercedes, on his way to getting it serviced. Roland never bothered with mundane matters like oil changes and lube jobs, leaving them to his son, who kept meticulous records to ensure such details were attended to on schedule. Jackson introduced Leanna and observed the other man's reaction as she tucked her notebook under her arm and shook his hand. Murray liked pretty women and he certainly appreciated Leanna's beauty, but Jackson didn't see any spark of attraction. He wondered if his friend was still reeling from Casey's rejection.

"Explosions and fires are funny things," Hank explained. "People expect them to destroy the evidence of how things got started." He took off his hard hat and laid it on the hood of his official vehicle. "Yet we're often able to locate the exact source of the disaster, find the overloaded electrical wiring that short-circuited, the gasoline can or even the book of matches that was used to light it. In this case, we've isolated the pipe connection that was loosened."

"Loosened. You mean on purpose? Could it have been overlooked or come loose on its own?" Jackson asked.

Hank ran a hand through his curly black hair. "Two reasons why not. First, we know who did the walk-through. Andy Breton is one of the most thorough and professional inspectors on the force. She would never make a glaring mistake like that. You said yourself, you escorted her and watched her use a sniffer on all the joints and connections. If this link had been inside a wall—" he shrugged "—it's remotely feasible it could have been missed, though our equipment is pretty darn sensitive. This particular connection, though, was out in the open. As for it coming loose on its own—'' he shook his head ''—we might have considered that possibility if the joint was in an area of high vibration and the inspection hadn't been so recent. Neither is true here. There's no indication of structural flaw. Furthermore, we found recent pipe wrench marks on the pipe.''

Leanna pouted over the rim of her cup before taking a meditative sip. Her fleeting glance at Jackson hinted at disappointment, regret. Suspicion.

Murray's brows rose in amazement. ''You can tell all that?''

The inspector chuckled. ''You'd be surprised what we can figure out. There's a strong likelihood we'll be able to identify the actual wrench that was used— if it ever turns up.''

''I'm impressed,'' Murray acknowledged.

''Maybe if people realized how transparent their actions were, there wouldn't be so many arsons, but I guess trying to beat the odds is human nature.'' He shook his head, his expression sour, but then he smiled at Jackson. ''On the brighter side, your brother-in-law, Nick Devlin, would be out of business if people didn't like to gamble.''

Except this wasn't recreational gambling, Jackson mused.

''Any indication who might have done this?'' Leanna asked, speaking up for the first time.

The inspector bunched his lips and looked again at Jackson. ''I was hoping you might have some idea.''

He shook his head, resisted the temptation to concentrate on Leanna and stared, instead, at the damage in front of him.

''You might give it some thought, because whoever it was doesn't like you very much." Having delivered that understatement, he picked up his gear and moved to the cab of his truck. "I'll be filing my report this afternoon." He turned to Leanna. "You'll be receiving a copy, Ms. Cargill, but you already have my conclusion. Arson by person or persons unknown."

"I don't mind telling you," Murray commented, as the fire department vehicles rumbled down the shell road to the highway, "I'm glad we sold this place."

Jackson snorted. "Your father didn't seem very happy about it at the time, as I recall."

"Dad just didn't want to admit this place had become an albatross around his neck."

Jackson laughed. "And now it's around mine. Thanks a lot."

Murray flashed a grin. "Don't give me that. You love it. This is the biggest erector set you've ever played with."

He was right in part. One difference between the two men was that Murray, like Casey, enjoyed working with the earth, while Jackson was more mechanically minded.

"I know this place like the back of my hand, so if you want help getting the repairs and renovations done on this white elephant," Murray said, "I'm available. With the harvest in, I'm sort of at loose ends."

"Thanks, I just may call on you."

They shook hands. Murray said goodbye to Leanna, climbed into his father's car and drove away.

The lingering smell of burned sugar and charred wood was cloying and unpleasant.

"Shall we go back to the house?" Jackson asked.

LEANNA FOLLOWED HIM to Bellefontaine. From the back porch they could hear Betty using the vacuum cleaner inside. The weather was pleasant; they decided to stay outside.

"What now?" he asked.

She walked beside him in the garden behind the west side of the mansion. "I don't really have a choice. You must realize that. I'll submit my report—"

"Which will hold up my damage claim," he muttered.

She wished she could be more encouraging. "Until this matter can be resolved." The process could take months.

"You think I had something to do with this?"

He was angry and disappointed. Under the circumstances, she would be, too. She just hoped he appreciated her position.

"Personally, no. But facts are what count for insurance companies. The big one in this case is that your sugar refinery was sabotaged, and you are in a position to profit from the loss."

He ushered her to a park bench facing the fountain his parents had built. They sat, but not too close, as if the space symbolized the gap between them.

"I gain nothing from this, Lee. If anything, it throws me into a tailspin. I don't have the capital it'll take to rebuild, much less expand the refinery, and now I have the added expense of repairing the mess that's been created."

"Maybe," she said pensively.

"Maybe? What does that mean?"

One of the things she'd come to despise about the relationship she'd had with Richard was the way they'd danced around issues. Not until the very end of their marriage had she expressed herself frankly. Richard contended that her argumentativeness had destroyed their marriage. Maybe if she'd been more assertive from the beginning, they would never have gotten married in the first place. On the other hand, she wouldn't have Elise, either.

From what Jackson had told her yesterday, the only thing that had saved the refinery itself from being destroyed was the fire wall between the warehouse and the plant.

"What would have happened," she asked, "if this attempted sabotage had gone in the other direction?"

"You mean into the refinery?"

She nodded. "You would have been compensated by the insurance company."

"Go on." He spread his arms against the back of the bench, his posture an obvious attempt to be casual. His tone, however, was a challenge, forced between his teeth.

"You would have been paid for a three-centrifuge sugar refinery."

"An obsolete refinery," he pointed out.

"Exactly. Your policy provides for recovery of full replacement cost. Your premiums were high for that reason, but you only paid them for a few months. The insurance company wouldn't have compensated you for the original value of the plant, minus depreciation. You'd have gotten all new equipment. I haven't done enough research yet to determine how that would price out, compared with the value of the current setup. In the end, though, you'd have a totally new, modern facility for significantly less than it would have cost to tear down the old structure and replace it on your own.''

He straightened, took a deep breath and rose to his feet.

''You forget,'' he said, hands in his pockets, ''I was planning to add on to the existing design, not replace it.''

''So you say. Have you got any documentation to substantiate that?''

His brows rose precipitously and his blue eyes seemed to get darker, ominous. ''I did a cost-benefit analysis, weighing the two options.''

''And what did you conclude?''

He stared at her. ''That it would be better to tear down the entire plant and start from scratch.''

She looked up at him. ''But you asked for bids from contractors to modify the existing design. Why?''

He paced, digging in his heels as anger began to work itself to the surface. ''Because I don't have the capital to invest in the larger project.''

''And the bank turned down your request for the additional money.''

He stopped, whirled, his glare intense. ''How do you know that?''

She wanted to jump to her feet, but to do so would have meant bumping into him, touching him. She didn't feel threatened by him exactly.

''I may be new to the culture of Louisiana, Jackson, but I'm not incompetent at my job—'' she stared back ''—regardless of what you told Mr. Spruance.''

The air stirred between them.

He held her gaze. ''You're saying that since I

couldn't raise the funds to completely overhaul my refinery, I tried to blow it up?''

"I'm not saying that at all." This time she did jump to her feet. Brushing past him, she took several steps toward the fountain. A shaft of sunlight slanted through the trees, turning the fine water droplets to crystal prisms in rainbow colors. "It's what the evidence suggests, and until it can be proved otherwise, the company is not going to pay out your claim."

"And in the meanwhile I sit on my hands and do nothing?" He huffed. "I don't think so."

She came up beside him and placed her hand on his forearm. The lean muscles were tight, hard. "I wouldn't expect you to. I'm not going to, either, Jackson. My job isn't to deny claims. It's to make sure they're valid. That means I need to get to the bottom of this, as well."

That marginally calmed him, but he was still troubled. "I'd hoped this was all behind us. I'm sure you know about the other insurance claims we've made over the past few months. The kitchen fire. The theft of the harvester."

"I read the reports. Apparently, you had a disgruntled employee—"

"Former employee," he corrected. "Harold Broderick. He got caught when Casey found him trying to destroy computer records. He later admitted setting the fire and stealing the new harvester. I was out of town when it happened, and Casey had a dog of a time convincing the bank to loan her the money for another new one right away. Harvest was about to begin and missing her cue in the lineup at the mill could have been disastrous, especially with her experimental cane coming in. Losing it would have destroyed her reputation with LSU."

"We traced the harvester to Mexico."

Jackson nodded. "Harold Broderick claimed he was paid by someone to burn down the house, steal the harvester and destroy Casey's records, but he couldn't identify who."

"How credible is that?"

"He said he only talked to the guy who'd hired him on the telephone. Remember the TV star who was accused of having his wife murdered in a parking lot a couple of years ago? Supposedly, he and the hit man never met face-to-face. Their only contact was by phone. So, yeah, I think it's possible. The point, though, is that Broderick's in jail, so we can't blame him for this latest episode."

"You think they're related?" she asked, though she, too, believed they were.

"We're not talking about mere accidents or an isolated coincidence, Lee. There was this other incident," he noted, "one you might not be aware of. During the harvest, Noelani was attacked in the sugar mill by Denise Rochelle, another so-called disaffected employee. She claimed to be working alone, that it was purely a personal vendetta because she blamed Duke for ruining her father. Now I'm beginning to wonder if she acted alone or if someone put her up to it."

Leanna hadn't heard of that episode. "Where is she now?"

"Also in jail." Jackson came up behind her, placed a hand on her shoulder and pointed with his finger to a blue jay perched on the edge of a thin oak branch. His touch was light but decidedly masculine.

She wasn't prepared for her impulse to roll her shoulder up into the caress. The bird fluttered away, he dropped his hands, and she let out her breath.

"Denise pleaded guilty to aggravated assault and malicious destruction of private property and was sentenced to two years."

"Maybe if I go see her she'll tell me something."

"A waste of time." Jackson circled the small of Leanna's back and guided her to the bench they'd deserted. "She was given every chance to implicate an accomplice, might even have gotten out on probation if she'd named a co-conspirator, but she had no one to fink on."

Leanna didn't doubt him, but Denise had been locked up for a month or so now. That experience could have changed her mind if she was shielding someone. The danger was that it might also compel her to make wild accusations in an attempt to shorten her sentence. Either way, any information she gave would have to be carefully evaluated.

"If there is a conspiracy," she said as she settled at one end of the seat, "there must be a mastermind. Who do you think it is?"

To her relief and disappointment, he sat at the opposite corner. Being touched by him was distracting.

"I wish I knew," he said.

"So far you've identified two ex-employees who were willing to put Fontaine lives at risk. Are your employee relations that bad?"

Jackson shook his head. "Duke was a shrewd businessman, but he wasn't a fool, and he wasn't stingy. We pay well, Lee. It's one of the ways we gain loyalty. You'll find people who've been working for our family all their lives, some of them going back several generations. The problem with Broderick wasn't us—it was him. He was a heavy drinker. Casey gave him every opportunity to straighten out his act, but he chose the bottle, instead. She had no alternative but to let him go.''

"Does he have a family?"

"Two, actually. Divorced both wives. Wasn't much of a breadwinner for either of them.''

"And this other employee, Denise Rochelle?"

He took a deep breath. "She's a different matter. Her father was a small cane grower who eventually found it impossible to make ends meet and had to put his land up for sale. Duke bought it at auction, just as he had several other small farms in the area. Denise became very bitter and blamed us for her father's failure and her loss of status. She worked for several local plantation owners, eventually getting a job in our sugar mill. It was Noelani who noticed that actual sucrose yields of Casey's experimental cane didn't match the core-sample readings Denise took. The new variety appeared to be a failure, when in fact it was producing eight percent more sucrose. Then Adam Ross showed up. Denise had had a crush on him in high school. When he started paying attention to Noelani, Denise went over the edge and attacked her.''

"Obviously, she isn't responsible for the current situation, either, so the question remains, who is?"

Jackson hunched over and rested his elbows on his knees. "I have no idea," he muttered.

"Excuse me." Neither of them had noticed Tanya's approach. "Your aunt wants to know if Ms. Cargill will be staying for dinner.''

He straightened. "Yes."

"No," Leanna said at the same time.

"We'll pick up her daughter on our way back from the mill," he continued, ignoring her. "Tell Aunt Esme we should be back in time for the cocktail hour."

The downturned corners of the nanny's mouth made it clear she wasn't pleased with the answer. "Okay." She retreated to the house.

"We've imposed enough."

He smiled. "Aunt Esme wouldn't have invited you if it was an imposition. I really would like you to stay. Elise is good for Megan and... I enjoy your company."

A simple phrase, a pleasant sentiment, but one she hadn't heard in a very long time. It conjured up warmth and friendship. Nothing more. So why did her face suddenly feel flushed?

"You haven't seen all of the house yet, anyway."

She wondered what more there could be, except a few bedrooms. "I'll think about it," she agreed, "but right now I have an appointment in the city...."

"I'll meet you back here at two, and we'll tour the sugar mill."

"THEY'RE STILL REFUSING to pay?" Nearly four months had gone by since Jackson's parents were killed in the crash of their private plane in the Italian Alps, and the insurance company continued to balk at forking over the death benefits. "They were quick enough to cash the premium checks we sent them over the years."

"As you know," Shelburne Prescott said quietly from behind his impressive mahogany desk, "the conclusion of the authorities is that it wasn't a simple accident, that your father's plane was sabotaged.''

Jackson got that sick, sour taste in his mouth whenever he thought of his parents falling helplessly from the sky. He could see his father fighting desperately to save the crippled plane, assuring Angelique that everything was going to be all right. He pictured his mother gripping the arms of the seat with white-knuckled fists, confident to the very last second that Duke would pull them out of it. When did they realize they were going to die? He could only hope the end had come quickly. He still had trouble comprehending that they would never be coming home from their long-delayed, well-deserved vacation.

''The insurance company has to rule out the possibility that the beneficiaries are in any way mixed up in their deaths,'' the family lawyer continued.

Jackson gave him a cold stare as the implications of his words penetrated. ''Are you telling me the insurance company is accusing Casey and me of killing our own parents?''

Shelburne fingered his coffee cup. ''Not accusing—''

''The hell they're not.'' Jackson jumped up from his chair, paced toward the picture window and peered at the towering capitol. The earlier downpour had slackened marginally, but it was still duck weather. He turned and scowled at the white-haired, senior partner of Prescott, Walters and Simms. ''The only justification for withholding payment from my sisters and me, the rightful beneficiaries of those policies, is if they have reason to believe we're culpable in our parents' deaths. That constitutes an accusation.''

"They have a fiduciary responsibility—"

"I don't give a damn about their rationalizations, Shel." He recognized the knot of bitterness in his words, as well as outrage and fear and vowed to stanch them, but he'd never been this scared in his life, never felt so helpless…or so ashamed. He'd been so eager to be his own boss, to prove he could get along fine without his father in the background, that he'd practically given them the bum's rush out the door. He'd imagined his parents coming home, suntanned and rejuvenated and pleased with how their son had handled the family's affairs in their absence. His mother would resume her social life with a smile on her face, and his father would buzz around the parish bragging about how Jackson had improved things so much while he was gone that he was going to turn everything over to him and retire. They'd never do any of those things now. Not ever.

The truth was, if Jackson didn't receive an infusion of money—a lot of it—damn soon, the Fontaines were headed for bankruptcy, and Bellefontaine, the plantation that had been in their family for five…no, six…generations would be lost.

"File a writ or whatever you guys do and force them to pay up," he went on, sitting down again. "Then I want to sue them for defamation of character. Nobody accuses me or mine of murder and gets away with it."

The older man watched him with patient, imperturbable brown eyes. "You're upset, Jackson, and you have every reason to be," he drawled, "but let's approach this rationally and carefully."

"Don't patronize me, Shel." Jackson hated this

feeling of not being in control. Fontaines led; they didn't follow.

Everything he and his family had ever worked for was at stake. Over time, he might be able to regain the family's good name, but once Bellefontaine was lost, it would be gone forever. Of that, he was absolutely convinced. There were too many vultures out there ready to tear it into little pieces and devour it. His sister Casey's beloved cane fields would be corporate owned. The sugar mill his half sister, Noelani, had improved with her advanced computer program would be swallowed up by someone else. Aunt Esme would have to leave the home where she'd been born and had lived in her entire life. The antebellum mansion, with its centuries-old magnolia trees and famous fountains, would become a museum, a relic of another time. No, he wouldn't have it.

"You don't seem to understand." Jackson picked up his coffee cup, took a generous mouthful of its cold contents and set it down. He had to force himself to speak moderately, temperately. "Without that insurance money, we're in serious trouble. I don't have to tell you Duke left us cash broke. Because of all the things that have been going on since his and Maman's deaths, we're in a serious financial bind. Nick—" who a few short months ago had been well-heeled "—has investment problems of his own since the buyer of his riverboat casino defaulted." He threw up his hands. "We've had one disaster after another. I had to borrow money to restore the kitchen after the fire—"

"Insurance paid for the repairs," Shelburne reminded him.

''But not all the extras that had to be done—the additional safeguards against fire and theft, sophisticated sensors, alarms, direct telephone hookups.''

''At least you can rest easy, knowing the threats of fire and vandalism have decreased.''

''At a price, and that's more to the point. There was the harvester that was stolen—''

''Insurance covered that, too,'' Shelburne said.

''Yeah, but again they took their sweet time, and they didn't reimburse me for the interest I had to cough up until then.'' Jackson fingered his cup. He would have preferred something stronger, something with shaved ice. ''To add insult to injury, our insurance premiums have almost doubled.''

Shelburne nodded sympathetically. ''I know this seems overwhelming to you at the moment, Jackson, but your father was in tight situations more than once, and he always managed to find a way out.''

Being compared with Duke didn't feel all that complimentary. He loved his father, but that didn't mean he always liked him or agreed with what he did.

''You were always there to help him, Shel,'' Jackson said smoothly. ''Is there anything you can do to help me now?''

The older man pursed his lips while he stroked his chin. ''I'll call Leland Kirk, the president of the insurance company. We've worked together before. I'll see what he can do to nudge the process along.''

Jackson tried to calculate how much time he had before his creditors started getting obnoxious. Quarterly payments for their coalition cane crop were due in soon, but accumulated bills, end-of-year bonuses and overhead would eat them up in no time. Thus far the family name had spared him the kind of harassment most people experienced when they were late with payments.

Institutional patience didn't last forever, though, even with the help of crafty lawyers. Once word got out that the Fontaines were suffering from major cash-flow problems, the house of cards his father had built would quickly come tumbling down. You could borrow from Peter to pay Paul just so long.

"I'll give you a week, then I want action, either on their part or ours." Jackson rose. "I'm dead serious about this, Shel."

The aging attorney pushed to his feet. "I know you are."

Jackson moved across the Aubusson carpet. The portly man joined him at the door. They shook hands.

"I'll be in touch with you in a day or two," Shelburne assured him.

Jackson had the feeling he shouldn't hold his breath.

CHAPTER FIVE

LEANNA'S APPOINTMENT on the east side of Baton Rouge didn't take as long as she'd expected, so she arrived back at Bellefontaine at one-thirty. She frowned at the sputtering sounds the Toyota made when she switched off the engine and started walking toward the mansion. Tanya was sitting on the veranda.

"I just got Megan to sleep," she said, as Leanna mounted the steps.

Leanna nodded. "I'm supposed to meet Jackson here at two."

"He called a little while ago to say he'd been delayed," the younger woman informed her. "Said you could wait, or he'd get with you another time."

"Did he say how long he'd be?"

"Nope. He was at his lawyer's office."

Leanna had shuffled her calendar so she could spend the afternoon with Jackson, which meant she'd be burning the midnight oil tonight and maybe tomorrow night playing catch-up. She didn't mind. She enjoyed his company, and it wasn't as if she was neglecting her work. Learning as much as she could about every aspect of the sugar industry was part of her job. Pleasant surroundings were a bonus.

"Where's Esme?"

Tanya snickered. "Taking her nap, too, though

she'd never admit it. The old bag thinks no one's onto her. Figures anybody whose pedigree doesn't match hers is stupid.''

Leanna didn't like the tone of disrespect. Her place wasn't to correct Tanya, but she couldn't let it pass. Jackson's aunt did like to wear the purple cloak, but she had treated Leanna with generosity and graciousness.

"I suggest you don't talk about Jackson's aunt that way in front of him," she advised. "He wouldn't appreciate it."

For a moment, the young woman looked ready to make a snide comment, then seemed to think better of it.

"How about Betty?" Leanna asked. "Is she around?"

"In the dining room polishing silver. With the holidays coming up, everything's got to be bright and shiny. Esme runs the poor woman ragged. Do this. Do that. I don't know why Betty puts up with it."

The girl had an attitude, and from a comment Casey had made, Tanya tended to be lackadaisical about her duties if Jackson didn't keep on top of her.

She spied the mug on the glass-topped iron table. "Is that cocoa?"

"It's Betty's Cajun coffee with chicory." Tanya's eyes narrowed. "If you're going to wait, I can get you some."

"Thanks. I would like to try it." She'd sampled the muddy brew only once since she'd been at Bellefontaine and hadn't decided if she liked it.

Tanya sprang up and strolled into the kitchen.

Leanna stood at the rail of the porch. It had rained hard in town, but there was hardly a drizzle here, though the sky was overcast. She gazed out over the grounds of Bellefontaine. Even at this transitional time of year, the landscape was beautiful. Upkeep must be enormous, but allowing the grounds to deteriorate seemed sacrilegious. The red-brick walks and sculptured gardens were drawing cards for tourists, who visited three days a week. She wondered if the family made much money from letting strangers parade through their home. Esme seemed to regard it as a civic duty.

Tanya emerged a minute later carrying a steaming mug. Leanna accepted it gratefully.

"This must be an ideal place to live and work." Leanna sipped. The rich brew already had generous amounts of milk and sugar in it, giving it a bittersweet flavor.

"I couldn't believe it when I saw the ad for a nanny on the bulletin board at school. I mean living here, getting paid and still being able to go to school in the evening."

"That must really keep you busy."

"Megan can be a handful sometimes, but mostly she's pretty easy."

"Where's her mother?" Leanna asked. "Are she and Jackson divorced?" He didn't wear a ring, and he certainly didn't act like a married man, even around his family. "Does she live around here, visit very often?"

"You don't know?" Tanya's lips curled in sly amusement. "Megan's illegitimate. Jackson got permanent custody of her when her mother was sent to prison."

"Illegitimate?" Leanna's eyes went wide. "In prison? Why?"

"Don't you have studying to do for your exams?"

They both turned to find Betty standing in the doorway. She was wearing baggy jeans today and a tasseled hide shirt that could have come directly out of the sixties. As usual, she held an unlit cigarette between the index and middle finger of her right hand.

"Why don't you go crack the books or strum your guitar or something. I'll entertain our guest."

"Hey, thanks." Either Tanya was completely oblivious to the cook's put-down, or she was a darn good actress. "I'll go get my notes." She practically flounced past Betty and disappeared inside.

"It'll take more than a college degree to give that girl an ounce of sense. She talks too much." Betty looked at Leanna's coffee. "Let me get a cup and I'll join you."

A minute later she was back. "What do you think of this stuff? Didn't get anything like it up North, I bet."

Leanna laughed. "You're right. Actually, it's not bad." She took another sip.

"Since Ms. Airhead let the cat out of the bag, I guess you might as well hear the whole story. Better from me than someone else. I'll give it to you straight."

Leanna knew she should protest that it was none of her business, but her interest was definitely piqued.

"Six years ago Jackson got engaged to Paige Paturin. If you haven't heard of the Paturins, you will. They own Sweet Meadows Plantation about twenty miles upriver. Old family. Old money. Noses in the air. Paige was definitely to the manor born, with her fancy clothes, fine education and impeccable manners. So it came as a complete shock when, two months before their wedding, she eloped with a professor at LSU.''

Leanna lowered her cup to the saucer. ''While she was still engaged to Jackson?''

''Took everyone by surprise, including her parents. The prof was almost twenty years Paige's senior and had recently divorced his wife of fifteen years. No kids, thank God. Anyway, Jackson took it pretty hard.''

''Who wouldn't?''

Betty toyed with her cigarette, bits of tobacco spilling out the end onto the table. ''He went a little wild after that. He was always popular, liked to have a good time, but I wouldn't exactly call him a party animal. After Paige, though, he started drinking too much, staying out all night, hanging around with people who weren't going to do him any damn good. That's when he met Janis Donagan.''

Leanna sipped her coffee and waited.

''She was a cocktail waitress at one of them fancy lounges in the city. Jackson brought her out here once.'' Betty laughed, a throaty whiskey-voice sound. ''Angelique was appalled. Esme practically had the vapors.'' She chuckled gleefully. ''And Duke had a fit. Told Jackson it was time to get over Paige. If he wanted to keep a piece of fluff on the side, it was his business, but he was not to bring women of that sort home.''

''Wow.''

''Yep. A real stink. Jackson didn't take it kindly, but it sobered him up. A few weeks later he broke up with Janis. More coffee?''

Leanna declined. Betty went inside and refilled her cup.

"About a month after that, she called Jackson," Betty said after sitting down. "She was pregnant and claimed it was his kid."

"Megan," Leanna contributed.

Betty nodded. "When the paternity test came back positive, Jackson was ready to marry her. Duke told him he was crazy, that within a year, two at the most, they would be at each other's throats, and that would make it even worse for the baby. He wanted Jackson to pay her off and get her to move out of state."

"But she refused?"

Betty pursed her lips and shook her head. "He did. He and Duke had the worst fight I ever heard them have, and they had had a few over the years. Duke was no angel, and...well...maybe Jackson isn't, either, but he used to really get furious at the way his father manipulated people."

"I heard Duke was quite a wheeler-dealer."

"In spades." Betty chuckled. "I could tell you some stories... Anyway, Jackson agreed not to marry her, but he insisted on his name going on the birth certificate, and he made a legal arrangement to pay child support in exchange for visitation rights."

That was a twist. Most unwed fathers had to be forced into supporting their offspring.

"He fell in love with that kid," Betty went on. "I don't think he expected to. He just wanted to do the right thing. But when he'd bring her here—without Janis, of course—you could see it, the love and pride in his eyes."

Leanna had seen it when they were together, too. "How did his parents react to their granddaughter?"

"At first, they weren't particularly receptive, but they weren't bad people." All of a sudden, Betty's voice tightened, and Leanna realized that, in spite of her posturing, this woman felt a deep emotional bond with the family.

"Tanya said Megan's mother is in prison. Is that true?"

Betty twisted her mouth and nodded. "Last year Jackson was getting concerned about the company Janis was keeping. She'd just left the lounge and started hustling drinks in a topless bar. Maintained that the tips were a lot better. Probably were, too. She was also keeping company with one of the owners of the place. Jackson met the guy a couple of times. Fancy dresser, drove a new BMW. Megan called him Uncle Frank and seemed to like him, but Jackson didn't think it was a good environment for the kid. He was getting ready to petition the court for custody of Megan when Frank was picked up for drug dealing and Janis was arrested as an accomplice."

"So she was into drugs, too?"

"Claimed she wasn't, that she never allowed anyone to use them around the kid. Thanks to Judge Sarratt, Jackson got immediate and permanent custody. That was almost six months ago. Janis pleaded guilty a month later to distributing a controlled substance and was sentenced to five years in prison."

"Poor Megan."

"She's a Fontaine. She'll come through just fine, especially with Jackson to protect her."

Leanna smiled, remembering his comment that Fontaines have steel for backbones. She hoped it was true. Little girls needed strong daddies, but they also needed good mommies.

Leanna toyed with her coffee cup and was mulling Jackson's conduct as a father, when the man in question showed up.

THEY DROVE to the sugar mill in his Jag. He enjoyed owning the luxury car, the mild pungency of its fine leather. Even more, he liked the feel of Leanna sitting beside him and the smell of her. Nothing heavy, just a delicate feminine scent.

He pulled up alongside the entry station. There several huge wire-sided wagons loaded with cut cane sat lined up, waiting to be weighed and to have samples taken from the core to determine their sucrose contents.

"Noelani runs the mill now," he said. "I used to, but I'm tied up with the refinery these days. She's made major improvements in the computer system. Production is up more than ten percent."

Over the next hour, Jackson and Noelani escorted Leanna through the milling process, starting outside where billets—six-to-eight-inch lengths of cut cane— were stacked fifteen feet high. Inside they climbed pierced-steel steps and marched along catwalks overlooking the entire operation.

"The smell keeps changing," Leanna noted as she rose to the third level, where the control panels were located. "At the beginning it was sort of sour, then it grew sweeter and now it smells like molasses."

Jackson nodded. "We try to move those mountains of cut cane as fast as we can—within twenty-four hours—but stored in piles like that, there's a certain amount of fermentation that naturally begins. That's the sour smell you noticed.''

"As we go through the process,'' Noelani continued, "pressing the cane, separating and clarifying the juice, we remove a lot of the impurities, producing a cleaner smell, a little like sugar, but not quite.''

"Then we crystallize it—'' Jackson again took up the narrative "—by evaporation. That's when you start to get that cooked-sugar smell.''

They moved to the last stage of the process. "These centrifuges,'' Noelani explained, "extract as much of the molasses as possible. The results are two components—raw sugar and blackstrap, which is used in sweet feed for animals.''

They proceeded to the warehouse, where fat-tired, front-end loaders scooped up huge piles of the tan granulated raw sugar and dumped it into trucks for transport to refineries.

Leanna looked around. The building was industrial, a tin cavern with a concrete floor, but it was also very clean. "How do you control bugs and vermin?'' she asked.

Jackson smiled. "We don't have to. We have no ants, no mice or rats. Apparently, sugar in these quantities is too rich for them. They're not interested. Even bees don't come in here. They sometimes fly through the open doorway, but never penetrate more than about six feet. Occasionally, they'll build a hive outside, but not often. When they do, we call an apiarist, who comes and removes them safely and gives them good homes elsewhere.''

The sky had cleared and the sun was shining when they emerged outside.

"Almost time to pick up Elise,'' Jackson said,

glancing at his watch. "You will join us for dinner, won't you?"

She grinned. "Yes."

"HOW'S THE CLEANUP at the refinery going?" Nick asked, over the rim of his beer glass several evenings later.

"We're making progress. Billy Doyle got the bid."

"Billy Doyle? Doesn't he work for Woody Stevens?" Casey asked.

"Used to," Jackson replied. "He set up his own construction company eight months ago."

"He's a gambler then," his sister commented. "Woody's a charter member of the good ole boys' club. That's tough to buck."

Duke had been tight with Woody and would probably have given him the job without even asking for a second bid, but Jackson was determined to be his own man.

"Stevens gets every road-building contract in the parish," Casey pointed out, "often without competition."

"Is that legal?" Leanna asked.

Adam grinned. "It's called politics. It paves a lot of roads."

"Stevens has been growing complacent and lazy," Jackson pointed out, "and Billy's young, smart and ambitious. He's playing it low key, not trying to compete with the old man for now, bidding on the marginal jobs Woody isn't particularly interested in. As long as he performs well, on time and on budget, he has a fair chance of carving out his own niche and getting stronger."

"What are you going to do about the plant itself?" Nick asked.

"Murray and I have been reviewing several options. I'd like to replace the existing centrifuges and install new, high-efficiency ones, but I don't have the capital right now. Murray's located a couple of used centrifuges of essentially the same design and capacity and found three contractors who are willing to bid on the expansion project."

"He's been busy," Adam said. "Let me know who the contractors are and I'll do some checking through my channels to see what kind of reputations they have."

"I'd appreciate that," Jackson told him.

Esme finished the last mouthful of her julep. "You're making a mistake, depending on a Dewalt," she insisted. "They're not trustworthy."

Casey took a sip of her beer. "You have reason not to like his father, Roland—"

"Jackson—" Esme cut off her niece "—may I have another julep, please?" She rarely had two.

"Coming right up." He took the crystal glass from her outstretched hand and walked to the bar, casting his sister a warning glance.

Casey scrunched up her mouth. "I understand my brother has been showing you around Baton Rouge," she said to Leanna. "How do you like it?"

"It's a beautiful city," Leanna agreed. "We went to the old capital yesterday afternoon. Elise had never been in a real castle before."

Noelani chuckled. "I hadn't, either. I don't know why Mark Twain hated the place so much. I think it's neat."

"He considered it decadent," Adam said. "I have

to agree with him. Still, it's an interesting landmark.''

Tanya appeared a minute later with the two girls.
Betty was right behind her to announce supper was
ready. They proceeded to the dining room.

The meal that followed was leisurely, and the discussion had now turned to architecture. Leanna listened, only occasionally chiming in with an obser-
vation or a question. Later, she helped clear the
dishes and let Elise go up to Megan's room to play
with the new tea set Jackson had brought home that
afternoon.

"Am I being too nosy if I ask what was behind
Casey's remark to Esme that she had a reason to
dislike Roland Dewalt?" Leanna asked. She and
Jackson were walking through the garden.

He snickered. "You picked up on that, huh?"

"Sorry. I shouldn't be asking," she apologized.
"It's none of my business."

All families had secrets and were entitled to their
privacy. In her case, it was a great-aunt who'd been
married six times, always to men old enough to be
her father—in one instance, her grandfather. She was
something of a legend, rather than a hidden secret,
and, Leanna suspected, an object of unspoken envy,
since she'd survived every one of her husbands and
inherited their considerable fortunes—all of which
she left to an animal shelter.

"You want the family dirt, eh?" Jackson led her
to their usual bench in the rose garden. "You'll find
it out eventually, being the outstanding investigator
you are—"

He was mocking her. Remembering their initial
encounter, she could take offense but chose to laugh,

instead. "That wasn't your first evaluation of my skills, if I recall."

His grin could have been a smirk. "One must guard against snap judgments."

He sat beside her, not exactly touching but near enough for her to be aware of the heat of his body. Close enough for him to reach for her hand. This probably wasn't a good idea. She ought to pull away, but she didn't. Her hand felt comfortable in his.

"The story goes back more than thirty years," he said, "to Esme's salad days. She's what I guess you would call a handsome woman now, but the pictures of her back then show her to have been…maybe not exactly beautiful, but very pretty. Her features were soft. They hadn't yet acquired their sharp edges. Still, she had a firmness in her expression that spoke of strength."

Some people Leanna couldn't imagine as young—like her old piano teacher, who seemed to have been created at some indeterminate age with tortoiseshell combs in her battleship-gray hair. Esme was like that. Timeless and unchanging. An institution rather than a person.

"Roland Dewalt," Jackson went on, "was a handsome eligible bachelor back then, and he was engaged to her. Their impending marriage was considered an excellent match for both of them. Old money, class."

Having not met Roland, Leanna tried to picture his son, Murray, in the role. Thirty-plus years ago, the late sixties, early seventies. Did he wear bell-bottom trousers, turtlenecks and a nickel-plated peace medallion? She glanced up at Jackson. Leather, she decided. Sexy black leather, soft, tight fitting and shiny. The image was tantalizing and made her chuckle.

He cocked his head, unsure what he'd said that was so funny.

"Sorry," she muttered. "I'm just having a hard time picturing them in the Age of Aquarius."

His expression was skeptical. "I never thought of that." After a pause, he went on. "Esme followed the old tradition among the Creole of Louisiana—went to France, attended the Sorbonne and majored in French art and literature." He looked over at Lee. "I'm sure that if you ever want to discuss de Maupassant or Mauriac, she could satisfy your wish. And you would probably make a friend for life."

Leanna grinned. "I'll keep that in mind."

"Anyway, she was finishing her last year there and brought her roommate, Angelique Rabaud, home for the Christmas holidays—apparently, with a bit of matchmaking in mind for her brother."

"Angelique? Your mother?"

"Uh-huh." His thumb stroked the back of Leanna's hand. "But we're getting ahead of the story. Esme introduced her friend to all the eligible young men at the Christmas ball."

"Did your mother speak English?" Leanna asked.

"Perfectly, but with a British accent at the time. People around here were enchanted with her exotic English and, of course, her impeccable French and she became the absolute hit of the social season. Esme's real hope was that Angelique and Duke would hit it off. They did. But Roland also took an unexpected shine to the visitor. The holiday season turned into a good old-fashioned flirting contest.

Both men strutting their stuff in front of the beauty from France.''

''But you said Roland was engaged to Esme.''

Jackson frowned. ''Their wedding was planned for the spring, but he not only started making passes at Angelique, he asked Esme for his heirloom ring he'd given her so he could offer it to Angelique.''

''What a hideous turn of events. Esme coming home bubbling and happy, doing her best to share her happiness with her best friend, only to be betrayed by the man she'd expected to spend the rest of her life with.''

''Exactly,'' Jackson replied. ''In fact, Roland did ask Angelique to marry him, but he was too late. She'd already accepted my father's proposal. Roland was enraged. A century earlier, he would have challenged Duke to a duel. Esme was crushed and humiliated. My grandfather was furious, and so the great family feud began.''

''A regular Hatfield-McCoy,'' Leanna observed.

''This one is better,'' Jackson observed. ''Theirs started over a pig. Ours was over a woman.''

He could make light of it now, Leanna thought, but it obviously wasn't funny to Esme, the innocent victim in the intrigue. ''And so, Esme never married.'' How sad.

''I understand she had several opportunities after that, but declined all suitors.''

''Does she still love Roland, do you think?''

Jackson let the question linger for a minute before he answered. ''I've heard that love and hate are kissing cousins. If I had to attribute an emotional response on her part to Roland now, I'd say she loathes him.''

"He certainly seems to have done a number on her psychologically...destroyed her confidence as a woman."

"More like destroyed any hope that a man could be faithful. Esme adored her brother, Duke. She maintains she didn't know about Noelani until the reading of my father's will, but I wonder. It would help explain her unwillingness ever to commit herself to a man. For his part, Roland was convinced Duke had stolen *his* woman. He seemed to forget Angelique was the one who made the decision not to marry him. Maybe it all would have died down, if over the years, Dewalt fortunes hadn't gradually declined while ours rose."

"Why was that?"

"Roland's got more pride than intelligence. My father was proud, too, but he was also a pretty slick businessman. Technically, he didn't do anything illegal—that I know of—but he came darn close sometimes, and Duke wasn't shy about taking advantage of a situation."

The next question seemed so obvious Jackson must have asked it himself. "Could Roland be behind all the problems you've been having?"

He shook his head. "The wind went out of his sails years ago. He's pretty much settled down into a harmless, if somewhat premature, dotage. Were he motivated to do anything against us, it would have been years ago when there was something for him to gain."

"I gather from Casey's comments that Murray doesn't share his father's dislike of the Fontaine family."

"He and I have always gotten along fine. Casey

likes him, too—as a friend. A strain developed between them a few months ago when he asked her to marry him. By then she'd met Nick. The irony is that Roland not only approved but encouraged the union.'' Jackson chuckled. ''I guess he figured if you can't beat them, join them. The combination of our two estates had the potential for a very profitable alliance.''

Leanna cocked her head in thought. ''How has Murray handled Casey rejecting him?''

''I'd say a lot better than his father did under similar circumstances.'' Jackson stood up and, still holding her hand, pulled her gently to her feet. ''Enough about other people and other times. Let's talk about the present.'' He led her along the brick path that hemmed in a small square garden on the east side of the house.

''Casey and I are considering building our fountain here at the end of Whistle Walk. What do you think?''

''Why do you call it that?''

He chuckled softly, close to her ear, or it seemed that way. ''I guess we can't escape history.'' He put his arm around her shoulder. She hadn't been aware of how chill the night had become until she felt the warmth of his body. She had to fight the temptation to snuggle against him.

''In the old days, kitchens were outbuildings, because of the heat they produced and the danger of fire. When the slaves carried platters of food to the house, they were ordered to whistle so the master or mistress would know they weren't sampling it. The path they used was, therefore, called Whistle Walk.''

Leanna shook her head. ''Fascinating...and sad.''

He turned so they were facing each other. "The only thing that's left is the walk and the garden that replaced the kitchen."

His hands had moved down to her hips. Trying very hard to concentrate on the discussion, she asked, "Have you picked out a design for your fountain yet?"

"Noelani is helping us with it. You can be sure it'll incorporate pineapples."

"The symbol of welcome." Her voice was barely above a whisper. "Appropriate."

"The moon is out," Jackson murmured. "In the moonlight, it's appropriate for a man to kiss a woman."

The night grew still. He angled his head and captured her mouth. Her breath caught and something inside her trembled. She heard a soft sigh and realized it was her own. The kiss was sweet, gentle, not shy as much as patient. An invitation rather than an invasion. When he slowly wrapped his arms around her, she settled into the embrace, entwined her arms under his and felt the lean muscles of his back. It had been so long since a man had held her. She had no right to this, but just for a minute, she wanted to savor his touch.

"Moonbeams become you," he muttered, when at last he broke off. He wasn't normally a patient man in his relations with women, but with Lee, even though his urges were strong, he was willing to take his time. Leanna Cargill wasn't just another woman. What he felt for her wasn't only the craving to have sex, though that was embarrassingly obvious. It was a desire to mate, to bond, to join in a way he'd never experienced.

He wanted her differently than he'd ever wanted another woman, yet—or maybe because—he wanted her so completely he was willing to wait until they were both sure. There was a word for the yearning he was beginning to experience, but he wasn't ready to use it. After all, he'd felt this way once before, and the affair had ended in disaster.

CHAPTER SIX

LEANNA SPENT the following morning on the west side of Baton Rouge inspecting the ruins of a mobile home. The fire investigator was satisfied that the blaze that had destroyed it had been accidental, the result of an overloaded, aluminum-wire electrical circuit. The family had barely managed to get out with their lives. All their possessions had been lost, including the brand-new car in their carport. Relief and charitable organizations were already on the scene, offering temporary housing and other assistance.

She decided to go home, fix herself a sandwich, write her report and file it from her laptop before setting out on her next assignment. A plumbing repair truck was stationed in the middle of the parking lot when she pulled into her apartment complex. She paid scant attention to it. In low-income housing, things were constantly breaking down. The landlord, who lived on the property, fixed most of them himself, often with chewing gum and baling wire, but Leanna couldn't really complain. The rent was cheap, and after splurging on a couple of gallons of bargain paint, the place was relatively comfortable and clean.

Gilbert Alain, the landlord, came out to meet her in a dirty T-shirt, wisps of gray hair standing on end. His jowly face was flushed with perspiration.

"Ms. Cargill," he said anxiously, "I tried to reach you, but you didn't answer your page."

"I was probably out of range," she explained. "What's the matter? What's happened?"

"A little problem." From the way he kept his eyes averted, she suspected it was probably more than little. "You know the Johnsons moved out last week."

A nice family, just getting started. They had a baby boy. Lew had finally received his degree in business administration from LSU and taken a job in New Orleans with an advertising agency. They were moving up, and Leanna was happy for them.

"Nobody scheduled to move in till Tuesday. Well, since the place was empty, there was no way of knowing the commode was running constantly. Can't understand it. I did a walk-through with them just before they left. Everything was fine. Anyway, it overflowed and flooded the bathroom and half the bedroom."

Leanna swallowed. Their apartment was directly above her.

"The Garnets called me a couple of hours ago." Leanna's next-door neighbors were an elderly couple living on social security. "Said they heard a crash in your place and wondered if everything was all right. Since you weren't home, they thought maybe someone broke in."

Burglary? What would anybody possibly want? She had so little. The TV maybe. Well, she and Elise could live without it if they had to. But replacing other things, such as clothes, would be another nail in her financial coffin. Then she remembered the plumbing repair truck and the malfunctioning toilet and waited for Mr. Alain to get to the rest of the story.

"I'm afraid...well, the ceiling in your bedroom and kitchen caved in."

"What?" Her stomach roiled.

"It's a mess, Ms. Cargill. I'm real sorry."

Leanna rushed past him to the half-open door of her apartment. Dirty footprints had beaten a path from the entrance to the alcove that separated the kitchen from the single bedroom she shared with Elise. The ceiling in the bathroom was buckled. Water was still dripping down the front of the cabinets. Stepping gingerly across the sodden carpet, she found even worse devastation in the bedroom. There the ceiling had actually collapsed. Soggy plasterboard curled around a yawning gap that exposed aged wooden joists. The orange shag carpet, the dressers—everything was covered with gray dirt and wet grime. Her bed was a total disaster, as was Elise's single trundle on the other side of the room. Leanna opened the closet door. Thin wire hangers sagged under the weight of drenched garments. Several had fallen to the floor. Even her shoes had pools of water in them.

"Mr. Alain, what am I going to do?" She was heartsick, an overwhelming sense of defeat gnawing at her.

He shook his head. "If I had another vacant apartment, Ms. Cargill, I'd give it to you rent-free for a month, but the Johnsons' place was the only one available, and it's nearly as bad as this. It'll take forever to get everything dried out. I'll have to redo the ceilings and floors—"

"I need a place to live." She really wasn't interested in his problems at the moment. He still had a dry home to go to, and he didn't have a young child to care for.

"I got some friends with apartments," he said, with more hope than encouragement. "I can check to see if they have any openings."

"You'll have to put us up in a motel until I can find something suitable," she told him.

"I don't know about that, Missus."

"I do. Your insurance will cover this, so I better start calling around."

Alain grumbled, as if the money were coming out of his own pocket.

"Well, I guess that's right," he conceded. His mind seemed to be adding up nickels, dimes and dollars. "Get yourself settled. Send me the bill, and I'll reimburse you."

Her husband had suckered her with promises to repay bills in the future if she'd just take care of them now. She wasn't about to fall into that trap again. "No," she said adamantly, "the bill will be in your name, not mine."

He was flustered. "I'm not sure I can."

"You can and you will, Mr. Alain. This situation is a direct result of your negligence. If I have to take you to court to resolve the matter, it'll cost you a lot more than the price of a few nights in a motel, I assure you."

"No need to make threats, Ms. Cargill." He was acting offended, but she could also see he was worried.

"I'm simply explaining the consequences if you don't fulfill your responsibility. We can handle this in a friendly manner, or it can get ugly." She soft-

ened her tone. "I'm not trying to take advantage of
you, Mr. Alain, but I have my rights and you have
legal obligations. I also have a young daughter to
think about."

He was angry, but plainly, he was in a box. He
stared at her. She stared back, hard and unflinching,
just to let him know she had no intention of backing
down. Not one inch.

"Who's your insurance carrier?" she asked.

The question agitated him, his eyes shifting before
he named a prominent company.

"I'll be glad to look at your policy, call the claims
department and help you get this settled expeditiously."

"That won't be necessary. I'll call them myself."

She wasn't sure if the notion of a woman handling
his affairs irritated him or the general implication that
he couldn't deal with them himself. Either way, he
clearly didn't want her meddling—even if it might
be helpful. She shrugged off his rejection. Dealing
with adjusters was his problem this time, not hers.
Her predicament was how she was going to find another place to live on such short notice. Elise's life
had been disrupted enough in the past couple of
months; she didn't need this, too.

She surveyed the miserable condition of her meager belongings and would gladly have lain down on
the bed for a good cry, had the bed not been such a
calamity of its own.

Over the next hour, she bullied Alain into cough-
ing up a credit-card number to pay for a room in a
nearby motel until she could find another apartment.
When she'd come down to Baton Rouge at her own
expense for her interview she'd stayed at the Star-

light. It wasn't luxurious by any means, but it was decent and reasonably clean. Closer to Elise's school, too, so she could walk her there and back. That would save a little wear and tear on her already worn-and-torn car.

She needed to salvage enough clothing to get them through the next few days. One would expect an insurance investigator to have renter's coverage, but she didn't. It had been an expense she didn't think she could afford, especially with all the other bills she was trying to pay off. Bad gamble. What she couldn't browbeat out of her landlord or his insurance company, she would have to bleed out of an already anemic budget. The next task was sorting through soggy clothes.

Water had even seeped into the cardboard dresser she'd gotten for Elise's things. Fortunately, they were all washable. She loaded a basket and hauled it to the laundry room, where she counted out quarters for the washing machines and dryers. Her own undergarments had survived the flood, but the few good outfits she'd kept, those that she'd stopped wearing because they required dry cleaning, were history. She made a careful inventory of the ruined items and the expenses she was incurring on redeeming the rest. As soon as she was permanently settled somewhere, she'd submit her list of damages for reimbursement.

Between transferring jeans from washers to dryers, she began the daunting task of locating another permanent place to live. She found a one-room, efficiency apartment that, based on the newspaper descriptions, would do, but when she telephoned, the rent was nearly double what she was paying here.

Any hopes she'd had of getting out from under her debts were as damp now as her bedroom carpet.

Not until nearly three o'clock did she remember Jackson's invitation for dinner at Bellefontaine. Elise and Megan were getting along famously. Even Esme had commented that her grandniece seemed to be coming out of her shell.

Esme answered the phone. "My dear, that's simply dreadful," she said when Leanna explained what had happened. "I'll inform Jackson immediately. I'm certain he'll want to help in any way he can."

"That's very kind of you, and him, but everything's pretty much taken care of." She explained that she'd already tracked down another place to live, not bothering to mention that she hadn't made a commitment on it yet. Perhaps in the next few days something better, or at least less expensive, would miraculously appear.

She was carrying a plastic bag full of Elise's pajamas and underwear from the laundry room to her Toyota when Jackson showed up. His shiny maroon sedan, with its gleaming chrome trim, looked totally out of place, making her conscious of just how shabby her surroundings were.

"How did you know to find me here?" she asked, when he greeted her. She hadn't told Esme where she was, and had pointedly not given him her address. People who lived in the style of Bellefontaine didn't visit run-down rentals in this part of town.

"I called Ripley Spruance." His eyes swept her as if he were making sure she hadn't sprouted gills. "Are you trying to hide from me?"

"Why would I do that?" She shoved the still-warm garments into a corner of her trunk, all the time doing her best not to show him how glad she was to see him.

"No reason you should. Pretty messy?"

She took a deep breath and let it out. The fact was, she was ashamed of having to live like this, in poverty, scrimping and saving every penny she could to pay debts she'd never incurred. Not just ashamed, angry. But being angry was better than being bitter. She wouldn't give in to that temptation, strong as it was. In spite of everything, she still had Elise. She'd live in sackcloth if she had to for her daughter.

"Yeah. Pretty messy."

"Can I take a look?" He glanced at the open door to her apartment.

She didn't want him to see where she lived…how she lived. With cardboard dressers and sparse, battered furniture. "There's nothing you can do. Everything is under control."

"Let me help with the rest of your stuff," he offered, studying her.

Go away, she wanted to tell him. *Don't add to my humiliation by pretending everything is fine. Everything isn't fine. I want to cry, but I can't do that with you standing here.* Instead, she said, "I'm just about finished. I have to pick up Elise in a few minutes."

"Where are you going to stay?"

"We've got temporary accommodations."

"Where?"

Why wouldn't he go away? Why did he insist on embarrassing her like this?

"Where are you staying?" he repeated, his tone more insistent this time.

Temper flared. He had no right to make demands of her. She managed somehow to keep her voice casual. "At the Starlight, until I sign the lease on a new place."

She saw the frown of disappointment, but he quickly replaced it with a neutral expression. *I'm doing the best I can,* she wanted to yell at him. *Leave me alone.* But she didn't say it, and she didn't tell him that at the moment she wanted more than anything for him to take her into his arms. Then, of course, she'd be lost, all hope of dignity vanished. She turned as if to retrieve another bag of clothing, but it was really to retreat from his searching eyes.

"I'll help you move in."

Move what in? she almost blurted out. They'd be living out of cardboard boxes and sitting on beanbag chairs for the foreseeable future. She didn't need Jackson Fontaine to help her cart them in.

"Thanks," she said, "but I—"

"Have everything under control." He completed her sentence for her. "Where's your new place?"

"I haven't made a final selection yet. I want to check out a few options before I decide."

He nodded. "You're wise to not jump at the first thing that comes along."

As if she had many choices.

"Why don't you leave this stuff here for the time being. We'll go pick up Elise, then I'll help you transfer your belongings."

He really was trying to be helpful, she supposed. But it still made her uncomfortable. Or rather, he did. She felt frumpy, dowdy, like Cinderella after midnight, standing beside a pumpkin, surrounded by mice.

"Thanks, Jackson, but I know you have other

things to do. Elise and I can handle this fine. It'll be another adventure for her.''

"Hey," he said, brightening, "I like adventures, too.''

It was no use. He was going to stick around, unless she got rude. Even that might not work. "Let me lock things up first.'' She barked out a laugh. "There's isn't much to steal, but—'' She shut up. Why draw attention to her meager belongings.

He nodded and leaned against the side of his car. She could feel him watching her as she reentered her apartment. She wanted him to go away, but the truth was she was glad he stayed. It was the idea of having another adult to share her problems with, she told herself, but she knew it was more than that. She and Jackson Fontaine hadn't known each other long enough to call themselves real friends, even though he had kissed her and she'd kissed him back. Maybe she was simply being naive. Heaven knows, she was good at that, but somehow their relationship seemed to have gone beyond the realm of their being mere acquaintances. Or was he just playing with her?

She found a box of crayons behind Elise's dresser. Soggy, but it would dry. Clutching it triumphantly, she returned to the parking lot. Jackson opened the passenger door for her. She smiled wanly and slid inside.

The soft, luxurious interior of the Jaguar mocked her as they drove the half-dozen blocks to the school.

"The *garçonnière* is still available," he pointed out casually, his eyes straight ahead. "We can move your things there.''

"Thanks, but no.'' She fluttered her hands to

punctuate her polite refusal. "We're going to be fine."

"It would be a perfect setup," he continued. "Our two kids get along so well. Elise has been wonderful for Megan. She seems to open up more every time Elise comes to visit. I know Megs is lonely for companions her own age. Next year she'll be entering kindergarten, too. Was it hard for you letting her go?"

Torment would be a better description. Elise had been eager to start school, like a big girl, but when the time came and she had to release Leanna's hand, the child had displayed hesitation and uncertainty. Her first time away from her mother, and it had scared them both.

She gave a half shrug. "As you say, kids need to socialize with others their own ages. The first day was difficult, but it got gradually easier after that." Leanna still worried, though. She would home-school Elise if she could, if she didn't have to work full-time outside the house.

"So, how about we pick up Elise, go back and get your things and move you into the *garçonnière*? You won't have to worry about day care, either, because Tanya can baby-sit her along with Megan. A win-win situation." He smiled over at her happily, proud of himself for solving her problem.

His plan had merit, but a woman had her pride. "I appreciate your offer," she said. "It's very generous, but I'll manage."

"Why not let me help?" He sounded disappointed, offended.

She wouldn't allow herself to cry, so the only emotion left seemed to be anger. "Because I'm perfectly capable of taking care of my daughter on my own,'' she said harshly. ''Thank you very much.''

He didn't say anything for a moment, and she thought—hoped—he'd let the matter rest. No such luck.

''I'm not asking you to abrogate your responsibility,'' he replied calmly, almost pleadingly. ''I'm just offering you an opportunity to improve the circumstances for your daughter and mine. Those kids deserve every chance we can give them.''

''Please don't use the guilt-trip technique on me, Jackson. I've had it tried by the best. You're good— I'll give you that—but you don't hold a candle to my ex.''

His jaw tightened. ''I may not be the best father in the world, and maybe I'm coming to it later than I should, but I love my daughter. I won't use her, and won't allow her to be used.''

''I...I didn't mean it that way.'' She lowered her voice.

''How did you mean it?''

She wasn't accustomed to this kind of conversation. Richard blamed; he didn't discuss. And now, put to the test, she wasn't sure she could explain how she felt or exactly why, especially to a guy who never had to worry about money, about where to live; a man who had no idea what it was to survive from one paycheck to the next.

''I don't like being manipulated,'' she finally declared. ''You made a generous offer, one I thank you for, but one I've declined. That's my right, and I'd very much appreciate it if you'd respect it. As kind as your offer is, I don't owe you an explanation why I choose not to take it.''

Jackson turned his head and stared at Leanna, stunned for a moment by the forcefulness of her argument. He didn't like being compared with her ex-husband, but ever since he'd kissed her, he'd found himself comparing her with Paige, noting how different the two women were. In a situation like this, Paige would have acceded to his request without a second thought. *Whatever you say, Jackson. Oh, you're so clever, Jackson. How sweet of you, Jackson.* He thought he'd liked the superior role, being the *man* in charge.

He looked over at Leanna. She didn't play the helpless female. She had a mind of her own. He found that much more stimulating, much more challenging.

Halting at a stop sign, he reached across the back of the seat and touched her shoulder, then wormed his fingers over to caress her neck. He could feel the taut muscles there and the pulse throbbing under the smooth, warm skin.

"Lee, I'm sorry. I didn't mean to insult you. You're right, you don't owe me an explanation."

A horn beeped behind him. Reluctantly, he withdrew his hand, clutched the steering wheel and stepped on the accelerator. The school was halfway down the next block. He located a spot at the curb not far from the front door, shifted the transmission into park and swiveled to face her. She was biting her lips, on the verge of tears. He wanted to take her into his arms and soothe her, but instinct told him this wasn't the moment for that kind of intimacy.

"Can I propose a compromise? If you won't take the *garçonnière* for free, pay me the same rent you've been paying at the Cane Billet Arms."

She shook her head. "The *garçonnière* is worth a lot more than that." People were willing to cough up big bucks for addresses like Bellefontaine Plantation.

"We don't normally rent it out. It's a guest house for friends of the family." He couldn't resist. He reached over and began to gently massage her neck again. "And you and Elise are friends of the family." He'd put the money she gave him in a special account for Elise's education. "Plus," he added, "Tanya can mind Elise just as easily as she does Megan. They all get along so well together."

"I'll pay for baby-sitting my daughter," Leanna insisted. "Not you."

She was weakening. Now, if he could find a way to cinch the deal and not offend her. "How about this? I don't expect Tanya to baby-sit two for the price of one, but I wouldn't expect her to charge twice as much, either. Let me find out what the going rate is for two kids, and you pay the difference."

"Even if it's more than what I'm paying Mrs. Peltière?"

"Absolutely." He'd have to find out what Peltière was charging and be sure this didn't come out higher.

"You're very generous, Jackson," she finally admitted, her voice small and humble, "but—"

"Lee," he coaxed sympathetically, "I'm not being completely unselfish. This gives me an advantage, too. As I told you, I like the idea of Megan having someone to play with, especially Elise. I think this will be good for both of them."

He could see her weighing the pros and cons. In the end, he knew, her daughter's best interests would be the deciding factor.

"Aunt Esme might not be too happy with two kids running around the place," she argued weakly.

He chuckled. "Don't tell her I said this, but dear sweet Esme is beginning to mellow in her old age. You've seen the way she is with the girls. She may not be willing to admit it yet, but she loves having them around." He chuckled. "Especially if she can teach them proper manners."

Leanna laughed, and a sense of relief invaded him. At the sound of the school bell, kids exploded through the front door. She got out and waved when her daughter appeared. "Let's see how Elise feels about it," she suggested.

Jackson smiled. He had no doubt what her response would be.

MOVING INTO the *garçonnière* took less than an hour. All they had were clothes and a few of Elise's toys. Leanna found the building fascinating. In the nineteenth century, the compact octagonal, two-story structure had constituted bachelor quarters for the plantation owner's teenage boys. It had been renovated over the years, amenities added. Downstairs she found a comfortably furnished living room and half bath, as well as an efficiency kitchen, complete with a microwave and refrigerator. The upstairs was comprised of a single large bedroom and full bath. Sharing the bedroom with Elise was no problem. They were used to it. They'd stay here a month, two at the most, until Alain's insurance paid up, then she'd find them a place of their own.

Two days later, Leanna came home from work and freshened up. She only barely managed to resist the temptation to stretch out on the bed—for just a minute to rest her eyes—knowing one minute would turn into five and five into a nap she couldn't afford to take. She was already late for the cocktail hour. Not that she craved a drink. She'd had one glass of white wine the evening before, and it had made her so sleepy she'd vowed not to take anything stronger than orange juice again, not with Elise around.

Dinner with the family had not been part of the deal she'd made with Jackson, but when the invitation was extended, it was hard to say no under the circumstances. Elise had bounded off to the mansion this afternoon as soon as they'd gotten home. Now, passing through the garden, Leanna mounted the steps of the back porch. No longer regarded as a stranger, she let herself in and started toward the drawing room.

"Mommy, Mommy—" Elise clattered down the stairs with something blue in her hand "—Mommy, I got a letter from Daddy. See."

Leanna had put in a change of address card the previous morning and was surprised the mail was already being rerouted. Pasting on a smile, she tried not to let her anxiety show. Elise was always excited at the prospect of seeing her father. Well, at least she didn't have to worry about that. He was in New York. They were in Louisiana. A card couldn't upset the child nearly as much as one of his visits. She was just reaching for the envelope when Jackson appeared in the doorway of the drawing room a few feet away.

"Somebody seems awfully excited," he said with a smile on his face and a glass of beer in his hand.

"My daddy's coming to see me," Elise blurted.

"Oh, honey," Leanna said. "I don't think so."

"He is. He is," the girl insisted. "He says so right here." She fumbled to get the letter out of the already crumpled envelope. "I can read some of the words. Tanya helped me with the rest."

Leanna looked up at the nanny, who'd padded down the stairs with Megan. "You read her this?"

"It was addressed to her," Tanya said with a roll of her eyes. "I didn't see why I shouldn't."

Leanna wanted to rail, but not in front of her daughter. "In the future," she said dryly, "please hold all our mail until I've had a chance to examine it."

"Sure," the young woman said with a flippant shrug. Which further set Leanna's teeth on edge.

"Is something wrong?" Esme asked from behind Jackson.

"Everything's fine," Leanna assured her. She took the letter from Elise and tried not to let her hands shake as she read it. "He's coming to Baton Rouge next week," she announced.

"Is he going to live with us?" Elise looked up eagerly.

Leanna was sure her heart was going to break, or explode. Richard was doing it again. Coming into Elise's life. He'd offer her all sorts of promises and false hope, then he'd disappear for long stretches, leaving Leanna to deal with the emotional pain that would follow.

"He's just coming for a visit," she said, attempting to sound neutral, if not enthusiastic. She again read the brief note, carefully printed so his daughter could read it herself. It didn't say how long he'd be staying. She hoped not for long. Perhaps he was going to New Orleans on a junket and was just passing through. Maybe he wouldn't show up at all.

CHAPTER SEVEN

JACKSON WATCHED Leanna's face very carefully as she read the letter to her daughter. He didn't expect her to be ecstatic about the news, but he was surprised to see the look of fear and defeat that shadowed her face. He knew enough about her by now to understand only one thing truly frightened her, and that was a threat to the welfare of her daughter.

He waited until after dinner before saying anything. She had pitched in with the rest of the family to clear the table, and the girls had gone up to Megan's room to play for a while before bedtime. The evening was cool, but not too chilly for a stroll in the garden.

"You're upset about this upcoming visit by Elise's father, aren't you?"

She crossed her arms in front of her and drew the sweater she'd thrown over her shoulders a little tighter. He didn't think it was the night air that had her shivering. He slipped his arm around her waist and held her to his side.

"You're safe here. Tell me what's bothering you."

"Richard isn't...a good influence," she said quietly.

Jackson had the impression she was so used to not saying anything bad about him for Elise's sake, that even now, she couldn't bring herself to condemn the man she'd married. From friends who'd gone through divorce, Jackson knew it often left permanent scars on people, robbing them of their self-confidence and self-esteem.

"Elise is a smart kid, Lee. Eventually, she'll catch on," he tried to reassure her.

"He can do a lot of harm between now and then. She's the innocent victim in this mess, Jackson. It isn't fair for her to have to go through these disappointments over and over."

He snuggled her closer and was rewarded by her putting her arm around his back and holding him tight. The comfort was short-lived.

"Staying here is a mistake," she mumbled against his chest, as much to herself, Jackson suspected, as to him. "Richard will take it as a sign that I'm doing well and try to get his child support payments lowered or canceled. I can't do it all by myself," she admitted. The pain in her voice, the hint of failure, was palpable.

"Surely he wouldn't do that."

"You don't know Richard. I won't put anything past him."

Jackson drew her over to the bench and sat beside her, his arm still wrapped around her shoulders. He gazed down into her mournful face. "All you have to do is explain to a judge how much you're paying here, and his premise is defeated."

"He'll make it look like our living on the plantation, in a house that should rent for so much more than I'm paying, means I'm doing something wrong, that I'm an unfit mother."

"We have plenty of people to say just the opposite,'' Jackson countered. ''I can assure you, my witnesses will carry a lot more weight with a court than anything he says.''

When she didn't respond, he tipped her head up and peered into her sad eyes. ''It's not as if we were living together, Lee,'' he said, then smiled. ''We're actually farther apart than if we were next-door neighbors at your old apartment house.''

''I hadn't thought of that.'' She smiled, showing the first signs of a positive attitude.

''Now, I don't want you to worry about this anymore.'' He touched his lips to hers. As much as he wanted to linger, to pursue, he pulled away. ''Go help Elise with the letter she wants to write to her daddy, then relax and get a good night's sleep. If you think Richard is formidable, you haven't seen Fontaine forces in action.''

She did her best to put on a happy face.

''That's my girl.'' He took her hand and led her back to the house.

RICHARD CARGILL SHOWED UP the following Sunday afternoon. He came, not to the *garçonnière*, but to the front door of the mansion. Esme, aware of who he was and the disruptive influence he might have on his daughter, greeted him politely, showed him into the drawing room, then went to Jackson's office to tell him ''that man'' had arrived.

''Give me a minute alone with him,'' he said. ''Then buzz the *garçonnière* and let Lee know he's here.''

Jackson donned his suit coat and straightened his tie. Being overdressed had a certain intimidating quality. Confident, he walked resolutely into the drawing room.

Lee's ex-husband was standing over by the Steinway, his back to the door, studying an oil painting of Angelique.

"Mr. Cargill," Jackson said as he crossed the oriental carpet. "I'm Jackson Fontaine. Welcome to Bellefontaine Plantation. We've been expecting you."

Richard spun around. Jackson pegged him at about five-ten, a little shorter than he was and several pounds heavier. Not muscle, either, judging from the padding girding the belt line.

"Mr. Fontaine." Richard stepped around the end of the grand piano, his hand extended. "Thank you so much for letting me visit. You have a beautiful home." His handshake was firm and aggressive. "May I ask who the woman in the portrait is?"

"My mother," Jackson said.

Richard glanced back at it once more. "She's very beautiful."

"Thank you." Lee had warned that her ex could be charming and disarming. "My aunt is calling over to the *garçonnière* right now. Lee and Elise should be here momentarily."

"*Garçonnière?* What's that?"

Jackson waved him to the couch and took the dominant position in the wingback on the other side of the coffee table. "It's our guest house. It means boy's place. In the nineteenth century, the teenage males in the family lived there to keep them from getting underfoot."

Richard chuckled. "Sounds like a smart idea. And they didn't even have boom boxes back then."

He was wearing a brown tweed jacket, pale-yellow shirt, conservative tie, sharply creased tan slacks and tasseled loafers. Jackson was disappointed. He would have preferred a flashy or inappropriate dresser, rather than one tastefully and expensively attired. Leanna was forced to pinch pennies, while this guy went around in Armani threads and Gucci footwear.

"Is this your first visit to Baton Rouge?" Jackson asked, in his best Southern manner.

"Yes." Richard crossed one leg over the other, totally at ease. "I was in New Orleans a few years ago. An interesting city. Now I'm looking forward to seeing more of your state capital."

A clatter arose at the back of the house, drawing both men's attention to the doorway. They were climbing to their feet when Elise burst into the room. "Daddy!"

Richard opened his arms, swept the girl up and gave her a big hug. He kissed her loudly on the cheek. "How's my honey bunch? Has my baby missed me?"

She leaned back, her little hands on his shoulders. "I'm not a baby anymore, Daddy. I'm in school now."

"School? My, you have grown." He looked past her to Leanna, who was standing in the doorway.

"Kindergarten," she explained quietly, her face unsmiling.

If there was any lingering affection on his part for the woman who had borne his child, Richard Cargill didn't display it. Instead, he telegraphed mild disdain.

"Well, that's wonderful, munchkin." He rubbed

noses with Elise. "I bet you're the smartest kid in class."

"Except for Bobby Philips. He knows the albabeth by heart."

Richard's face glowed with delight at his daughter's mispronunciation. "The whole alphabet?"

"Mommy is helping me and I'm going to know it, too," the child said proudly. She had her legs around Richard's hips and was leaning back in the bow of his outstretched arms.

"Well, maybe I can help."

Esme wheeled in her tea cart. "I thought we'd have some refreshments. Elise, child, why don't you go upstairs and invite Megan down. Then you can introduce her to your father."

Elise was about to protest when Richard started lowering her to the floor. "I'd like to meet all your friends," he said, encouraging her.

"Oh, okay." Clearly, though, she would rather have stayed there and bathed in the radiance of her daddy. She scampered out of the room, her feet racing up the stairs.

"She looks good," Richard said to Leanna with a pleasant smile. "How are you? I went by the address you originally sent me. This is definitely a step up."

The only time Jackson had seen her so stiff, so ill at ease, was when he'd yanked her car door open at their first meeting. She'd been afraid of him, and she was plainly afraid of Richard Cargill. She said her ex-husband had never been physically abusive, but without a doubt he had been emotionally.

"Our apartment got flooded," she explained simply. "The Fontaines have been kind enough to let me rent the *garçonnière*."

"I'd like to see the place. Jackson was telling me about its history. Sounds fascinating."

The words were innocuous enough, making Jackson wonder if he was reading innuendo and a veiled threat in them only because of what Leanna had said about him.

"I have tea, Mr. Cargill," Esme interrupted. "Perhaps you'd prefer something stronger. I'm sure Jackson will get you whatever you want from the bar."

Jackson suspected she herself would much prefer having a mint julep, but propriety dictated otherwise. After all, it wasn't even two o'clock yet.

"Tea will be very nice, Ms. Fontaine. Thank you." For all his vices, Leanna said alcohol wasn't one of them, though he had a good nose for French wines. Perhaps that discriminating palate gave him his ruddy complexion.

At the older woman's behest, they sat down. Jackson considered putting Leanna in the power throne but decided it would give the wrong impression. Instead, he pulled up a straight-back upholstered chair for her beside Esme.

Elise raced into the room, this time pulling Megan by the hand. "Daddy, this is Megan. She's my best friend. She doesn't go to school yet, but she will next year, except I'll be in a different school then, but after that—"

"Slow down, sweet pea," Richard said with a laugh. He extended his hand slowly, palm up, to the timid four-year-old. "Hello, Megan. I'm very pleased to meet you."

The little girl was shy with the stranger and didn't seem to know what to do.

Jackson got up and crouched beside her. "Shake hands with Mr. Cargill, sweetheart." He took her hand and placed it in Richard's. "Say hello to him."

"Hello," Megan mumbled.

"Megan, dear," Esme said gently, "would you like some orange juice?"

She nodded meekly.

Jackson gathered up his daughter and sat her on his knee in the wingback while Esme shook the two bottles she'd included on the tray, twisted off their caps, inserted straws and offered them to the girls.

Elise jumped into her father's lap. Richard winced, then smiled with some discomfort at the room at large.

Esme continued serving tea. "How long are you going to be here in Baton Rouge, Mr. Cargill?"

"Please call me Richard. I'm relocating here permanently," he announced.

"You're going to stay here with us?" Elise was clearly ecstatic at the idea.

"Not at Bellefontaine," he said. Jackson had the feeling if he'd been offered the other *garçonnière* he would have accepted without a moment's hesitation. "But I'll be living in town—" he tickled her under the chin "—so I can come and visit you every weekend, just like I used to."

Elise threw her arms around his neck. She obviously didn't remember that, according to her mother, he missed his visits back home at least as often as he kept them.

Leanna found her tongue. "You have a job here?"

His free hand swirled the silver spoon in the teacup on the end table. "I've accepted the position as second chef at the Sugar Belle." He winked at his daughter, who giggled. "So I can be close to my munchkin here." He looked at Jackson. "You may be familiar with it. It's just across from the riverboat, the *White Gold*."

Jackson knew it quite well. The restaurant served some of the best French cooking in the city. He'd been planning to take Leanna there for a quiet dinner one evening. Candlelight, soft music, good food, ambience. Well, that plan was shot to hell.

"A very fine restaurant," he said dryly. Cargill must be a damn good cook for Henri Gaudage to hire him. The Sugar Belle had a reputation to maintain. "It was there long before the riverboat came in. I imagine they're busier now than ever."

"So it would seem."

"Is that your specialty, Mr. Cargill?" Esme asked, ignoring his request that she address him by his first name. "French cuisine?"

"French and Italian."

"I assume you're not referring to pizza," she said without a hint of humor.

Richard laughed easily. "I make an individual Pizza Florentine as an appetizer that I think you might enjoy, but you're quite right, Ms. Fontaine. Pepperoni-and-pineapple-supreme isn't one of my featured offerings."

"Where are you staying?" Esme asked.

"At the Beauregard Court," he said.

"I've been by there a few times," Jackson commented, casting Leanna a glance. She was trying not to show resentment, but the flash he caught in her eyes told him otherwise. "Looks like a nice place."

"It's adequate," Richard remarked, "for the time being."

"We dine early on Sundays, Mr. Cargill," Esme said. "At five o'clock. Will you be able to join us?"

"That's very kind of you." It was also obvious he was going to accept. "Thank you."

"Perhaps in the meantime, you'd like to tour the grounds."

"You can see my room," Elise volunteered.

LEANNA CRINGED. She felt as if she were being stalked. At least the *garçonnière* was presentable. What would Richard say about her and Elise having to share the same bedroom? Well, she had nothing to be ashamed of. She couldn't help wonder, though, how he could afford to stay at the Beauregard Court. It had been way above her price range when she'd been hunting for a place to live. But then, she hadn't gotten out from under a load of debt by declaring bankruptcy. Evidently he hadn't altered his lifestyle. She wondered if his creditors were starting to bug him again, if that was why he'd come down here. Well, his new bills were his own now, not hers. She had enough of his old ones to pay.

Taking a deep breath, she vowed to suppress her resentment. Her main concern was how to keep Elise from being further hurt by this man. The news that he was coming for a visit had been bad enough, but the announcement that he would be living in Baton Rouge was devastating. A one-time social call would have been a temporary setback in the stable world Leanna was trying to establish for Elise, but the prospect of his coming around regularly—or even worse, irregularly—would keep the child permanently off balance. Yet what could Leanna do? The court of jurisdiction in their divorce was in New York. She couldn't afford to travel back there to petition for a change in visitation rights or pay an attorney to represent her, even if she had provable justification—and she didn't. Richard had been very careful in that regard.

What were her options? There didn't seem to be many. Relocating again would be of no avail, even supposing she could find another well-paying job. Richard had made it plain he'd follow her wherever she went. Denying him access to Elise would only give him ammunition to use against her, and in the long run, she might end up losing custody.

There was one possible route, the one she'd shunned for pride's sake. She could declare bankruptcy, as Richard had. It would free up more money to do what needed to be done, which was fight Richard. Instead of paying the merchants who had sold Richard products and services in good faith, a lawyer would get her money—with no guarantee of the results. A lose-lose situation.

That night, as she slipped into her nightgown, crawled into bed and turned out the light, Leanna thought of Jackson's comment about the formidable host the Fontaines could be. She had no doubt it was true, but the trouble his family had suffered over the past six months was also an indication of the forces that could be aligned against them. They had that much in common: powerful enemies.

Jackson had vowed to protect her. She'd agreed to help him identify his adversaries. They had a pact, but so what? He was in no position to insulate her against the man she'd divorced. She was equally impotent to uncover his opponents.

Then he'd kissed her and the magic of that moment erased all thoughts of foes and conflicts. She'd kissed him back, and desires she'd so long suppressed came bubbling to the surface. What, she wondered, could Jackson Fontaine possibly see in her? She wasn't beautiful. Not anymore. There were too many worry lines marring her once-smooth features. She had nothing to offer him—except access to information that might or might not help him identify his nemesis. Is that what this was all about? Was he using her for his own ends?

Exhausted by the day's overload of emotions, she fell into a fitful sleep.

NOW THAT THE FIRE MARSHAL had completed his investigation of the explosion and turned in his report, Jackson set Billy Doyle to work on cleanup—which meant out-of-pocket expenses until the insurance company decided on their course of action. He'd have to keep very careful track of the expenses involved, since there wasn't much cash available. Jackson wondered if his father had had any idea what he was getting into when he'd bought the old Dewalt refinery. Probably not. He wouldn't have gone off on vacation if he had.

"Billy's charging ahead," Murray said, as he sat down opposite Jackson in the office at Bellefontaine Thursday afternoon.

"He'll do a good job."

Jackson usually had good instincts about people and was able to sum them up quickly. Had the contract gone to Woody Stevens, Billy's former employer, Jackson would be more circumspect. Stevens did acceptable work, but he wasn't averse to padding expenses or double billing. He graciously conceded accounting errors and clerical mistakes when he got caught, but the point was you had to catch him.

"He probably won't make a lot of money," Murray went on, "but if he does well and manages to at least break even on this project, he'll pick up more work and the real profits will start rolling in."

Despite his quiet, almost nerdy disposition, Murray had a good head for business. Had his father let him run things on his own, the Dewalts might not have ended up in the pickles they perpetually found themselves in. Roland loved playing the business tycoon, but he wasn't very good at it, not like Duke.

"How long does Billy think cleanup will take?"

"A couple of weeks. Removing the debris will be fairly easy, but he has to make sure the structure is sound before he can repair the damage."

"Safety first," Jackson declared. "I can't afford any more mishaps."

"I'M IN AWE of the job you did in this kitchen," Leanna told Adam Ross the following Saturday morning. Betty had insisted she come over for her hot beignets, made from scratch. "Aunt Esme showed me the pictures of the damage done by the fire. Walking into the house now, I'd never know there'd ever been a fire."

Adam smiled broadly. "Like a car body shop," he said, "I aim to make sure no one ever knows I did anything."

"I should think that would be hard on the ego,"

she commented. "Most of us want people to notice what we accomplish."

"Ah—" he held up a finger for emphasis "—the two most important people do know. Me and the person who pays me."

"You should see the job he's doing on Magnolia Manor," Noelani offered proudly.

"Can I?" Leanna asked. "I heard you mention putting in a cypress floor. I'd love to see it."

MAGNOLIA MANOR WAS three miles down Old River Road, and like the other plantation houses, it faced the Mississippi. A section of wrought-iron fence was missing between a couple of the stone pillars, and the lopsided gate was fixed open. The grounds were overgrown with weeds; several large shrubs had died of neglect.

Leanna's car putted up the narrow driveway toward a broad, two-story house that was enshrouded in scaffolding. Workmen were nailing shingles on the roof. She parked behind a glazier's truck and mounted the four wooden steps to the front *galerie*. The outside of the house was still in dire need of fresh paint, but she could see where boards had been replaced, others filled. The inside of the building was flooded with light.

Noelani stepped into the wide central hallway from a side room. "Welcome to Magnolia Manor."

Leanna knew this had been Adam's home before his father had gone missing in Vietnam. Unable to manage the family's affairs on her own, Mrs. Ross had been forced to sell the estate. She was now residing in a sanitarium.

For the next hour, Adam and Noelani took turns

showing Leanna the work he'd done. Again, she was impressed by the meticulous attention to detail. The building had been abandoned for more than ten years, and by all accounts was in terrible condition before then. It wasn't as big as Bellefontaine, or as lavish in its appointments, but it still contained an atmosphere of history. Perhaps a truer one, for Bellefontaine and the other big houses that had been preserved were exceptional even in their day.

Adam had carefully replicated the wood moldings and ceiling medallions. Shutters that had been removed or nailed closed had been replaced or restored to their original functions.

"We're going to air-condition the place," Noelani explained. "Installing it in a way that it doesn't distract from the original design has been a fun challenge." She pointed to columns flanking the doors of the dining room. "The one on the right was badly scarred, so Adam replaced it with a metal reproduction. It's hollow and serves as an air duct."

"Ingenious," Leanna commented. As hard as she stared at the two fluted columns, she couldn't detect any difference.

The loud noise and choking dust of an electric floor sander finally drove the two women out the back door. Before leaving, they snagged a couple of bottles of water from an ice chest.

"How often does your ex-husband visit Elise?" Noelani asked, when they were outside and conversation was easier.

"Too often and not often enough," Leanna replied. To the inquiring expression, she explained, "When we still lived in Ithaca, he promised to come every weekend, but only showed up about half the time. Elise would wait excitedly for him, then make excuses for as long as she could. Finally, she'd just go to her room and cry. When he did appear, he showered her with so much attention, I had a hard time getting her back on track.''

Noelani shook her head. "That sounds cruel."

"I'd hoped when we moved down here, we were getting away from him."

"I never met my father," Noelani said between sips of water. "And he never saw me."

"How sad. I'm sorry." Leanna said. Her own father had been such a positive influence in her life she couldn't imagine growing up without him. It added to her frustration with Richard. She wanted her little girl to have the same happy childhood she'd enjoyed. Clearly, that was not to be.

They settled on a long wooden crate under a sprawling live oak tree. Cables supported several of the long thick limbs. As a result of the recent rain, tree ferns feathered the upper surfaces.

"I've often wondered if I would have liked Duke," Noelani said.

"He seems to have been an interesting character," Leanna offered on a light note.

"My mother loved him. He left her pregnant, never saw her again, yet she continued to love him till the day she died. Hard to fathom."

Either he was one hell of a man, Leanna mused, or she was a fool. Judging by her daughter, Leanna didn't think it was the latter. "I haven't met anyone yet who can explain love. Wars have been fought over it, lives lost, and still understanding eludes us."

"He was a complex man," Noelani acknowledged. "That much I've learned." She plucked a wild columbine and examined its delicate blue flower. "He never came back to Hawaii, but he sent child support to my mother every month, even though she never asked for it, and he set up a scholarship fund for my college education. I didn't learn that he'd established it specifically for me until after he was dead."

"A regular wheeler and dealer." Leanna remained silent for a minute, mulling the information over. She felt compelled to ask what seemed to her an obvious question. "What about Jackson? Is he like his father?"

Noelani's face softened. "Yes and no." She laughed at Leanna's wry expression. "That doesn't help much, does it?" She held the colorful bloom gracefully in her lap. "One comparison is obvious. They both fathered illegitimate daughters."

Leanna said nothing, sensing a pain that wasn't rational or controllable, only inescapable.

"I think the parallel ends there, though," Noelani went on. "Duke kept his daughter a secret, except to his wife and a trusted friend in Hawaii, who turned out to be more of a father to me than Duke ever was."

She put the flower aside and drank from her water bottle. "I wish I had gotten to meet Angelique. You've seen her portrait. She was such a beautiful woman. Esme tells me she was also smart, and in some ways as cunning as her husband. Auntie E is convinced Angelique was the one who prompted Duke to set up the child-support payments and scholarship fund."

She must have been quite a woman. Not many wives would be that understanding or compassionate.

"Jackson, on the other hand," Noelani continued, "embraced Megan from the beginning and made sure he was involved in her life. From what Casey tells me, Janis was a real gold digger who tried to snare Jackson into marrying her. I feel sorry for Megan, but she's better off without the kind of mother who would get involved with drug dealers."

She examined the flower for a minute.

"Jackson's a good man, Lee, and a great daddy. Megs will be all right."

That was essentially what Betty had said, and though the two women were generations and worlds apart, they had both said it with absolute conviction and affection.

"How else does Jackson take after his father?"

"He's a sharp businessman." Noelani hastened to add, "I mean that in the good sense. He's not afraid to use his influence when he thinks it's the right thing to do. Like when Nick Devlin wanted to dock his riverboat here in Baton Rouge. A city ordnance forbade it, but Jackson persuaded the council to waive it for Nick. He didn't gain anything personally, just did it to help a friend." She laughed. "A friend who later became his brother-in-law. A lot different from his father, who wasn't afraid to create the situations he could profit from."

"What do you mean?"

Noelani pursed her lips. "The refinery. The Dewalts owned it for years. From what I gather, old Roland fancied himself lord of the manor, the kind that doesn't believe in getting his hands dirty. He's perfectly content to pay other people—his son, for instance—to do the real work, while he makes all the decisions. Then he complains when things don't go his way."

"Sounds like my ex-husband," Leanna said on a laugh. "Brilliant at planning, scheming and dreaming. Lousy at execution."

Noelani smiled. "He was a charming man at dinner Sunday."

"Yep. Richard never fails to make a good first impression. The lasting impression is another matter. But I don't want to talk about him. You mentioned Murray…"

Noelani nodded understanding. "A couple of years ago, after Roland kept complaining about refinery profits declining, Murray decided to get personally involved. It didn't take him long to figure out the plant needed serious overhaul. The old man hadn't upgraded anything in years. Equipment was constantly breaking down, and safety was becoming an issue. Murray fixed what he could, but the place needed to expand if it was going to compete with Sugarland, where most of the refineries are located now. When he finally convinced his dad to put some capital into the place, Roland went to the bank for a loan."

Leanna thought she could see what was coming, but she let the other woman spell it out.

"Duke was on the board of governors at the time," Noelani went on. "When the loan application came up for consideration, he argued against granting it. The loan was denied. The plant continued to deteriorate, business dropped off. Old man Dewalt was already late on several earlier loans. Eventually, the bank forced him to sell the refinery."

"And Duke bought it," Leanna concluded.

"For about fifty cents on the dollar. It was a good investment, except Duke then got himself killed in a plane crash. Whatever plans or schemes he had up his sleeve died with him. Jackson has been struggling ever since."

An interesting irony, Leanna ruminated. Both she and Jackson had been saddled with debts of someone else's making.

CHAPTER EIGHT

JACKSON WAS FRUSTRATED. Cleanup at the refinery was taking longer than he'd expected.

"What's the problem?" he asked Murray. "This first phase of the project was supposed to be completed in two weeks, but Billy still hasn't finished removing all the debris."

"He's run into a few snags," his man-in-charge said. "Doyle's equipment isn't exactly new, and he's been having trouble with some of it."

"If he didn't have the resources to do the job, he shouldn't have accepted it."

"Give the guy a break, Jackson. He's just starting out and doing the best he can. One of his two dump trucks broke down and he's been having trouble getting parts. He tried to borrow a truck from Woody Stevens, but the old man isn't cooperating, claims all his equipment is committed."

"Is it?"

"Not when you drive by his yard. He has a bunch of trucks sitting there. Could be out of commission, I guess—"

"Stevens is worried about the competition," Jackson said. "Maybe I ought to talk to him."

Under other circumstances, he would probably have rolled with the punch. A week or two slippage on a project of this magnitude wouldn't be catastrophic, but holdups so early in the process, it didn't bode well for the work ahead.

"Delays cost money. You know the bind I'm in." He was trying to sound reasonable. With anyone but Murray acting as his overseer, he'd be less candid. "I don't like squeezing nickels, but it may come to that."

"Things will work out," his friend said philosophically. "Actually, the situation isn't as bad as it appears. The place looks chaotic, but Billy's cleared the immediate work area and has completed the structural inspection. He'll start putting up scaffolding tomorrow, then he can begin reconstruction. The only real delay is getting the debris moved off-site. He's promised to put his drivers on overtime—at his own expense—to meet the timetable we agreed on."

Overtime wreaked havoc with profits, and Jackson knew Billy was running a close margin on this job.

"I'm not interested in bankrupting the guy," he said. "He needs to get his feet on the ground. Tell him to remove the waste as economically as possible, provided safety isn't compromised."

Murray smiled. "You're a real softy, Jackson."

He laughed. "Yeah, right. Don't confuse the velvet glove with the iron fist."

Murray snickered.

"ARE YOU SURE putting Murray in charge of things is wise?" Leanna asked that evening as they walked through the garden. Jackson had just told her about the problems creeping into the refinery project.

He laced his fingers with hers. "Has Esme been bending your ear again?"

These strolls in the garden after dinner were becoming a nightly ritual, one she looked forward to. She felt a little guilty at the pleasure she took in holding hands with him. Not so conscience-stricken, though, that she was willing to pull away. It wasn't just his hands, either. Being with him at the end of the day had become important to her, and that worried her even more. Her stay here was transient, but even temporary pleasure was better than none, she consoled herself. She was being selfish, of course. Getting too close to Jackson wasn't a good idea. She couldn't let it happen, especially now with Richard back in the picture.

"It's not just Esme," she said. "You've explained where she's coming from. But look at the situation objectively. The refinery belonged to the Dewalts. Murray ran it—"

"Which is why he's the best person to oversee the repairs and later the renovation and expansion."

"He would also have been in the best position to sabotage the place."

Jackson halted the swinging of their hands and turned to face her. His eyes were almost black in the scant light flowing from the house behind them and the little electric torches dotting the perimeter of the footpath.

"Why should he do that?"

She arched her eyebrows. "Revenge?"

"For what? I've never done anything to him. If you mean because the refinery used to belong to his family, forget it." He resumed their walk, their fingers still joined. "That's not Murray's style. Besides, if he really wanted to blow the place up, he would have done the job right."

The sound of crickets and splashing water filled

the night. "Maybe he didn't want to totally destroy it," she observed.

They circled Duke and Angelique's fountain. "What do you mean?"

"Murray knew the fire wall was in place because he was the one who had it installed. He would also have known that an explosion in the utility room wouldn't have done any serious damage to the refinery portion of the building, but that it would definitely have destroyed your stored sugar."

Jackson mulled over her hypothesis. On one level it made sense, but there were problems, too.

"Let's take this a step at a time." He led her to their favorite bench, but instead of sitting beside her, he paced in front of her.

Steepling his fingers, he brought them up to his lips. "Let's assume, for the sake of argument, that Murray found out from a mill driver that raw sugar had been transferred to the warehouse, rather than sent directly to a refinery in Sugarland. The logical conclusion would have been that it was coalition sugar and was just being held until the refinery had capacity for it. Destroying it wouldn't profit him and it wouldn't harm me, because his assumption would be that it was insured."

"The anonymous tip said it was illegally being stored," she pointed out.

"If it were illegally stored," he went on, "why destroy it?"

"The evidence would have been rendered useless," she admitted, "but it would still have cost you a large investment."

He had to admit that was true.

"There's something else," she added. "The police

and fire inspector found no evidence of a break-in. Whoever got into the refinery and loosened the gas line had a key.''

He shot her a glance that lingered for several seconds.

''Did you change all the locks when you took over the plant?''

Jackson pursed his lips, his eyes still intent on hers. ''I didn't take physical possession of the place. Duke did. I got the keys from him. Just before he went on vacation.''

Leanna cocked her head. ''So you can't be sure the locks were ever changed.'' It was a conclusion, rather than a question.

He shook his head unhappily.

''Murray had access to the keys before they were turned over to your father. He could easily have had duplicates made.''

Jackson considered the possibility. ''I don't believe it.''

''Since we're examining possibilities, let's look at this from another angle,'' Leanna suggested. ''The explosion destroyed two-and-a-half-million pounds of raw sugar. If it was illegally stored, you're in trouble. If it was legal but uninsured, you're still out big bucks. Murray knows your predicament. He has the most to gain, the least to lose. If you're forced to sell the plant for one reason or another, he'd be in the best position to buy it.''

''Buy it back?'' Jackson laughed. ''I don't think so. Murray ran the place the last five years it was in operation, but only because his father was so lackadaisical about it. Murray has a small trust fund from his late mother, and he's doing pretty well with his computer programming, plus what his father pays him to grow their sugarcane. Murray may not be rich, but he isn't poor, either.'' Jackson shook his head. ''No, he's not interested in getting the refinery back. Besides, he'd be in the same pickle I am—strapped for the capital to do anything with it.''

''How about Roland, then?'' Leanna asked.

Jackson chuckled. ''Same problem. He'd be in even less of a position to make it a profitable operation now than he was before. I don't know how much of what we paid him for the place he got to keep. The old man's been tightfisted with that money, much to Murray's disgust. He wanted to put some of it into improving their cane operation and fixing up the house, which had steadily deteriorated over the years.''

Jackson sat down, intent on distracting her from refineries and sabotage, but first he had to put her mind at ease. He took her hands and slowly massaged her knuckles.

''The old coot has the personality of a porcupine and entertains delusions of grandeur, but he's harmless. He wouldn't have the nerve or expertise to sabotage the place, and he's too cheap to hire someone else to do it. As for Murray, he's much more interested in growing cane and playing with electronic gadgets than he is in sugar refining.''

''Then why is he so eager to help you on this project?''

''Because he's a friend,'' he said, and wondered if that was the complete answer.

LEANNA AND ELISE WERE having dinner with the family every night now. Leanna loved the sense of belonging, the feeling of comfort and security she felt when she and Jackson shared time with their two girls.

Elise was comfortable with everyone—even Aunt Esme, who seemed indeed to be warming up in her own way. Perversely, her smooth transition into this environment disturbed Leanna. This was someone else's household, someone else's family. She and her daughter were outsiders, guests who had no permanent status. What would happen to Elise if...when that bond had to be severed? At five, she'd already suffered the divorce of her parents, separation from her father and relocation to an unfamiliar part of the country. Elise was a bright child, but Leanna wondered if she was helping or hurting her daughter by letting her develop an attachment to people who might quickly disappear from her life.

Then there was Jackson. Leanna's feelings for him, instead of leveling out, were intensifying, and she was pretty sure his for her were, as well.

After supper one evening, the girls elected to play outside rather than upstairs in Megan's room. It was already December, but the weather was mild, the night air cool but not cold, a sharp contrast to what it must be like in Ithaca, Leanna ruminated. She wouldn't miss the brittle winds that swept upper New York State. The warm breezes that drifted in here from the Gulf were much more pleasant. While Esme tidied up the spotless kitchen, Leanna helped Casey and Noelani stack the dishwasher, then she wandered out onto the back porch to wait for Jackson and their evening constitutional in the garden.

The girls had tied the end of a jump rope to a banister. One of them turned the rope, while the other girl jumped. Leanna had just sat down to watch when Jackson joined her from his office.

"Can I play?" he asked. "I haven't jumped rope in a long time."

"I'll show you, Daddy," Megan replied.

Leanna watched Jackson's face light up. His little girl was coming out of her shell. What setback would she suffer when Elise left? Jackson had meant it when he said Elise was good for her. Decidedly the extrovert, the five-year-old seemed to be a born leader—or maybe that should be instigator.

"You can jump with us, too," Megan told Leanna.

Jackson gave her a playful wink.

"Right after dinner? I don't know..." The crestfallen expressions on the two girls brought out a big grin. "Oh, all right. But just for a few minutes."

She descended the porch steps while Jackson untied the rope. Leanna took the other end. They spread out, started turning and invited the girls to jump in. Elise naturally was the first. Megan came in two rotations later. Jackson and Leanna began counting. One...two...three... They got up to nine before Megan tripped.

Jackson scooped her up and brushed off her knee. "You okay, sugarplum?"

"Can we do it again?" she asked, clearly unconcerned about the dirt on her bare legs.

"Sure. Maybe Elise and Miss Lee can turn the rope and we can jump together. Would you like that?"

Megan nodded, her eyes bright and happy.

He bent and held both her hands as they jumped facing each other. By the count of ten they were giggling. Megan slowed, and Leanna gauged the speed of the rope to accommodate her. Elise, of course, had other ideas. On the next swing, the rhythm of the two ends didn't match, and the rope collapsed down around Jackson's shoulders.

They switched places. He and his daughter turned the rope for Elise and Leanna. Mother and daughter got to sixteen and immediately declared themselves the winners.

"I demand a rematch," Jackson insisted, and tickled his daughter under the chin.

This time he held the four-year-old in his arms.

One...two...three. He joined their foreheads and rubbed his nose against hers, making her giggle.

Seven...eight...nine. He tickled her under the chin, and she began to laugh.

Fourteen...fifteen...sixteen. He dragged his knuckles along her ribs. She squirmed and cackled.

Twenty-three...twenty-four...twenty-five. By now, Megan was guffawing so hilariously she could hardly hold on to her father's neck. He held her to his chest, his face as jubilant as hers, aglow with pure delight.

Thirty-one...thirty-two...thirty-three. He missed a beat and stepped on the rope.

Everyone was chuckling at his antics.

"That was fun, Daddy." Even as she laughed, she clung to his neck.

Jackson beamed and rubbed her small back. "Yes, it was," he said, trying to catch his breath.

"Wow, that's the mostest anyone has ever jumped," Elise said in awe.

"I guess we're the champs," he told his little girl. "You think we ought to give them a chance to catch up?"

She smiled from ear to ear and shook her head.

"It would be fair," he coaxed her. "I bet they don't get to thirty-three, though."

Reluctantly, she agreed to let them try.

Leanna and Elise held hands as they jumped. They got to twenty-six, then Leanna missed the beat. "Whew. That was exhausting and fun."

"Can we do it again?" Elise pleaded.

Leanna was winded. "I need to rest. Why don't the three of you jump and I'll watch."

Jackson awarded her another wink.

Leanna mounted the steps of the porch, still breathing heavily, and joined Casey, who had come out to watch. Grinning, she handed Leanna a bottle of water.

"Thanks." She collapsed onto the cushion of one of the wrought-iron chairs.

They watched as Jackson turned the rope with each of the girls while the other one jumped. He couldn't seem to get the smile off his face.

"Elise has so much energy," Casey said a couple of minutes later. "How do you keep up with her?"

Leanna finally caught her breath. "It isn't easy, and I don't have trouble sleeping at night." Of late that wasn't totally true. Worry about what was going on in their lives sometimes left her staring at the ceiling, and Jackson tended to invade her dreams. The former was exhausting; the latter, strangely invigorating.

"I envy you. You have a bright, healthy baby."

There was something wistful, even sad, in the way the compliment was delivered. Leanna didn't want to pry but felt the other woman was inviting an inquiry. "Is something wrong?"

Casey gulped from her own water bottle. "I had a miscarriage not too long ago."

"I'm so sorry," Leanna said. "Was the doctor able to determine the problem? Is everything all right?"

"Supposedly."

"But it has you scared."

"I want to have kids. I never thought much about them before I met Nick, but now that we're married, I want children more than anything else in the world."

"You've been through a very difficult time," Leanna reminded her. "The kitchen fire, the threat to your cane crop, the terrible tragedy of your parents' deaths, discovering you have a half sister. Now all this turmoil with Nick having to take over the riverboat again, in addition to this business with the refinery. I'm sure when things settle down, you'll be fine."

Casey wiped a water mark from the table. "That's what the doctor said. Tension. My body was just telling me it wasn't ready yet."

"I'm sure that's right. You have to have faith."

Casey gave her a crooked smile through tears she fought to hold back. "I will. Thanks."

Leanna opened her arms; Casey accepted the comfort.

Leanna was so grateful to have Elise. She wondered, though, if the little girl would ever have a sister or brother. Jackson laughed at something the girls did. He was still glowing. A proud papa. A good daddy.

LATE THE FOLLOWING DAY, after a particularly frustrating session with his banker—they were continu-

ing his line of credit but refused to raise the limit,
even to pay off interest-accumulating bills—Jackson
decided to drop by the refinery. In addition to wor-
rying about Leanna, he'd been considering her res-
ervations regarding Murray. Jackson didn't really believe his friend could be involved in his troubles, but
he did need to check on the progress of the work.
The raw sugar stored in the warehouse had been his
ace in the hole. He'd been counting on its sale to
bankroll the expansion and upgrade of the refinery.
Even if he'd been forced to sell it at depressed prices,
it would have yielded enough cash to at least get
them out of their immediate financial bind—until
Duke's and Angelique's life insurance policies paid
off. But the sugar was history, and in its place he'd
inherited another liability—what his friend had aptly
called a white elephant.

Murray had phoned that very afternoon to report
yet another delay. A shipment of building materials
had been lost somewhere en route. No telling how
long it would take to get the matter straightened out.
Jackson had wanted him to reorder. The problem was
that these were specialty items in short supply. Billy
Doyle was examining alternative materials and
thought he might have come up with a solution. Naturally, it was more expensive, but delay was costly,
too.

The crew had left for the day by the time Jackson
arrived at the job site. He'd been hoping to talk to
Billy, get his personal evaluation of the situation. Not
that he didn't trust Murray to give him the straight
skinny, but face-to-face discussions were always
preferable to secondhand.

Doyle was doing a good job, as far as Jackson could see. The grounds were neat and orderly. After several items, including tools, had gone missing, Billy had constructed an exclusion area using chain-link fence and heavy padlocks. At night, two German shepherds patrolled it. Their barks were intimidating when Jackson approached, so he retreated.

The sun was already set, the last traces of twilight fading in the west. Security lights illuminated the perimeter of the galvanized-tin building. Jackson used the key Murray had dropped off when they'd finally installed the replacement doors. They rolled smoothly back on their runners. He entered the building.

The inside was dark. He fumbled and finally found a light switch. Jackson could see temporary stairs fifty yards to his left leading up to the catwalk. The original iron staircase had apparently been damaged in the explosion. He decided to climb to the top for a bird's-eye view of the work in progress.

The stairs were not as solid as the ones that had been removed, but they felt safe enough. He stepped onto the catwalk proper. Was it his imagination, or did it sway slightly? He was moving to his left, facing the fractured wall when he heard a voice call out, "Jackson, what are you doing up there?"

In the echo produced by the shouted question, he couldn't be sure who it was. He moved to the rail and leaned over it. "Is that you, Billy?"

"Dammit, get down from there. Immediately. It's not safe."

A grating sound was followed by a sharp crack. The next thing Jackson knew, he was skittering sideways as the gangway shifted, creaked and finally jolted to the right. Jackson's legs slid out from under him, and his hand lost its grip on the rail. He scrambled for anything but found no purchase. In a matter of seconds, he was rocketing feet forward like a child on a playground slide. Except this chute was rough. He could feel the nubs of the pierced steel abrading his butt. All of a sudden, his feet hit bottom and his knees practically came up to his chin.

Billy Doyle was instantly at his side. "Jackson, you all right? You hurt? Should I call an ambulance?"

He took a moment to collect his wits. "What happened?"

"Didn't you see the red flags on the scaffold?"

"Red flags?" Jackson slowly extended his legs. He felt what might be a bruise or two, but no broken bones.

"Sure you're okay?" The worry in Billy's voice was unmistakable.

"I think so." He rolled his shoulders, flexed his arms.

"Here, let me help you." The burly construction worker put an arm behind Jackson's back and practically lifted him in his arms.

"I think I can make it from here," Jackson said, and stood on his own two feet. "What's this about red flags?"

"At the bottom of the stairs. I put them there to remind everyone the catwalk wasn't safe yet. You would have had to duck under them to go on up."

"I didn't notice any flags. I certainly didn't duck under any."

"But they were there." Billy's face was a mask of confusion.

"When did you see them last?"

He looked suddenly frightened. "I put them up this afternoon. I'm sure they were still there when I left."

"Was anyone else here?"

"Murray and I closed up together." Billy started scouting around. He found the flags tossed in a heap in a corner. "I don't understand this." He held them in his hand. "I know they were there when I left."

"By the way, what are you doing here now?" Jackson asked. "I thought you'd quit for the day."

"I came back to check on the dogs. I worry that I don't leave them enough water."

Jackson realized he hadn't heard the dogs bark while he was inside the building, but then, if they were Billy's dogs, they wouldn't bark at him.

"I'm glad. No telling what would have happened if you hadn't shown up when you did."

"Isn't Jackson here yet?" Leanna asked.

After greeting Elise and Megan in the playroom upstairs, she'd come down to the drawing room, where the cocktail hour had already begun. She'd expected to find his Jaguar parked in its regular spot.

"Must be running a little late." Nick had assumed the bartender role. "Wine or juice?"

"Juice, thanks. Did he call?"

"I'm sure he'll be along presently," Esme noted from her armchair, mint julep in hand. Straight-backed as always, she looked regal in an elegantly simple gray rayon dress. "He's usually quite punctual, but there are so many things going on these days, it's difficult to maintain a schedule."

The sound of the back door opening and closing

drew everyone's attention. A moment later, Jackson appeared in the hallway. Leanna's heart raced.

"What in the world happened to you?" Casey asked, sounding unsure if she should be alarmed or amused.

"Are you all right?" Leanna's voice wobbled—at least, in her own ears.

He chuckled. "I'm too old for slides."

"Jackson, whatever are you talking about?" Esme seemed both annoyed and appalled by his appearance. His white shirt was torn and his khaki slacks were badly stained.

"You look like you could use a drink." Nick had already removed the cap on a bottle of beer. He handed it over.

"Thanks." Jackson took a mouthful of the cold brew. "I went by the refinery to see how work was progressing and made the mistake of climbing a scaffold. Billy Doyle stopped by to check on his watchdogs just about the time it collapsed. Apparently, someone had removed the red flags he'd put up."

Leanna's stomach jittered with anxiety. The idea immediately came to mind that this couldn't be just another stroke of bad luck. "On purpose?"

"No telling. Murray was the last one on the site. I called him. He insists the flags were still in place when he left."

"Do you believe him?" Leanna asked. Murray seemed to be lurking in the background whenever something unfortunate happened. The house fire. The refinery explosion. Now this incident.

"I've never known Murray to lie," Jackson said. "He's as worried about what's going on as I am."

"He's a Dewalt," Esme noted, as if that were statement enough.

"So who did it?" Casey asked.

Jackson shook his head. "I have no idea."

Leanna couldn't dismiss the notion that Jackson was in imminent danger. "Whoever did this...was he out to get you?"

The expression on his face as he turned toward her didn't suggest she might be paranoid, though the question probably came across that way. He shook his head. "No one knew I was going there this afternoon. It was a spur-of-the-moment decision, unplanned. I think whoever is behind it just wanted to cause trouble. Even if a workman hadn't realized the scaffold was unsafe and tried to climb it, like I did, he wouldn't have been injured any more than I was."

Esme sipped her mint julep and silently eyed them both.

"This was more a prank than a serious threat," Jackson continued, though he didn't seem as convinced as his words suggested.

"You're not just going to forget about it, are you?" Leanna asked.

"I called Detective Bouchard. He's going to look into it, but I don't expect him to find anything."

"Have you considered putting on a full-time guard?" Adam asked.

"I was hoping I wouldn't have to. Security services get expensive."

"Death and injury are more expensive," Leanna reminded him.

"Point taken," Jackson said. "Now, if you'll excuse me—" he set his empty bottle on the side of the armoire "—I'll go upstairs and get cleaned up for dinner."

CHAPTER NINE

JACKSON WASN'T NEARLY as sanguine about the minimal threat posed by his tumble at the refinery as he'd pretended. True, the incident could hardly have been targeted at him personally, but the idea that someone was willing to hurt blindly, simply to get back at the Fontaines, kept him tossing and turning for several hours that night. That was not the exclusive cause of his restlessness, of course. He kept picturing Leanna playing with the girls, jumping rope, her face flushed with effort, her breasts rising and falling. The image had a stimulating effect that definitely frustrated sleep.

Early the next morning, he made two telephone calls, one to a contact he'd developed in Italy shortly after his parents' deaths, the second to a friend at the airport, who furnished him the current address of one of her charter pilots.

Chuck Riley lived in a duplex in a part of town that was in transition—in other words, going downhill. The development had looked inviting ten years earlier, but time had not been in its favor. From all the reports Jackson had received, Riley was not doing well, either. Nick had thrown him off the riverboat twice for insulting behavior and disorderly conduct, finally banning him from the premises altogether. The airline owner also informed him that the licensed commercial pilot had been arrested twice, once for DWI and another for starting a barroom brawl. The charter service had suspended him indefinitely.

For his part, Riley had steered clear of Jackson, even though at one point he'd claimed Duke owed him back pay. Jackson could find no record to verify that services had been rendered beyond those he'd already been paid for, and Riley could show no personal records to verify his claim. Riley had since dropped the issue, making Jackson wonder if it had been valid to begin with.

At eight o'clock that morning, Jackson rapped on his door, then did so a second time. He was about to pound still harder when the door finally flew open and Chuck Riley stood before him in skivvies and a rumpled gray T-shirt.

"What the hell are you doing here? What do you want?"

"To talk to you." Jackson didn't wait for an invitation, he simply barged past him into the cluttered living room.

"Get out," Riley demanded, his hand still holding the doorknob.

"Close the door." Jackson parked himself on the tattered couch. "I don't think your neighbors want to see you in your underwear."

Scowling, Riley slammed it shut, strode into the center of the room and crossed his arms over his chest. "Say your piece and get out."

He was a big man, taller and thicker boned than Jackson and a decade older. Riley hadn't treated those ten years with respect, however. His nose had been broken at least once, its capillaries ravaged. His dark-amber eyes were bloodshot.

"For someone who claims I owe him money, you're not very hospitable."

Riley snorted. "I suppose you're here to give me my back pay."

Jackson put his booted feet on the pile of newspapers covering the coffee table. "Actually, you probably owe me money."

"What the hell are you talking about?" He picked up a pair of wrinkled chinos that were draped over the back of a nearby chair and stepped into them, leaving the T-shirt hanging out.

"I called Italy. They gave me a slightly different version of what happened between you and Duke. According to Inspector Signorelli in Milan, Duke fired you for your drinking two days before he and my mother were killed."

Riley had returned from Europe a day before the funeral, claiming Duke had insisted on flying Angelique around alone that day.

"I don't know who told him that. It's not true." He mellowed his tone. "Your dad and I got along fine. That's why he took me along on their trip."

Riley maintained eye contact, but it wasn't in defiance, more nervous gauging to determine if his lie was being bought. It wasn't. Ever since the overseas call, Jackson had been wondering if he could be responsible in some way for the plane crash. What Riley said was essentially true. He and Duke had gotten along. Back then, Riley had a reputation as a damn good pilot. He also performed a fair amount of the routine maintenance on the plane. Signorelli admitted that what looked like sabotage could have been gross negligence. The Italian authorities were still examining that possibility, but it would take months before they reached a final conclusion—and the insurance company wasn't likely to pay off until then.

If Riley was drunk when he serviced the aircraft... Guilt might explain why he'd been in a state of nearly constant inebriation since his return home.

"Look," Jackson said, moderating his approach, "the investigating team says the accident could have resulted from carelessness when the plane was last serviced. If that's what happened, Chuck, for God's sake, just say so, and we can get this matter settled once and for all. There'll probably be sanctions against you, but I'm willing to testify at a board hearing that Duke had every confidence in you, that we, the family, hold no grudge. Mistakes happen. They're unfortunate and tragic, but it's time for us to move on. If money's an issue—"

Riley had cocked an eyebrow during his visitor's speech. Now he burst into laughter.

"You Fontaines are all alike. Figure you can buy anybody. Well, sonny-boy, you can't buy me. No one can. You think I don't know what this unexpected social call is all about?" He snorted. "You want me to cop a plea of negligence so the insurance company will pay up." He grinned broadly. "Well, guess again, *Mr.* Fontaine. I don't know what happened to that Cessna, except that I had nothing to do with the crash. Better look somewhere else. Now, get the hell out of here."

Jackson took his time lowering his feet to the floor and rising from the couch. "Thanks for your hospitality, Chuck," he said sarcastically, as he sauntered to the door. He halted and faced the man. "Oh, by the way, where were you yesterday between five and six?''

Riley had started to move up behind him but stopped dead in his tracks, his mouth open. ''What?''

''Where were you late yesterday afternoon?''

The other man's eyes flitted. ''What's it to you?'' He was clearly stalling for time. Jackson wondered if it was because he was at the refinery or because he couldn't remember where he'd been.

Jackson stared him down.

Clearly, the guy would have liked to throw him out on his tail. Instead, he answered the question. ''I spent all yesterday afternoon at La Grenouille.''

The Frog was a popular bar in a rough part of town. Jackson might check it out, but it probably wouldn't do any good. If Chuckie-boy had friends there, they'd vouch for him. Still, it wouldn't hurt to pass this bit of information on to Detective Bouchard, who'd been investigating the other incidents at Bellefontaine.

''Have a nice day.''

LEE DROVE through the swampland on the long causeway that connected Baton Rouge with New Orleans. The car thumped on the uneven surface and bobbed like a rocking horse with each beat. The shocks were shot, and she didn't even want to think about the condition of the tires. She'd rotated them just before driving down to Louisiana, leaving the worst of the lot in the trunk as a spare. Her breathing grew shallower with each passing mile on the elevated roadway; the rhythm of the ba-bump jostled her already tense nerves. It was beginning to rain, which made matters worse. Her windshield wipers operated at only one speed—slow.

Investigating the damage done to a warehouse by a lightning strike in a recent rainstorm in New Orleans had given her a chance to visit the city for the first time. She'd seen enough of the Big Easy to know she wanted to bring Elise there to explore the French Quarter, to sit under the awning at the Café du Monde, sip café au lait—did they serve milk for children?—and bite into sugar-drenched warm beignets. She wouldn't be able to hire a horse-drawn carriage, but they could explore St. Louis Cathedral on Jackson Square.

Jackson. Without realizing it, he'd slipped into the picture, sitting with them at the famous open-air café, laughing in the park in front of the cathedral, standing at the rail of the *Delta Queen* as it paddled up and down the muddy Mississippi River.

The acrid smell of burning rubber assailed her nostrils. She looked to see if someone had suffered a blowout, but traffic on both sides of the divided highway was moving steadily. No cars were pulled over to the guard rails. Surely it wasn't her. Please God, don't let it be her car. Please.

The stench grew stronger. She checked her dashboard. Oh, no. The temperature gauge was pegged on "hot." Wisps of smoke and steam were slipping now from the edges of the hood. The end of the causeway was another forty miles away—forty miles to help.

With a muffled curse, she steered the car onto the wide right shoulder and shut off the engine. What should she do? No use looking under the hood. Whatever the problem was, she couldn't fix it. Cautiously, she got out of the vehicle. The rain was slow but steady. She didn't have a raincoat. The engine was crackling. Not an encouraging sound.

On the trip into the city, she'd seen telephone boxes on poles every mile or two along the causeway, and she'd prayed she wouldn't have any use for them. Now she scanned the concrete guard rail ahead and behind her. The only one she could make out in the misty downpour was about half a mile ahead. She gathered her handbag and started walking. A car pulled over in front of her. She came up on its passenger side.

The window slipped down. "Trouble, I see." The man who leaned over from behind the wheel was probably in his late thirties, with sandy hair and a pockmarked face. "Jump in. I'll give you a lift."

She was tempted, if only to get in out of the rain, but a single woman getting into a car with a complete stranger wasn't a smart idea, even if only for half a mile.

"I appreciate the offer," she said, "but you would be doing me an even bigger favor if you would stop at the next call box and let the emergency service know I'm stranded out here. I'll wait for them in the car."

"Okay," he agreed readily. "Wait." He reached behind his seat for something, and for a moment Leanna felt a twinge of panic. If he had a weapon...if he attacked her, there wasn't much she could do in the circumstances. Maybe another car would stop to investigate and give assistance. Maybe not.

He pulled out an umbrella and passed it to her through the window. "Here—take this."

Reflexively, she reached for it, then paused. "How will I get it back to you?"

"Keep it," he said. "It's an old one. I don't need it."

"But...are you sure?"

"Lady, it's raining. Stay as dry as you can. It might be a while before a tow truck gets out here."

She opened it. One of the ribs was bent. Still, she felt instant relief and an encouraging sense of hope under its protection. "If you give me your address, I'll send it back to you."

"Don't worry about it," he said, put the car into gear and rolled up the electric window. With a wave, he pulled back into the lane of traffic.

She couldn't believe it. A total stranger had done this.

In fact, the umbrella didn't do a whole lot of good, except to keep her face and shoulders dry—and raise her spirits. The downpour grew worse as she retreated to her crippled vehicle, and the spray from passing cars splashed her legs and feet. Back at the Toyota, she opened the door, quickly folded the umbrella and climbed inside.

Nearly an hour went by before a tow truck showed up. The time gave her an opportunity to take stock of her situation. None of it seemed very positive. She'd moved to a new city—one in which she felt very much a stranger—to earn more money and get her daughter away from her ex-husband's bad influence. The added income was about to be sacrificed now to car repairs. Her ex had established residence in the same community, and to make matters worse, she was living in a place on virtual charity, for the small rent she was paying was less than half what the *garçonnière* was worth. She and Elise ate at least half their meals with the Fontaines. Even her baby-sitting fees were subsidized. So much for independence.

The tow-truck driver was a burly man in a torn and stained T-shirt, and he had a sour disposition. He seemed offended when she asked about his charges. She had no choice about the tow, he huffed. The police would insist the vehicle be moved. Her only option was where she wanted it hauled to. New Orleans was nearer and would cost less, but she didn't know any garages in "Nawlins," and she'd have the added problems of where to stay and how to get home. She was confident Jackson and his family would take good care of Elise, but she didn't want her little girl to be upset by Mommy not coming home.

"Baton Rouge," she told him. "Take me and the car there."

He wasn't happy. "Look, lady, a friend of mine runs a real good place in the city, and it's a lot closer."

"I don't live in New Orleans," she explained patiently. She could see he wanted to argue with her, so she met his eyes and held them.

"Whatever you say," he finally declared.

She stood in the rain, clutching her handbag under the gift umbrella, while he hoisted the car onto the tow bar. He didn't open the cab door for her and she had a difficult time climbing up the metal steps in her skirt, which was now wet and clinging. The cab was overheated, smelled of stale cigar smoke and greasy food. She'd used her lunch hour to drive around the city, and her empty stomach clenched at the nauseating stench.

His next question, a dozen miles down the road, was where to deliver the car. She didn't know. Jackson, no doubt, would. She hated having to admit the bind she was in to him, but there was no way she could keep this secret. When they got to the outskirts of the city, she asked the driver to pull into the first gas station so she could make a phone call.

"Look, lady, I'm not a taxi service."

"But you are a service," she snapped back, fed up with his attitude and the not-so-subtle looks he'd been giving her across the cracked-vinyl bench seat. Thank heavens it was wide. She'd been relieved to see he didn't have power door locks. She was careful to keep her button up. "And you are being paid by the mile," she reminded him. "Pull into the service station in the next block and wait."

"I'll drop you off there," he snarled belligerently.

"Then you won't get paid. Which is it going to be?"

"The hell you say." Now he was angry.

"And I'll have you arrested for kidnapping and auto theft," she stated firmly, facing him down.

"Th—that..." he sputtered. "That's bull. You called me."

She almost felt sorry for him. Apparently, it hadn't dawned on him that she would fight back. "Look, Mr. Spence," she said, having noted his name on the license tag displayed on the dashboard, "why don't you just let me make my phone call. I'll get you an address where you can drop my car and me off. I'll pay you for your time and courtesy, and you can be happily on your way, richer and wiser."

He mumbled something and pulled into the station she'd indicated.

"Don't take all day," he said as she climbed down into a puddle that came up almost to her ankles.

She considered telling him she'd take as long as she damn well pleased but decided against it. Rummaging for change in her purse, she also got out her address book and made a note of the license-plate number of the tow truck and the name of the driver, for future reference, if necessary. She half expected him to leave her stranded, but he didn't.

Betty answered the telephone. Leanna explained her dilemma.

"You need a new car," the woman stated, as if it were an order.

Leanna could picture her standing at the wall instrument, an unlit cigarette hanging from the corner of her mouth. "Gee, why didn't I think of that?" she retorted, then caught herself. "Sorry," she added. "It's been a trying day."

"And I'm not helping," Betty replied, with the mildest hint of apology. "I take my Harley to Luszte's."

"Lusty?" Leanna asked.

"Get your mind out of the gutter, girl." Betty snickered, and spelled the name. "Hal works on cars, too." She gave the address. "Tell him I sent you. He'll do a good job, and he's honest."

"Did Tanya pick up Elise?"

"She'd require painful surgery to give me back my boot if she didn't. The kid's fine. Relax. If you're not here for Miss Frou-frou's cocktail hour—she's resting her eyes now," Betty mocked, "I'll let them know why. Jackson will probably bring the cavalry."

Leanna laughed. The image held a certain appeal. "Thanks, Betty. I owe you one."

"Nuts." She hung up.

The rain had stopped. Not that it made much difference. Leanna was soaked to the skin and feeling absolutely miserable. Her chauffeur was tapping his fingers impatiently on the steering wheel when she finally managed to climb back into the cab, her skirt restricting her like shackles. She gave him the name and address of the garage.

Judging from the expression on his face, he was about to say he didn't know where it was, but she glared at him so hard he only grunted, then put the truck into gear and drove on.

Less than ten minutes later he pulled into what had once been a filling station. The pumps were gone. The overhead awning was peeling. The windows of the office were painted black. A variety of vehicles— cars, vans, trucks, motorcycles and farm tractors, were parked in haphazard rows on the side and in front of the four garage bays. She did notice, however, that among the sedans was a late-model Cadillac, a BMW, a Mercedes and a Lexus.

Spence was removing the security chains after lowering the hitch, when Jackson drove up in his Jaguar. He shut off the engine, jumped out and strode toward her.

"You all right?"

The wave of relief at seeing him nearly overwhelmed her, and for a moment, she had an irresistible urge to fall into his arms. Except she must look like a soggy rag doll. She certainly felt like one. Contenting herself with a smile, she said, "I'm fine.

You didn't have to come down here." Her smile broadened. "But I'm glad you did."

"That'll be two-fifty," Spence said.

Leanna flinched and turned. "How much?"

"Two hundred and fifty dollars, lady," he said flatly.

Jackson started to say something, but she stopped him with an up-raised hand.

"Explain that, Mr. Spence. It seems a bit excessive."

A man in greasy overalls came out of one of the garage bays and joined them. He and Jackson exchanged what appeared to be familiar nods of greeting.

"There's a fifty-dollar service charge and a per-mile rate of a buck out and back."

"It isn't a hundred miles—"

"Let me handle this, Jackson, please." Her voice was firm with outrage. "It's seventy-five miles between Baton Rouge and New Orleans, Mr. Spence. According to the sign in your cab, fifty dollars is the minimum charge, not a service add-on. You towed me less than fifty miles. I'll write you a check for one hundred dollars. Not a penny more." She started to get her checkbook from her handbag.

"Two-fifty and it's cash or credit card."

"I don't have a credit card," she informed him, "and it's one hundred or I call the cops."

"Cash," he said, trying to sound both belligerent and put upon.

"Check, or you spend the night at your own expense until I can go to the bank in the morning to withdraw the money. Which will it be?"

"I'll pay it," Jackson offered, and started to reach for his wallet.

She spun on him. "No, you won't," she said angrily. "I'll take care of this. Which is it, Mr. Spence?"

The driver glanced at the two men facing him. "Give me the damn check. It better not bounce."

She retrieved her checkbook and a pen and used the hood of her car to write. "If it does—" she handed it to him with a tight smile "—sue me."

He started to make an obscene gesture, saw the expressions on the faces of her companions, thought better of it, got in his truck and roared away.

Leanna turned to the man from the garage. "Are you Mr. Luszte? My name's Leanna Cargill. Betty recommended you."

He smiled at the mention of Betty's name, and put out his hand. "Call me Hal. What seems to be the problem?"

She stood by, tense yet resigned, as Hal examined her engine. The adrenaline of the emergency had run its course. Exhaustion was creeping into her bones.

"Busted radiator hose," he said, straightening up.

Leanna's head began to throb. Was this nightmare starting again? The day after her divorce became final, she'd gone out to her car and found a puddle under the engine. Richard had come by during the night and slashed the radiator hose. A neighbor had seen him. When confronted, he denied doing it, but it was the kind of petty vindictiveness he practiced. The question was whether he had done it again. Her Toyota was a derelict, but it seemed too coincidental that its newest part was the one that failed.

"How long were you running on hot?" Hal asked.

She shook her head. "I don't know. I didn't pay any attention to the gauge until I saw smoke coming out from under the hood."

"It was too late by then." His tone was matter-of-fact, rather than accusatory.

"Can you fix it?"

"The hose is easy." He checked his watch. "It's after five, though, too late to get parts today, but I can have them here first thing in the morning."

She sighed with relief.

"Might be more to it than that, though," he added, before she got too comfortable with the idea of an easy solution. "If the block isn't cracked, the head might be warped from the heat. In that case, I'll have to get it remilled, provided it isn't warped too badly."

"What would that cost?" she asked.

"A few hundred bucks. I'll know when I get a better look at it."

JACKSON HAD WATCHED HER as she explained what had happened. She was a mess. Her clothes were wet and wrinkled. Her hair curled into damp tendrils that would have done Medusa proud. Her lipstick was gone and there were smudges on her cheeks where her mascara had run. And she was absolutely beautiful. He wanted to scoop her into his arms and kiss her.

"Come on. It's the cocktail hour," he said, putting his arm around her damp waist. "You deserve a double orange juice tonight."

She let out a sigh and rested her head against his chest for just a minute, then she pulled away.

"Let's see if Hal has a piece of plastic for your car seat, so I don't ruin the leather."

"Don't worry about it." It amused him that with everything that was going on, she was worried about his car's upholstery.

She ignored him and approached Hal. He nodded, went into his office and came out with a black plastic garbage bag. She ripped it up the sides and spread it over the back and seat on the passenger side before climbing in.

Jackson closed the door for her, slid behind the wheel and took off.

"Why don't you have any credit cards?" He kept his eyes straight ahead and tried to make the question sound casual.

"Richard ran up gargantuan bills on the ones we had, and I'm determined not to fall into the same trap." She turned toward him. "It's also none of your business."

Defensive. Feisty. He wondered what she would be like in bed.

Jackson drove on for several blocks, waiting for her nerves to settle down. "What Richard did has nothing to do with you now."

"What Richard did has everything to do with me. I'm the one stuck with paying the bills." Brooding, she stared out the side window. The streets were shiny wet, but the sky was cerulean blue.

"You don't have to be."

"I made a contract, Jackson. Maybe you would renege on it like Richard, but I won't."

He didn't appreciate being compared with her ex.

"Those people deserve their money." Her voice

was tense with lonely determination. "No matter how long it takes me, they're going to get paid."

He admired her tenacity, her sense of honor and responsibility, but she was unfairly penalizing herself.

"You still can't afford to be without a credit card, Lee."

"What I can and cannot afford, Jackson, is my concern, not yours."

"For emergencies," he persisted.

"I can take care of myself."

He reached over and touched her hand. Her shoulders were rigid, trembling. Partially, at least, from the chill of being so wet. He'd wrap her in blankets as soon as he got her home. But half of the shakes, he suspected, came from pure rage and humiliation.

"I know you can, Lee," he said gently, then smiled. "You did a pretty good job on that Spence character."

He looked over and saw her lips begin to curl into a thin smile, before she caught herself and turned to stone again. But she couldn't maintain the stoic expression. A grin developed.

"I did, didn't I?"

"Remind me not to tangle with you." He squeezed her hand and felt her respond. *Except in bed,* he added silently. He imagined their arms and legs intertwined on rumpled sheets. Taking a deep breath, he tightened his grip on the steering wheel.

CHAPTER TEN

"I'M SORRY WE WEREN'T able to go to the zoo with the girls," Jackson said Saturday morning. He'd just come to the *garçonnière* from the mansion after his meeting with Remy Bouchard. The police detective had stopped by to further discuss the incident at the refinery and Jackson's subsequent encounter with Chuck Riley. Jackson could easily have put the detective off, but he didn't think it would be wise. Bouchard had been working with the family since the fire that Broderick had started.

"How did it go?" Leanna asked.

"Remy isn't eager to adopt a conspiracy theory, but he's also suspicious of coincidences. He promised to look into Riley's whereabouts, when I had my little 'accident' at the refinery."

"Do you think Riley's involved in what's been happening?"

"Something about him isn't right, Lee. First he claimed we owed him money, then he dropped the issue. Lately, he's been drinking awfully heavy, even for him, and getting into scrapes. He used to be a good pilot, now he's been suspended."

Leanna nodded, but he could see her mind was somewhere else.

He moved in front of her, blocked her way and placed his hands on her hips. "The girls are going to be fine.'' He drew her to him and touched his forehead to hers. ''We're going to be fine.''

''I just wish we could have gone with them,'' she said. ''Elise loves elephants.''

He grinned. ''So does Megan. You'd think small kids would be intimidated by such huge animals.''

''They're gentle creatures, and children sense that.''

''Have you heard from Hal yet?'' Waiting for his call was the reason she hadn't accompanied the girls.

She shook her head.

''Maybe after he does, we can catch up with them at the zoo.''

''They've been gone over an hour. Finding them won't be easy.''

Then the phone rang. Reluctantly, Jackson released her so she could answer it. He followed her into the kitchen.

''The block's not cracked?'' she said brightening. ''That's good news, anyway… Oh, but you still have to regrind the head. How much will this cost?'' She scribbled some numbers on a pad by the phone. After a sigh, she said, ''Yes, go ahead. Are the time payments we discussed still okay? Thank you. When do you expect it to be ready?''

She hung up a minute later. Jackson took a peek at the paper. She'd written $500-600.

''What are you going to do?'' he asked.

''Hal says the Toyota should be ready by the end of the week, so I'll have to rent a car for a few days. I just hope nothing else goes wrong.''

''My father's Town Car is sitting the garage,'' Jackson said. ''Nobody uses it. Why don't you forget about the Toyota and borrow it?''

She wavered, as he'd hoped she would. The trick now was to keep the momentum going. "Take my father's car for a few days. At least until yours gets repaired. It's not doing anyone any good parked in the garage."

"A Lincoln Town Car?" She quirked an eyebrow. "You must be joking. Can you imagine the expression on the faces of disaster victims when I drive up in a Town Car to pass judgment on their claims?"

"What difference does it make?"

"You really don't get it, do you?" She shook her head. "Anyway, there's a bigger problem. What do you think Richard's reaction will be when he sees me in a great big Lincoln? I'm already residing at an exclusive address in upscale accommodations. That car would be the clincher. I'd lose child-support payments, and probably end up paying him alimony."

"Don't be ridiculous," he said, dismissing the notion.

"Don't be naive," she countered.

He gaped at her, as stunned as if she'd slapped his face. "Naive? I think you've got it backward, sweetheart." Anger erupted into sarcasm. "You're living in a make-believe world if you think you can avoid debt by not having credit cards...if you think you can save the world by paying someone else's bills."

She stared at him, equally shocked by his outburst. Her eyes were dry, though she bit her lip. "I didn't realize you thought so little of me." She took her cup to the sink. "I'll find a place today and get out of your house. Thank you for your hospitality."

He grabbed her arm as she turned away. She swirled around, and for a fleeting moment, he saw genuine fear in her eyes. At that instant, he hated himself.

"Think that little of you? Are you completely nuts? I love you."

The words slipped out, surprising him as much as her. He hadn't intended to say them. After Paige's betrayal he'd vowed never to repeat those words to another woman, never make himself vulnerable to being hurt and humiliated like that again. Confused by his own admission, he dropped his hand and simply gazed at her.

"You love me?" she asked in a small voice.

He nodded. His gaze still intent on hers, he cupped her face with his hands, his fingers caressing the delicate skin beneath her ears. He could feel her pulse, the slow, heavy throb of her heartbeat. Holding eye contact with her till the very last, he brought his mouth down, joined his lips to hers and tasted.

His tongue found its way between her teeth. He savored and explored. Her body stiffened, resisted, relented, then surrendered, until she had accommodated herself to him. Hunger grew. Need took over. He had to have more of her. Racking his teeth against her lower lip, he reluctantly withdrew.

She kept her head lowered. High color mottled her cheeks. His hands still gripped her shoulders. Gently, he ran them down her arms until he had her fingers locked in his.

"I won't hurt you," he murmured. "I'll never hurt you. You mean too much to me." He pulled her against him, pressed her head to his chest so she could hear the impatient beat of his heart. "Let me make love to you, Lee."

When she didn't respond, he tilted her head up and gazed into her eyes. "Shall we go upstairs?"

The choice was hers. Leanna knew that. She could say no. Surely she had the strength to say no. Except it wasn't a matter of power but of will. She didn't want to reject him. She wanted Jackson, more than she'd ever wanted anyone in her life.

The muscles in her legs threatened to betray her as she moved to the spiral staircase and began the steep climb. He was right behind her, ready to catch her if she slipped, if she fell.

The open, upper room shimmered in the dreamlike aura as the cool afternoon light of December slanted through the windows on the southwest and danced on the walls. Jackson came up behind her, guided her to the bed and sat her on its edge. Crouching, he slowly removed her shoes and massaged her feet, his hands strong, firm, powerful. From his kneeling position, he released the buttons of her blouse. The warmth of his touch heated her already torrid skin. Erotic messages streaked through her body. With soulful eyes and careful deliberation, he slipped the garment off her shoulders and cast it negligently aside. She felt naked until he touched her, then she was bathed in his caress.

Her breathing slackened as his fingers danced along her skin. Slipping his hands behind her back, he unhooked the clasp of her bra and patiently withdrew the garment.

With trembling hands, Jackson cupped her breasts, brushed his thumbs delicately across her nipples, felt them peak under his touch. His mouth found one, then the other. She moaned, a hushed, ragged sigh as his tongue circled each pebbled areola. He tasted salt and skin and heat. He hardened painfully, joyfully.

"Let me," she murmured, the syllables cloaked in a smile.

Leanna ran her hands across his chest. Outlined the ridges of muscles, the small hard points, pressed her hand against the firm ripples of his belly, then pulled his shirt out of his pants. Insinuating her fingers under the cotton, she played in the dusting of body hair. His skin was warm under her palm. Warm and firm and tantalizing.

Patience spent, Jackson lifted his T-shirt over his head, pitched it in a corner and wrapped his arms around her. He thought he would lose it when her naked breasts made contact with his bare chest. He found her mouth and ravaged it. Heat rose to the explosion point. Pulling away, he grappled with the waistband of her jeans. She twined her arms between his and fought to unbuckle his belt.

Sweetness was transported into frenzy; patience, into raw, throbbing need. On their feet, they kicked off the last of their clothing and for one heart-stopping moment gazed at each other. Holding back with more determination than he ever knew he possessed, Jackson gently touched her silky skin. His mouth fell open; his eyes closed. He strained to maintain control.

She stretched out on the bed and raised her arms in a beckoning appeal. He settled beside her and explored the world of touch and taste until he could contain himself no more. His hands shook as he dove for his pants, groped its pocket and withdrew a packet. She took it from him, grinned mischievously as she oh so slowly sheathed him, then smiled up at him as he entered her. Wrapping herself around him, she smothered him in liquid warmth. Their mouths fumbled, fought and found each other.

He pressed down. She arched up. She gasped as the first wave overwhelmed her. She tightened her hold and held him captive. He pulled back. She thrust forward. The second wave nearly drowned her. She was sure she couldn't breathe. At last she opened her eyes to find his squeezed shut. She smiled, shifted, shuddered and took him with her over the crest.

THE ROOM WAS DARKER in the afterglow of the most extraordinary intimacy Leanna had ever experienced. Her life had taken a turn she hadn't planned and wasn't prepared for. She'd tried to resist her attraction to Jackson, but she'd never actually denied it. Not after that first kiss in the garden. She might have fought his invitation to have sex with him, too, if he hadn't said he loved her.

He loved her.

Such sweet words. She'd been starved for the sound of them, for the warm radiance they kindled inside her. Even now she wasn't sated. She wanted to hear them again, wanted to be sure he meant them.

Yet those three syllables frightened her, too. They could only complicate her life.

Did she love him? Or did she only want to love him? Want to be loved?

Oh, yes, she definitely wanted to be loved, and she wanted to make love with this man again, maybe forever. But sex wasn't enough. They were such different people. A Yankee and a Southerner. A woman strapped for money and a man used to living in luxury.

A foolish combination, one unlikely to succeed.

Except that he said he loved her. And God help her, she loved him, too.

"We'll be late for cocktails," she mumbled against his chest, her arm draped across his taut middle.

"I'm already intoxicated," he said dreamily.

"You need to get up." But she made no move to do so.

"Give me a minute to rest, then I'll be ready again."

She poked him in the belly and laughed. "You're insatiable."

He gave her a slow, delicious smile. "For you."

Rising up on her elbow, she awarded him a peck on the lips. His arms ensnared her and pulled her on top of him. "Kiss me."

She complied, then once more arched back. "The girls will be home soon. We really have to get cleaned up."

"I'll wash your back if you wash mine."

"Uh-uh. I'm taking a quick shower while you go over to your room and shower there." When he started to object, she pressed a finger to his lips. "Or we'll never get out of here."

"Spoilsport. I'll wait for you."

She ducked under the spray of warm water, lathered, rinsed and dried herself in five minutes. Jackson, fully dressed, was finger-combing his wet hair in the half bath when she came downstairs. "Ready?"

"As ever," he said, with a leering grin.

She shook her head and opened the entrance door.

"Insatiable," she repeated, as he passed by her and stepped outside. The door clicked shut behind them.

"Pleasant afternoon?"

She froze, the breath instantly sucked out of her. "Ri—Richard, what are you doing here?"

He did a slow survey of her damp hair, Jackson's disheveled appearance, and jumped to a logical conclusion. "Interrupting a tryst, it would seem. So this is why you sent Elise off with Tanya for the afternoon."

"You didn't answer the lady's question," Jackson informed him with cold unconcern. "What are you doing here?"

He gave Jackson a vicious smirk. "I stopped by to see my daughter but learned from Esme that the nanny's taken her to the zoo. That's something I would expect a parent to do, not relegate it to hired help. I can see why now."

"Richard..." She stopped, unsure what to say. He was so good at using her words against her. She couldn't deny what he was insinuating, because it was true. While the nanny was doing her job, she had spent the time making love.

"I don't think this promiscuous atmosphere is an appropriate environment in which to bring up a sensitive young child. I'm sure a judge will agree."

She wanted to fight him, to stand up to him the way she had the tow-truck driver, the way she challenged Jackson. But she was afraid of Richard, afraid of what he could do, afraid of what he would do. She'd tried to reason with him before, so many times, but he was too wily for her. She wasn't concerned about her own welfare or safety. Were she alone, she'd fight him every way she could, and accept the consequences. But she had Elise, and for her she would suffer any torment, even the intimidation and humiliation he seemed to take such pleasure in imposing.

"Get off this property, Mr. Cargill," Jackson said in a raised voice. "And don't come back. If you do, I'll have you arrested for trespassing."

"I'm going, Fontaine." Richard addressed his ex-wife. "I'll be filing papers to get full custody of Elise. You're not a fit mother."

"Richard—" she started to plead.

"Leave right now," Jackson interrupted, "before I also have you arrested for assault."

Richard chuckled, obviously enjoying himself. "Don't worry, I'm leaving. I've gotten all I want here." He took a step away and half-turned. "Please express my regrets to your aunt. She invited me to cocktails." With a laugh, he began walking to his Pontiac Grand Am parked next to Jackson's Jaguar. Again he spun around. "Oh, the reason I stopped by was to tell you I'd be picking up Elise next week for my court-approved visitation. Since I'm no longer welcome here, though, you'll have to bring her to me. One o'clock Sunday at my hotel. Don't be late."

Jackson's hands were fisted as he watched the man go. He then turned to Leanna. Tears were streaking down her face. For a moment, his hatred of Richard Cargill was white hot, but he quickly stanched it. Taking a deep breath, he gathered the woman he loved in his arms. Her whole body trembled against him. The thought crossed his mind that she might hate him for the position he'd put her in.

Fearful of the possibility or that whatever he said

might only make matters worse, he rocked her silently in his arms.

"I'm going to lose her," she moaned on a hiccup. "My little girl. He's going to take her away."

Her sobs tormented him. Gently, he lifted her face to him. "Listen to me, Leanna. He is not going to take Elise away from you. I promise. I'll do whatever I have to do, but I promise you, he'll never get custody of your baby."

"He's going to win. I can't bear the thought of losing her, Jackson. I can't."

"You won't. You have my sworn pledge."

"There's nothing you can do."

He shook his head. "Then you don't know me."

LEANNA WAS HAVING BREAKFAST in the kitchen with Elise and Megan Monday morning. She would have to rent a car today. As soon as business hours started she'd called around for the cheapest vehicle available. She didn't care if it had no fenders and four different-sized wheels, as long as it would get her where she had to go and back. She had three locations on her schedule for today and a dozen more lined up for the rest of the week; as luck would have it, they were in widely separated areas.

"Too bad you don't ride a bike. I could let you use my old flathead," Betty offered. "It's a beaut, even if it does rattle your teeth."

"I knew I should have let Boomer Hodgkiss teach me to drive his hog when we were in high school," Leanna replied playfully. "But my father didn't approve of the black leather."

"Nothing wrong with black leather," Betty snorted. "Specially on a hog. They're a natural."

Leanna chuckled. "Thanks for the offer, anyway, Betty. I appreciate it."

Elise looked up from her bowl of cereal, her eyes wide with wonder. "Mommy, are you going to ride a pig?"

Betty cackled. "Girlie, there's a big difference between a hog and a pig. Hogs are good. Pigs are bad. Dogs are even worse."

The girl wrinkled her nose, totally confused. "I like dogs. Daddy says he's going to buy me a puppy."

Leanna hadn't heard that before. She wondered when Richard made that promise—one he probably wouldn't keep, but that was sure to put her in a bind if he did. She'd love Elise to have a pet, but animals cost money to feed and maintain, and for the foreseeable future, all her cash was committed. For now, Toodles would have to be enough. Typical of Richard, though. But she wouldn't think about that now.

"We're talking about motorcycles, honey," she said, and sipped her coffee.

"Betty said she'll take me for a ride on hers."

The cook's movements jerked slightly, as she removed a pan of hot cinnamon rolls from the oven. Over her shoulder, she said, "Now, don't you go getting me in trouble." After depositing the rich-smelling buns on the top of the stove, she turned to the girl. "I said if it's okay with your mama, I'd take you for a spin around the plantation."

"Can I go, Mommy? Please."

Betty gave Leanna a measured glance, not quite sure if she might be in the doghouse. "I'll be real careful. You know I'd never do anything to hurt the child."

Leanna wasn't thrilled with the idea, but she did trust Betty. The woman was a maverick and a non-conformist, but under the bluster, Leanna was convinced, beat the proverbial heart of gold.

"You have to wear a helmet," she told her daughter.

"Absolutely," the other woman agreed.

"Can Megan go, too?" Elise asked.

"Go where?" Jackson strolled into the kitchen. "Smells wonderful in here."

Leanna explained that she'd just given permission for Betty to take Elise for a short motorcycle ride around the estate.

He smiled. "If Megs wants to go, I have no objection, but I'd like to be here when you take her," he told Betty.

"You're on," the older woman agreed, clearly relieved the matter was favorably resolved.

Tanya slunk into the kitchen, her usual bubbly personality subdued.

"Juice is in the fridge," Betty reminded her.

The younger woman ignored her. "Uh, Mr. Fontaine, can I see you a minute—privately?"

Mr. Fontaine? "Is something wrong?" he asked.

"I just need to talk to you—alone."

Jackson raised his eyebrows, then put down the coffee cup he'd just filled. "Okay. Let's use the dining room."

While they were gone, Leanna tried to figure out what might have happened. Had Elise done something she didn't know about? The child could get carried away in her enthusiasm sometimes, but why hadn't Tanya mentioned it to her, instead of Jackson? Or maybe it had to do with Megan. Elise wouldn't tattle on her new friend, but in her zeal, she wasn't very good at keeping secrets, either. She would have said something to Leanna.

"Finish your milk and go get your book bag, honey," she instructed her daughter.

Jackson returned as Elise was getting down from the table. His face telegraphed confusion.

"Is something wrong?" Leanna asked.

"Tanya just quit. Effective immediately."

Leanna was equally perplexed. "Why?"

"She refused to give me a specific explanation. Said only that it was for personal reasons. She already has her clothes loaded into her car."

Leanna wasn't sure she was particularly sorry to see the girl go. Tanya was a passably good nanny, but her heart didn't seem to be in it—a job she had to do, rather than one she enjoyed.

"Who's going to mind Megan and Elise after school?" Megan got out of preschool at noon every day, and Elise's kindergarten class was released at three. Even if Leanna managed to arrange her day so she could pick them up, there was no way she could stay with them. Her afternoons were crammed with appointments that often ran to six o'clock or later. "What are we going to do?"

Esme breezed into the kitchen, Toodles's toenails clicking on the floor behind her. "Good morning, all," she said, pleasantly. "Betty, you made your cinnamon rolls. Wonderful. A delightful way to start the day."

Betty looked at her askance. Esme wasn't one to throw compliments around, particularly at her.

"Why is everyone so glum?" Esme poured piping

hot coffee for herself and brought the china cup and saucer to the table.

"Tanya just quit," Jackson announced.

His aunt closed her eyes and clucked her tongue. "Good riddance, I say. Did she give proper notice?"

From beyond the back door they could hear the young woman's car pulling out of the shell driveway. Jackson glanced at his watch. "About ten minutes' worth."

"Quite unacceptable. I certainly wouldn't give her a favorable reference, Jackson. Is there an illness in the family?"

"She wouldn't say. The important question now is how we're going to handle her duties until I can hire a replacement."

Esme stirred cream and sugar into her cup. "I can take care of the girls in the interim."

Jackson's eyes widened. "Are you sure you don't mind?"

Esme waved her bejeweled hand dismissively. "*Mon cher,* have you ever known me to say something I didn't mean?" She didn't give him a chance to respond. "Of course I don't mind." She gave him her most determined expression. "You needn't hurry in selecting a new nanny…and this time, Jackson, do a better job."

"That was a surprise," Leanna said, as he escorted her back to the *garçonnière*.

He chuckled. "You can say that again. Six months ago, when I brought Megs home, she would have very little to do with her. Polite and considerate, of course, but there was no affection."

"Taking her negative feelings out on the child wasn't fair."

He agreed. "But she's come around. I should have realized she would."

"What was she like when you were growing up?"

He snorted. "Not the cuddly type." He paused. "But I never doubted that she cared deeply for Casey and me. In a crisis, she would have died defending us. Casey never developed into the lady Auntie E would have liked, and I've let her down, but don't kid yourself, the Dragon Lady loves us."

"It's too bad she never married."

They'd reached the *garçonnière*. "Life is about choices," he said. "She made hers. As for mine, I choose to kiss you. Will you kiss me back?"

She grinned at him. "Not out here, I won't. But come inside, and we'll see."

BY NINE O'CLOCK, Leanna had finished her phone calls to the car-rental companies listed in the Yellow Pages. The best deal she'd been able to find was for twenty-five dollars a day, plus tax and gas. The total would come to around a hundred and fifty dollars for the week—a hundred and fifty bucks she didn't have. The agent had wanted a credit card. When she said she didn't have one, that she would pay cash, he asked for a three-hundred-dollar deposit. Obviously, she didn't have that, either. She'd gone a year and a half without a credit card. It had been inconvenient at times, and she did worry about having to carry cash, but dammit, it had worked. There hadn't been any impulse buying, and she'd been able to make at least a little progress on her mountain of debt. But, as much as she hated to admit it, Jackson was right. She ought to have a credit card for emergencies and contingencies like this. She could apply for one at the bank where she had her checking account. However, it wouldn't be available immediately, and she needed it today. Borrowing the Town Car was beginning to look like her only option.

She shook her head. Not only didn't she want to drive the luxury sedan, she was terrified of what Richard would make of it in court. She could easily imagine him painting her as Jackson's mistress, a woman kept by the owner of a big, private plantation.

The phone rang. Since it was an extension of the one at the house, Leanna didn't normally answer it unless it rang three times, but she knew Betty was off buying groceries with Esme. Leanna wondered if they bickered in the car, too, or if in private they were civil, maybe even cordial, to each other. She suspected their mutual snarling and sniping was at least half for show. Esme might genuinely disapprove of Betty's unorthodox lifestyle, but secretly, the society woman might also envy the aging hippie's independence.

Leanna picked up the phone. "Bellefontaine Plantation. Leanna Cargill speaking."

"Ms. Cargill, this is Hal. Got some good news for you. That radiator hose of yours was on a recall list. Manufacturer's defect. So they'll pay for the replacement and labor necessary to install the new one. Not the damage it done, though."

That would at least save her a few bucks. The more important point, though, was that Richard hadn't had anything to do with this mishap.

"Hey, I just heard that you need a set of wheels till your car's fixed," Hal continued.

Betty must have called him or stopped by. "Yes, I do."

"I have one available. Ain't nothing fancy. The radio don't work, and the body has a few dents and scrapes, but it'll get you where you want to go and back again."

"Mr. Luszte, it sounds perfect."

"Call me Hal."

"What's your rental fee, Hal?"

"Hell, I couldn't charge you to drive that old thing. Just take it as a loaner."

"I insist on paying you something. Fair wear and tear, at least."

He laughed in a good-natured way. "Betty said you'd insist on paying something. Five bucks a day, you buy the gas and I'll supply the oil. Fair enough?"

"More than fair." The world was full of good people, she reminded herself. The man who gave her the umbrella and now Hal. Both were strangers who owed her nothing. "Thank you, Hal."

"I'll have Sonny come by. You can drop him off back here. Give him about fifteen minutes to get there."

"Thanks again, Hal."

"Betty says you're all right, and her word's good enough for me." He hung up.

Leanna bit her lip. Not everyone was like the tow-truck driver—or like Richard. She rose from the table and took her empty coffee cup to the sink. After washing it and leaving it on the drain board, she gathered up her papers, checked her calendar for the day and called her first client to tell him she'd arrive within the hour.

CHAPTER ELEVEN

By WEDNESDAY ELISE STOPPED talking about her father's visit. Leanna had hoped Richard would decide to leave town—disappear as abruptly as he'd appeared. Instead, he was demanding to take the girl out on Sunday.

What would he do with their daughter? See a movie? Go to an amusement park? Fill her tummy with junk food and her mind with lies and innuendos? Leanna's stomach turned sour at the prospect.

She tried calling him Sunday morning. He wasn't in his room. She left a message. She still hadn't told Elise she was supposed to spend the afternoon with her daddy, and now Leanna found herself with a dilemma. If she took their daughter to the hotel and Richard didn't show up, the girl would be devastated. But if she didn't take her to meet him, Richard would have a cause of action against her.

Leanna didn't know if she was relieved or upset when Jackson insisted that he and Megan accompany her and Elise to meet Richard at his hotel. Of course she was pleased that he wanted to be by her side in this minor crisis, and having Megan along would soften the disappointment for Elise if Richard failed to make an appearance. But she wasn't at all sure Jackson's presence was a good idea. Richard had caught them in a compromising situation. Wasn't bringing him along rubbing Richard's nose in it, reinforcing exactly what he claimed—that she was a scandalous mother? The worst part of it was that even though she wanted to continue to make love with Jackson Fontaine, she had no right to, not if it jeopardized her daughter's welfare.

"Where's Daddy taking me today?" Elise asked from the back seat, safely seat-belted in next to her playmate.

"I don't know, honey," Leanna replied. "He didn't tell me."

"Maybe you'll go to Blue Bayou Water Park," Megan offered. "My daddy and me went there in the summer."

Jackson smiled into the rearview mirror. "It's not open this time of year, sweetheart."

"Oh," Elise said unhappily. Leanna wondered if she had doubts about meeting her father, if she realized he might not show up. How often could a little girl be disappointed before she relinquished hope?

"But there are other fun places to go," Jackson assured her.

"Like what?" She sounded doubtful that anything could match a water park.

"Well, the Enchanted Mansion. It's a dollhouse you can walk through. Megan liked it, didn't you, Megs?"

The four-year-old nodded enthusiastically. "It was nice."

"Really?" The moment of interest quickly faded. "That might be all right, I guess."

"Maybe your daddy will take you on a boat to see alligators like mine did," Megan added.

Another summertime diversion. "They don't have

those tours this time of year, either, honey," he commented. "Sorry."

The Beauregard Court loomed, multistoried, Spanish tile roofed and almost elegant. Leanna tried not to be bitter that her ex-husband lived so well and apparently carefree, while she carried all the burdens. Life wasn't fair, she reminded herself, and dismissed the irritation as a waste of time.

Jackson left the Jaguar in the arched-entrance driveway and escorted Leanna and the girls into the lobby. Richard was nowhere in sight. Ashamed of the spark of hope she felt, she stepped over to a house phone and asked for his room. After three rings, he picked up. Clearly, from the huskiness of his voice, he'd been sound asleep. At one o'clock in the afternoon? She knew he worked evenings, but...then the thought occurred to her that maybe he wasn't alone.

"On my way," he said without explanation or apology.

"He'll be here in a minute," she told Elise, and gave Jackson a glance that he seemed to instantly comprehend. To know that he truly cared about her daughter's welfare sent a warm current washing through her. Fighting her battles by herself had been lonely. She felt stronger, more confident, with Jackson by her side.

The four of them sat on an oversize couch facing a splashing fountain, the two girls in the middle holding hands.

Intimidated by the silence and apprehensive about the scene to come, Leanna addressed Jackson over the heads of the girls.

"Have you and your sisters discussed the design of your fountain yet?"

He shook his head. "I found some preliminary drawings Maman put away, but I think we need to design our own. Casey and I didn't know we had a half sister then. Noelani deserves to be part of the decision-making process."

How generous of him to include her. After all, Bellefontaine was part of Casey and him, not Noelani. Over the past weeks, however, Leanna had come to recognize his inherent magnanimity. He liked to please people—a sharp contrast to her ex-husband, who was a taker, not a giver.

The elevator door opened and Richard approached. He was wearing casual slacks and an open-necked white oxford shirt with the sleeves rolled midway up his forearms. He scowled at the sight of Jackson and Megan, his step hesitating for a brief moment, then he strode forward defiantly.

"Hi, sugarplum." He held out his hands to his daughter, lifted her enthusiastically up into his arms and gave her a smacking kiss on the cheek. "Don't you look pretty. All set for your day with Daddy?"

"Where are we going?" she asked with the adventurous enthusiasm of an innocent child.

"It's a secret." He put his finger to his lips and made a *shh* sound.

Leanna nearly groaned. Richard had forgotten he'd asked to take Elise for the day. He had no plans. What would he do to entertain her? Leanna just hoped it wouldn't involve more than watching TV in his room and eating gallons of ice cream.

Elise pressed her finger to her mouth, too, and giggled at their little conspiracy.

"What are you doing here?" he asked Jackson. The question was simple, but the underlying animosity was unmistakable—at least, to the adults. Elise seemed perfectly happy in her father's arms. Megan clung to Jackson's hand.

"Playing chauffeur," he replied easily. "It's a great day for a drive."

"Please have her home by eight," Leanna interjected, trying to forestall any duel of words. "Tomorrow's a school day, and she always has a hard time getting to sleep after spending time with you."

He quirked an eyebrow in a smirk. "Does that mean I'm allowed on Bellefontaine property?" he asked Jackson.

"In this case, yes. Just don't make a habit of it."

"If you want to bring her back early, that'll be fine," Leanna offered, praying that his lack of plans might prompt a short visit. "I'll be home all day."

The corners of Richard's mouth curved up salaciously. "I'm sure you will."

The twist of a dull knife couldn't have hurt more. Leanna struggled not to let the pain show.

Richard chucked his daughter under the chin with his index finger. "Let's go up to my room, sweet pea. I'll get my coat and we can be on our way. Say goodbye to Mommy and your friend."

"Bye, Mommy. Bye, Megan," the girl said happily, her attention focused exclusively on her daddy.

"Have a good time, honey," Leanna said to her retreating figure, and fought the tears that were close to the surface. "I'll see you later."

THEY SANG NURSERY SONGS on the way home and Megan started giggling—a sure sign she was tired.

Jackson carried her directly to her room. The four-year-old asked Leanna to stay while her daddy read from her favorite Br'er Rabbit book. Three minutes later the girl was sound asleep. They crept quietly out of the room, leaving the door slightly ajar.

Leanna had been positive and upbeat with his daughter, but Jackson didn't have to be a clairvoyant to know she was upset.

"You're worried he won't bring her back, aren't you?" he asked, when they reached the foot of the stairs.

Her eyes went wide, as if shocked that he could read her mind. Then the corners of her mouth turned down in a quivering frown. Tears glistened, ready to trickle down her cheeks. "Every time she goes with him I'm afraid I'll never see her again." The words were strained, a cry of abject terror that tore at his heart. If something like that happened to Megan, he wasn't sure he could survive it. How much more devastating must it be for Lee, who had borne Elise and always been an active part of her life?

Should he tell her he had someone shadowing Richard, so that if he dared to make a run with her, he'd be stopped? Not to reassure her seemed cruel.

"He won't get far if he tries anything."

They moved toward the kitchen. Maybe Betty's Cajun coffee or a cup of tea would help relax her.

"A friend of mine is keeping him under surveillance," he said.

She gaped at him from the doorway. "You're having him followed?"

He nodded. "He's a retired cop who does freelance security work."

"Why didn't you tell me about this?"

He smiled. "I just did."

She wasn't amused. "Before you arranged it," she emphasized, a sudden chill in her voice.

He'd expected her to be glad, to be grateful. Was he missing something?

"I appreciate your doing this, Jackson. Really," she said softly. "I feel a lot better knowing someone is watching out for my little girl. But I do wish you'd told me beforehand."

What was the big deal? "Would you have objected?"

He wasn't sure where she was going with this. Maybe he should have kept it quiet, but he couldn't do that. She loved Elise too much for him to let her worry herself sick about losing her.

"No," she admitted. "It's just that I would have liked to be in on your plans from the beginning, an active participant in the decision, not a bystander."

"I only made the arrangements late yesterday afternoon. Besides—" he stepped toward her and brushed his knuckles along her cheek "—you know about the tail now. I hope it puts your mind at ease, at least a little."

She nodded. "It does." She clasped his hand. "Thank you." Then she pulled away and left the room.

THE WHOLE FAMILY—Jackson, his sisters Casey and Noelani, their husbands Nick and Adam, and Aunt Esme—spent the rest of the afternoon at the mansion, on one of the rare days when they all had arranged for time off from their busy schedules. Jackson dragged out the fountain designs his mother had filed away and everyone sat at the dining room table and reviewed them. He, Casey and Noelani were the ultimate decision makers, but the others, including Leanna, were welcome to offer ideas and suggestions.

The hours passed, but not nearly as rapidly as she had hoped. She played with Megan when the girl woke up, though all the time thinking of Elise, of how happy she always was to be with her father, how willingly she would go anywhere with him. That the two of them were being monitored was some consolation, but not enough. Elise's place was here with her, and Leanna couldn't relax until she was back.

Cocktail hour rolled around. She confined herself to juice and noted that Jackson limited himself to mineral water. Apparently, he wasn't all that at ease, either.

Esme popped the casserole Betty had prepared into the oven, since the cook was off this Sunday. It was ready on time, and was probably delicious, but Leanna couldn't even have said what it was. She picked at her food, afraid to eat, certain she would be sick if she did. Jackson watched her. His eyes straining to reassure her, but he wisely said nothing. Words were useless. Only one thing would relieve the ache in her heart, the pain in her belly, the insanity that threatened her mind—the safe return of her little girl.

Goddam Richard Cargill to hell.

The dishes cleared, everyone returned to the drawing room. Nick challenged Adam to a game of chess while they sipped cognac. Casey and Noelani paged through magazines on architecture and gardening in search of the perfect fountain. Esme read a French storybook to Megan, who was picking up the language with the unselfconscious agility that only a child possessed. Everybody but Leanna and Jackson had something to do.

"Let's walk in the garden," he suggested. It had become their retreat, their private refuge.

"I was to stay by the phone."

"There are five adults in the house to answer the phone," he pointed out with a reassuring smile. "You can use some exercise, some fresh air. We won't be a minute away from a call."

She wanted to shrivel up into a little ball and hibernate until Elise came home, but that was cowardice. Jackson was right, she needed to stretch her legs, inhale some deep breaths. He extended his hand. She took it greedily. The strength of his fingers and the warmth of his palm conveyed images of a cozy fire on a cold winter's night, as well as deep, mysterious, intriguing shadows in a summer woodland.

The chill, damp night air didn't bother her as they strolled hand in hand down Whistle Walk to the site of the future fountain. His touch, his closeness reassured her. This crisis would pass. The darkness would flee, replaced with sunlight.

"Just a little while longer," he said, when they reached their bench. It was already half past seven.

He turned to her, reached for her free hand and captured it. They faced each other, their bodies mere inches apart. He leaned forward and angled his head. His lips found hers. A soft, sweetly gentle bonding.

Suddenly, her control snapped and Leanna wrapped her arms around his waist and held on with a desperation that brought tears to her eyes. She pressed her head against his chest and wept. Only the warmth of his body, the smell of his skin and the murmurs of his deep resonant voice saved her from completely collapsing.

"It's going to be all right," he reassured her. "She'll be home, safe and sound, in a little while."

"If anything happens to her—"

"Shh." He tightened his hold. "I won't let anything happen to her or to you," he promised, and for the moment at least, she believed him.

He brought his mouth down to hers. This time their joining wasn't sweet but savage, not a union but a campaign, a crusade he won; she lost herself in his kiss. For just a little while the only world she knew was the one they shared. Lips fused. Tongues probing, teasing, taunting. His body was hard against her. Hot. Alive. Aroused.

She wanted more of him, wanted the clothes separating them to magically disappear so she could touch his skin, all of it and feel his hands caressing hers. Soft lights and string music played in her mind. He stroked her breast, sending liquid heat cascading through her. She felt the firm muscles beneath his cotton shirt, his heartbeat thumping in time with hers.

But reality had a way of intruding. Besides, they had to come up for air.

"I want to make love with you," he whispered in her ear.

She wanted to feel him inside her, too, but Elise could be home any minute.

With Richard.

She thrust herself away. Far more strength of will was required than physical pressure. Jackson acquiesced, and though she wished he wouldn't, she loved him for it. She was safe with this man who was looking out for her welfare…and Elise's.

"I'm glad it's cool this evening," she said idiotically.

He laughed, not at but with her. "A cold rain would be better. An ice-cold downpour. But it still wouldn't be enough to cool what I feel for you." He tilted her head up to him and kissed her briefly on the mouth. "Fire and ice. Fire wins every time."

She chuckled, bit her lip against the flow of tears and moved away, back toward the house. She helped him put Megan to bed.

"Is Elise coming back?" Megan asked. "Has she gone away like Mommy and I won't see her again?"

Leanna's heart broke. She hugged the little girl. "Of course she'll be back. She'll be here when you wake up in the morning. I promise."

She looked over at Jackson, whose face was stoic, but there was a painful sadness in his nod of approval.

"Now, why don't you let your daddy read you a bedtime story—"

"Daddy, can Miss Lee read me a story tonight?"

He grinned, but Leanna couldn't quite interpret the message. "You bet."

She selected an excerpt from Beatrix Potter while he sat on one of the small chairs near the window. Leanna felt the smile she knew was on his face as he listened to words he could probably recite nearly as well as his daughter. The atmosphere—just the three of them—was warm and poignant. He came up by her side.

"She's asleep," he said softly. "Thank you for being here for her." He kissed her on the top of the head, then bent and kissed his daughter on the cheek.

Together they pulled up the comforter and tiptoed out, leaving the door open a crack.

They went and sat on the cushioned chairs of the veranda.

And waited.

Eight o'clock came and passed.

Eight-thirty. Neither of them said anything.

Eight-forty-five. Leanna's hands were restless, shaking. She got up and paced.

Nine o'clock. So Richard was an hour late. So what. It was only an hour, and it wasn't the first time.

Her legs were so weak she had to sit down. "Maybe you could call your friend." Her voice trembled.

"It's going to be all right, Lee. He would have contacted me if there was a problem." He reached out his hand and covered hers. "But okay."

Jackson picked up the cell phone he'd earlier laid on the table and was punching buttons when the headlights of a car swept up the driveway. He closed the small instrument and rose. Unsure she could stand on her own, Leanna didn't move until he loomed in front of her with his hands out. Her whole body shook.

Richard pulled up in the driveway below them. Even before his car had come to a complete stop, Leanna was around the passenger side, tugging on the back door. Richard turned off the engine before hitting the door-lock release. Elise was half-asleep.

"Hi, honey," Leanna said, unbuckling the safety belt. "Did you have a good time?"

"Can I have a pony, Mommy?" Her eyes weren't completely open.

"A pony?" What had Richard promised her now?

A pony? Leanna could barely afford to buy her new clothes. Anger rose in her throat, but she swallowed it. Her argument was with Richard, not their daughter. She lifted the girl, who was nearly deadweight, out of the car and cradled her head on her shoulder. The warmth of her sleepy body was like a tonic, invigorating.

"What makes her think of a pony?" Leanna challenged him.

"We went to the Fair Grounds Race Course in New Orleans," Richard explained. "She got to pet some of the horses in the paddocks."

"The races." Leanna wasn't going to ask how much he'd lost. It wasn't her concern anymore. The only thing that mattered was having Elise back in her arms.

"Then we went to the Café du Monde for beignets."

Leanna had wanted to be the one to share that experience with her daughter; Richard had robbed her of it. Did he know? Had it been a calculated move?

"And there's a little shop down the street where they make a terrific sundae with marshmallows and peanut butter."

Fried dough and sugar overload.

"Mommy, my tummy hurts."

Great. Elise would be up with a stomachache, or, worse yet, vomiting half the night. But she was home. That was all that mattered. Elise would get over the indigestion, and Leanna's heart would quit making a punching bag of her chest. For now, at least.

"I asked you to have her here by eight." There

was no use in arguing over this, but she couldn't let it go by without comment.

"Sunday-night traffic. It was really heavy." He wasn't the least bit apologetic. Did he understand the torment he'd put her through? Leanna could forgive him if she thought he didn't, but she was afraid that had been precisely why he was late.

"Good night," she said, and started to make her way to the *garçonnière*.

"Are you coming back next week, Daddy?" Elise called out weakly.

"You bet, honey bunch. Next Saturday. We'll go to that dollhouse you told me about."

Contented, Elise snuggled into her mother's shoulder.

"Drive carefully," Jackson said.

The two men eyed each other in frosty silence, then Richard slid behind the wheel of his shiny Grand Am and drove away.

Leanna was upstairs when Jackson let himself into the *garçonnière* a minute later. He waited in the living room, listening to the cooing sounds of a mother putting her child to bed. He'd missed this warm atmosphere of home and family in Megan's early life. He'd do his best to make up for it.

Several minutes passed before Leanna reappeared at the foot of the spiral stairs. Her face looked stricken, like a war victim, shell-shocked, traumatized.

He went to her, spread his arms and gathered her to him. She curled up against his chest and the floodgates opened.

"I thought I'd lost her," she moaned, and her body shook against his.

''Shh. She's safe now, and so are you.''

In his heart, Jackson vowed that Richard would never again hurt the people he loved.

JACKSON SPENT a sleepless night. He and Leanna hadn't made love in the week since the afternoon Richard had shown up unexpectedly, but it hadn't been far from his mind—or hers, if he was reading her right. He'd never experienced anything to compare with those two hours of lovemaking with Leanna. He'd also said the words he'd foresworn. *I love you.* Words he'd said to Paige, too, but this had been different. With his former fiancée, he'd wanted them to be true. With Leanna, he had no choice. Even if she rejected him, he'd never be able to stop loving her. He was committed to Leanna in a way he'd never felt before. She'd filled a void in him he never realized existed.

He worried now about how he was going to keep his promise of preventing Richard from hurting her. That a man would use his own child as a pawn to punish the woman he'd promised to love and cherish was contemptible, but contrary to what Leanna thought, Jackson was not naive.

Somehow, Richard Cargill had to be taken out of the picture.

Bribery alone wouldn't work. It would only lead to blackmail, demands under threat, for more and bigger payoffs; the cycle would never end. Jackson had to think of something else, something more subtle and permanent. But what?

He lay on his back, staring at the ceiling. There were two ways people were brought down. By manipulating their strengths, and by taking advantage of their weaknesses.

What were Cargill's strengths, his virtues? He was charming, intelligent, a good talker, and apparently, an above-average cook. He was easygoing and seemed adaptable to circumstances and situations. Based on the way he dressed, he had good taste and a certain air of sophistication. What vulnerabilities did these assets disguise? He was vain and liked his creature comforts.

What were Cargill's weaknesses, his vices? Leanna had been pretty clear in that area. He was manipulative, vindictive, something of a control freak, yet he couldn't manage his money. He had expensive tastes, and he liked to gamble.

Bingo!

CHAPTER TWELVE

JACKSON'S FIRST STOP Monday morning was at the courthouse. Judge Sarratt was in the habit of coming in at eight o'clock to deal with the mounds of paperwork the law imposed on him.

The building was already bustling as lawyers, clients and clerks scurried to get administrative details taken care of before court sessions were called to order. Jackson could have gone to Shelburne Prescott for answers to his questions, but the law firm of Prescott, Walters and Simms was getting enough Fontaine money without adding another billable hour to the total. Might as well go to the man who could actually make it happen.

Harlan Sarratt's courtroom and chambers were in the east wing of the second floor of the art-deco courthouse, not far from the capitol—the only state house that was a skyscraper. The marble floors and wainscoting had the patina of age and lent a certain dignity that Jackson found pleasing. He'd entertained notions of going to law school when he was in college, but the prospect of the extra years in the classroom had dissuaded him. The concept of balance and justice still intrigued him, though, and that was precisely his goal this morning.

He walked down the corridor, turned the corner to the judge's private chambers and knocked on a door marked Private. A moment passed before he heard a muffled, "Come in."

The room he entered was large, the furnishings formal and reserved, but it was so cluttered that the atmosphere of quiet deliberation was missing, replaced with an impression of haste and confusion. The high-back, thickly upholstered leather swivel chair behind the chaotic desk dwarfed the old man. Jackson had observed him in action in the courtroom on a few occasions and was always amazed that a man of such diminutive size could command so much respect. But he did.

He rose now and came around the side of the desk, hand outstretched. "Jackson, haven't seen you since your folks' memorial service. It was a beautiful affair. Duke would have been impressed and Angelique would have been pleased. How is the family coping?"

Jackson shook his hand and accepted the visitor's chair. "We're moving forward."

"Of course you are." Sarratt settled back on his throne and lifted his coffee cup. "Can I offer you something?" When Jackson declined, he asked, "Now, what brings you my way? I doubt you're here to collect condolences." He never was one to waste time on small talk. "Surely Janis isn't pestering you." She signed away her parental rights when she was convicted. Jackson had sole custody. "Does she still want to see Megan?"

Jackson had visited Janis once in prison. She'd asked him to bring Megan next time. He'd refused but told Janis he'd allow access to their daughter after she was released, but he wouldn't subject the child to seeing her mother behind bars. Janis had remained silent for a long time, then she'd nodded her agreement.

"This isn't about me," he said.

Sarratt took a sip from his oversize coffee mug.

"A friend of mine is from Ithaca, New York. Moved here a couple of months ago. She's divorced and has custody of her five-year-old daughter. Her former husband pays child support and has visitation rights."

The judge nodded.

"Her ex has recently relocated here, as well. My friend is afraid he'll petition the court to lower his child-support payments, based on his perception that she's doing well financially and doesn't need them."

"Does she?"

"He declared bankruptcy immediately after their divorce. She refused to and got burdened with half his debts. She's financially strapped."

"What appearance would make him conclude she doesn't need his support payments?"

"She's living at Bellefontaine."

The little man quirked an eyebrow.

"Renting one of our *garçonnières*."

Again, the judge nodded without comment.

"Leanna is also concerned about visitation rights. Richard's appearances are erratic and very disruptive of the little girl's life."

Sarratt shook his head. "It happens in divorce cases. Parents use their children to get back at each other. It's vicious and cruel, but without credible evidence of physical abuse or overt intent to do harm, there isn't much that can be done. It takes more than hearsay to terminate parental rights, if that's where you're headed."

Jackson set his jaw. That was exactly where he was going. "Isn't the welfare of the child the court's primary concern?"

Sarratt's smile was a grimace. "Of course it is, but that isn't always easy to determine. I have two things to consider. Direct evidence and testimony. Evidence is rarely uncontested. Is a bruise the result of abuse or an innocent accident? Testimony is almost always he said-she said. Even witnesses can't agree. The most obvious conclusion to be drawn is often both sides will do or say anything to get their way. The worst part is when both sides sincerely think they're right."

Jackson mulled that over. He'd spent enough time with Leanna to know how devoted she was to her daughter, and he'd seen enough of Richard to recognize his suave vindictiveness. What played most prominently in his thoughts was the look of abject fear on Leanna's face when Richard had confronted them at the *garçonnière*.

The judge went on, "You said they were divorced in New York. Any adjustment to his financial obligations toward the child would go through family court there. The same for any modification the mother might seek in his visitation rights."

"They both live here now. Doesn't that make a difference?"

Sarratt stroked his chin. "It could. The parents can petition the court in New York to transfer the case. It doesn't have to agree, of course."

"But it is possible?" Jackson asked. He wanted earnestly to dispel the mood of helplessness he saw on Leanna's face when she had to deal with her ex-husband. Moving jurisdiction to friendly territory would empower her. He looked forward to watching her stand up to Richard in that feisty, take-no-prisoners way of hers.

The judge conceded the possibility with a nod.

"Could it be transferred to your court?"

Again a thoughtful nod.

"You said parents. Does that mean both parties have to agree to the transfer?"

Jackson was sure he could persuade Leanna to request the move here, but he was less confident about the prospects of Richard agreeing. He was single and apparently unconcerned about money. Making court appearances inconvenient for her was to his advantage, leaving him free to sway the court. There were ways to cajole agreement, of course.

"Either party can initiate the request," Sarratt said. "In this case, since both parents are permanent residents here, it shouldn't be a problem. The overriding issue, as you noted, is the best interests of the child."

"How long would it take?"

Sarratt frowned. "A month or two. Unless I'm given a compelling reason to expedite it. Then I might be able to assume jurisdiction sooner."

"What kind of documentation do you need?"

The man behind the desk studied him as he took another lingering sip of his coffee. For a moment, Jackson thought the old man was going to ask what he was up to, but he didn't.

"The clerk downstairs has the forms. He'll also notify the other party of the proposed action and give him ten days in which to comment."

"Thanks, Judge." Jackson stood up and offered

his hand across the desk. "You've been an inspiration."

Sarratt was leery. "Glad I could help. Say hello to the family for me. How's Esme doing?"

Jackson laughed. "Mellowing." She'd really taken to the kids.

"Give her my best." He escorted Jackson to the door. "Still having the Christmas ball this year?"

"Aunt Esme wouldn't hear of canceling it."

The judge laughed. "No, I don't suppose she would. Some traditions are sacred."

"BETTY, YOU NEED to start the fruitcakes, if they're going to be ready in time for *le bal*."

It was Monday evening. Betty had set the dining-room table and was getting ready to leave for the day.

"You're a slow learner, Esme. I've been doing this for nigh on to twenty years now and the fruit-cakes have always been ready on time, so why don't you just concentrate on your bridge game and let me do the cooking."

"Hmmph." Esme snorted.

"What's *le bal?*" Elise asked, doing a fair pronunciation of the French.

"Oh, *mes enfants,*" Esme said, her powdered face lighting up. She was wearing a frilly dress this evening that made her seem younger and almost flighty. "It is a long tradition here at Bellefontaine, one that goes back at least a hundred and fifty years. *Le bal* is a wonderful dance party."

"A party?" Elise grabbed Megan's hand. "We're going to have a party. Is it like a birthday party? My daddy gave me a birthday party when I turned four.

We had balloons and cake, and a real clown. Will there be a clown at this party, Auntie E?''

Esme's face broke into a rare, uninhibited smile. ''No clowns, my dear, but we will have a string quartet to play soothing music while we dine and—''

''I know what *dine* means, Mommy,'' Elise declared. ''It's a fancy word for chowing down. Betty told me.''

Esme rolled her eyes and shot the cook a withering glance. Betty blithely ignored it. Leanna smothered a chuckle.

''And we will have an orchestra afterward so people can dance,'' Esme went on.

''Instead of clowns, everybody dresses up like someone else. Can't be themselves.'' Betty removed an empty serving dish.

''Dresses up? How?'' Elise wanted to know.

''In period costumes.''

Elise looked up at her mother. ''What's that?''

''They wear old-fashioned clothes, honey, the kind people wore a long, long time ago,'' Leanna explained.

''Like in the pictures upstairs?''

''Precisely,'' Esme concluded.

''Ooh, neat.'' Noelani accepted her mint julep from Jackson. ''Christmas on the old plantation. Sort of romantic.''

''Noelani, dear, you did such a wonderful job arranging for the band at the *cochon de lait*. Do you think you might be able to get Luc Renault for the ball?'' The pork roast was part of the Sugar Fest held every year at harvest time. Setting up the luau-like barbeque had been Noelani's first project when she joined the family. ''I know it's awfully late to be requesting him," Esme continued, "but would you check to see if he's available for Christmas Eve?"

"Glad to."

"I've already spoken to Marc Antoine about his string quartet. They did a splendid job last year."

"Does *everyone* wear costumes?" Noelani asked.

"Oh, yes."

"What will you come as?" Casey asked her half sister.

"Not a hula dancer, I promise you." Noelani laughed. "But I'll think of something."

"Lee, my dear," Esme said. "I'm sure this catches you off guard—unless Jackson mentioned it to you."

Leanna shot him a mock sour expression, then curled the corners of her lips. "Not a word."

"In that case, I have a gown in the attic that should do nicely. It might need a slight alteration, but I believe it will suit you perfectly."

"That's very kind, but I really couldn't accept."

"If you prefer to get something of your own, of course—"

"It's not that. Actually I don't have anything—" and she couldn't afford to rent anything, either "—I don't want to impose."

"No imposition at all," Esme assured her.

"What can me and Megan wear?" Elise asked.

"Ah, I have just the things for you two. After we eat we can go up to the attic and find them."

LATER THAT EVENING, while the women were discussing clothes, Jackson gave Casey's husband a nod and invited Nick to join him in private conversation. The two men went to Jackson's office. He poured them each a snifter of the aged Napoleon brandy his father kept there, and they slipped out the back door. A generation earlier they would have lit cigars—a humidor on a corner of the credenza still contained several fine cheroots—but neither man smoked.

They proceeded to the east side of the huge house, toward Whistle Walk.

"I need your help," Jackson said.

"Name it," Nick replied readily.

Jackson led him over to where the new fountain would be built. "Has Richard Cargill been in your casino?"

Since it was right across the street from the Sugar Belle, where Richard worked, it seemed likely.

"He comes in every night after his shift around eleven."

No use asking *if* he gambled. "What does he play?"

"Blackjack, mostly. A little poker."

"Is he any good?"

Nick flipped his hand. "He wins a little, but he hasn't got sense enough to quit when he's ahead."

"How much has he lost?"

"So far he's down a few hundred."

Not enough. He'd have to be a big loser if Jackson's scheme had a chance of working. "You've kept track?"

"With the new security systems, we monitor everybody. Having met the man and seen the reaction he had on Lee, I made it a point to check on him."

The effect Cargill had on his ex-wife was apparent for others, too, it seemed. Jackson had wondered if he alone had noticed. "Does he have an open chit?"

Nick shook his head. "Strictly cash. We don't accept checks or credit cards. Not directly. We have ATMs located conveniently throughout the casino. He uses them, but when he runs out of the green stuff, the game's over for him.''

Sounded as if he was up to his old tricks. "I'd like you to grant him a line of credit.''

Nick stroked his chin. "I can do that if you really want me to, Jackson, but I'm curious why you would. We extend credit to people we trust to honor their debts. From what I know of this character, he doesn't have the dough, and he apparently doesn't feel compelled to pay his bills. Didn't Lee say he declared bankruptcy last year?''

Jackson nodded. "Which means he can't use that tactic to escape his creditors for another six years. I'll make good his losses.''

Nick cocked his head. "What are you up to, Jackson? This guy's a loser and hardly a friend.''

"I have my reasons.''

With an amused but wary chuckle, Nick said, "I'm sure you do. Perhaps it's just as well I don't know what they are. Not right away, at least. Maybe when the statute of limitations runs out.'' He studied his brother-in-law. "You're certain you want to do this?''

Jackson nodded.

"Very well, I can write off a few thousand as the cost of doing business.''

"I said I'll cover his debt. All of it.''

"No dice.'' Nick smiled in a brotherly, man-to-man way. "I don't know exactly what you're scheming—though I could probably figure it out if I put my mind to it, but I'm not going to. Whatever it is, it must be important to you, and it must be about Leanna. You're in love with her, aren't you?''

Jackson bowed his head. He'd hoped he hadn't been so obvious.

''That's good enough for me. I like her, Jackson. I like her spunk. I can see why you're attracted to her, and I have no doubt this is to help her. Before long, if my guess is right, she's going to be part of this family, so just chalk this up as my contribution to happily ever after.''

''Thanks, Nick.'' Jackson held out his hand. ''I appreciate this more than you realize.''

''Hey, what are brothers for?''

ELISE AND MEGAN WERE in their beds, sound asleep, when Leanna and Jackson took their walk through the garden.

''I spoke with a judge this morning about moving your case here from New York.''

''You what?'' She stopped, blinked and stared. ''You discussed my affairs with a judge without consulting me, without even finding out what I wanted?''

''You already told me what you wanted, Lee. Besides, I spoke in generalities, a friendly inquiry about what options might be available.''

She didn't thaw. ''You talked about me, about Elise, without telling me, without even asking me if you could.''

''Lee, please listen.''

She'd turned away from him.

There was no use trying to convince her his heart was in the right place. Maybe if she heard what he'd found out, she'd focus on that instead of him.

"Here's the way things stand. Tell me where I went wrong."

She stiffened her shoulders, but he knew she was listening.

"If Richard petitions the court in New York, you either have to hire an attorney to represent you there, or go there in person, or lose by default. That puts you in a spot. First, it costs money. Second, it means using vacation time or leave without pay to appear in person. That's time and money. And third, you would have to take Elise with you, disrupting her life—or leave her here, which would probably be even worse. She'd feel abandoned."

Leanna's posture sagged. Jackson wanted to put his arms around her, but she wasn't ready for him yet.

"The alternative is to have the case transferred down here. Not only would it make things cheaper and easier for you—and Elise—but you'd be dealing with them in a more hospitable environment. I have friends here, Lee, people who'll vouch for your character and testify to the shenanigans Richard will probably try to pull."

She shrugged, not quite as uptight as she had been, but still unhappy. But then, why shouldn't she be? Most of her efforts seemed to crash down around her.

"Judge Sarratt says all you have to do is petition him. The magic words are 'It's in the child's best interest,' and he'll have the case transferred here."

She swiveled. Her cheeks were wet with tears. How he wanted to kiss them away, to make this whole situation disappear.

"Richard isn't stupid, Jackson. Haven't you figured that out yet? He'll never agree to moving jurisdiction down here for the very reasons you mentioned. He wants to play this in his home court, not the visitor's.''

"He won't have a choice. Judge Sarratt is a friend of mine. He'll get venue changed, and he'll rule in your favor.''

She shook her head. "Wheeling and dealing.''

"Doing what's right.'' Jackson sucked in a chestful of air. "I'm not breaking the law. I'm simply using it to our advantage. Isn't that what Richard does?'' He tilted her chin up with the side of his index finger. "I told you I would never do anything to hurt you, and I meant it. I not only renew that pledge, I promise I'll do whatever it takes to protect you and Elise.''

She raised her eyes. They were shiny. He used his thumbs to gently wipe away the tears that ran down her cheeks. Then he kissed her softly on the mouth.

She wound her arms around his waist and rested the side of her head against his shoulder.

He inhaled the scent of her hair. "Do you trust me, Lee?''

"No…yes…I'm scared.''

"I know you are.'' He tightened his hold on her. "This is going to come out okay. You have my word on it.''

He just hoped he could keep that promise.

BY TUESDAY MORNING, Leanna made up her mind. Jackson had given her the chance to move her battle with Richard close to home—her home. Not to take advantage of it would be foolish. Even before Richard showed up, she should have explored the possibility of having the case transferred to where she and her daughter lived. She should have taken the matter out of her ex-husband's court, literally. She'd accused Jackson of manipulation and assuming control, which was true enough, but he was also thinking more clearly, more aggressively than she was. Well, he'd put a sword in her hand, and she was determined to wield it.

The clerk at the courthouse was a small balding man in his early sixties. The nameplate on the counter identified him as Stanislas Wyclowski.

"Mr. Wyc...clowski—" she stumbled over the name "—I'm Leanna Cargill." She extended her hand across the counter.

"Call me Stan," he said with a friendly smile. "Everybody does." His Southern drawl was mellow and pronounced. "It's a lot easier."

She smiled back. "Stan. I'd like to file a petition with the court to have jurisdiction for my child-custody case transferred from Ithaca, New York, to here. Can you help me?"

He pushed his wire-rimmed glasses up on his nose, reached under the counter and withdrew a series of forms. "Mr. Fontaine mentioned that you'd probably be coming in and asked me to expedite things for you."

Had Jackson talked to everyone in the parish about her? "How long will the process take?"

"I'll get the judge to sign the forms today and send them off this afternoon. Can't speak for the folks in New York, of course, but I believe Judge Sarratt plans to call up there and ask them to make it a priority. I'm sure that'll help."

Leanna found herself torn between two emotions. On the one hand, knowing so many people were aware of her situation was disconcerting; on the other, being recognized and so well treated definitely boosted her morale.

"I'll need a few documents from you," Stan went on. "Your divorce decree, a copy of the custody agreement..." As he rattled off several others, she produced them from her attaché case.

"You're well organized, Ms. Cargill," he said with approval. "Most people require two or three trips before they get it all together."

"If I'm going to call you Stan, Mr. Wyclowski, I think you ought to call me Leanna or Lee."

The paperwork took less than half an hour to complete, thanks to Stan's assistance. He was meticulous in checking all the boxes, making sure all the numbers and names were accurately spelled out. "I'll deliver these up to the judge right away and personally put them in the mail today, Ms. Lee," he said as he slipped them all into a manila folder. "And I'll notify Mr. Cargill that the petition has been filed."

"Can he hold things up?"

"That'll be the judge's call." He patted the folder almost fondly. "Everything's in order here. Don't you worry your pretty head. Mr. Fontaine's already talked to Judge Sarratt. This'll go through fine." He smiled reassuringly. "I'll phone you as soon as we get word back. Shouldn't take more than a couple of weeks."

Leanna left the courthouse with a feeling of relief and hope. There was something to be said for having friends in high places.

From there she went to the bank and applied for a credit card. She had no intention of using the card, but it was a form of emergency insurance. The interest rate wasn't very good, and the limit was low, but at least there was no annual fee.

The mood of liberation soon faded, however, as she contemplated the problems still facing her. Jackson and the parish clerk assured her that her petition to family court would go through expeditiously, and she didn't doubt them, but it also made her worry what vindictive maneuver her ex-husband, who didn't accept defeat gracefully, would take in retribution.

CHAPTER THIRTEEN

JACKSON WAS IN HIS OFFICE reviewing his dwindling account balances the following Thursday morning, when he received a call from the parish clerk.

"Mr. Fontaine, you asked me to let you know if Mr. Cargill came in."

"Has he?"

"He just left."

"What did he want?"

"He received my letter about Ms. Cargill requesting the move to family court here. Didn't seem real happy about it, but said he had no objection."

Richard was smart enough to recognize when the deck was stacked against him.

"Like you figured, Mr. Fontaine, he wanted to file a petition with the court, requesting full custody of his daughter—" there was a brief pause and the sound of paper being shuffled "—Elise Cargill. He says she's living in an unwholesome environment."

Jackson cursed under his breath. He'd hoped the reassignment to local jurisdiction would dissuade Richard from following through on his threat. "He came in alone? No attorney?"

"I suggested he might want to retain one, like I advise everybody, but he said all he needed to do right now was fill out the paperwork."

That was good news. A lawyer could really fog

the issue. Richard's acting alone also suggested he didn't have the resources to hire a lawyer—not yet, at least. Another positive note. Of course, putting out the word through Prescott that Cargill was a deadbeat might have foiled his attempts to get one.

"Did you let him?"

"No way I could legally prevent him, Mr. Fontaine, but I haven't processed the application yet. By law, I'm supposed to do so within twenty-four hours, but I thought I'd apprise you first."

"Thanks, I really appreciate this. Look, Stan, this is sort of a delicate matter, and I have to iron out a few details. Would it be possible for you to delay the process for a day or so, on a technicality or something?"

Jackson could almost see the man at the other end scratching his chin. "I might—"

"I'll be very grateful. You and my dad went back a long way. He knew he could always count on his friends and you were one of them. He taught me that friends help friends. That's what it's all about."

There was the briefest pause while Stan absorbed what Jackson was saying and what he was implying. "There is this one box," he muttered thoughtfully. "He was supposed to initial it, but he didn't. Normally, that doesn't make any difference and we just ignore it."

"I imagine that's with people you know, Stan," Jackson said helpfully. "Cargill's an outsider, from up North. I heard he had a real slick attorney there when he got divorced. I wouldn't be surprised if he didn't leave that little box blank so he could challenge the validity of the document should the case not go the way he wants it to. You know how litigation-happy some people are, and for the pettiest reasons. They just like to cause trouble.''

"You're right, Mr. Fontaine." Stan sounded more confident now, having been given the rationalization he needed for what he was about to propose. "It's my duty to make sure details like that are covered. I'll just hold on to this until he comes in to check the status, then I can have him initial that block the way he should have in the first place."

"There's a reason we keep electing you to the job, Stan. You're a good man. Say hello to Lainey for me, will you? She *is* still making her pecan fudge, isn't she? Aunt Esme was saying just yesterday that she needs about ten pounds for the Christmas ball, and no one makes pecan fudge better than your wife."

"She'll be pleased to hear that, Mr. Fontaine."

Jackson hung up, leaned back in his chair and steepled his fingers. So Cargill was making his move. Next step check, then checkmate. Jackson picked up the phone and called Nick at the *White Gold* floating casino. Less than a week had gone by since Cargill had been invited to join the inner circle of high rollers. He'd accepted immediately, as Jackson knew he would, and that night had lost almost a thousand dollars at poker.

"What's the tally so far?" Jackson asked his brother-in-law.

"You might want to reconsider this," Nick said. "He's already into us for more than twenty thousand."

Jackson whistled. "Whew, I hadn't expected him to run up a tab that big that quickly." He did some fast calculating in his mind.

"Jackson, I'm going to have to cut him off. I can absorb ten grand without too much trouble, but a sum this large will take some creative bookkeeping."

"I don't want you to do that," Jackson said.

"Not cut him off? That's crazy. There's no limit to what this guy can lose. Even doubling his bets, which he's been doing liberally, he won't make any real headway against this debt. He's not that good a player."

"I meant I don't want you to cook the books," Jackson clarified. "I told you I'd reimburse you for his losses."

"Jackson, I'm not asking you for the money. Besides, I know you haven't got that kind of cash, and if you did it would be going into the refinery."

"I'll get it."

"How?" Nick asked, concern in his voice.

"Leave it to me."

"So you're saying I should cut him off, right?"

The Jaguar was less than a year old, with fewer than ten thousand miles on it. He should be able to get at least sixty grand for it, though it was worth much more, but forced sales meant steep discounts—as Duke and Roland knew.

"Give him one more night," Jackson urged his brother-in-law. "Up to twenty-five thousand."

"You're sure?"

"Yep." He was amazed by how good it felt to be doing this.

"What's going on?" Nick asked, in spite of his earlier vow not to.

"I'll see you at cocktails this evening and fill you in then. And thanks for your help, Nick." Jackson disconnected, flipped through his Rolodex and dialed another number.

"Hal? I need to talk to you about selling my car. I'll be there in twenty minutes." He hung up, then hit his quick dial for the law office of Prescott, Walters and Simms. The senior partner was in.

"Shel, something important has come up. Are you free this morning?"

"Hold on." A minute later, the attorney was back on the line. "I was supposed to be in court in a little while, but one of our associates can handle it."

"I'll be there within an hour."

Jackson called the county clerk's office. "Stan, I could use another favor."

He hung up three minutes later and went in search of Aunt Esme to tell her to stop by Lainey's place and buy ten—make that fifteen—pounds of pecan fudge. He hoped the ten-dollar-a-pound confection could be frozen, because few people ate more than one piece.

NEARLY TWO WEEKS HAD PASSED since Tanya quit. With Esme taking up the slack, the daily routine had changed very little, but Leanna was still suspicious of the nanny's abrupt resignation. A sudden illness in the family would certainly explain the lack of notice, but why not say so? Why the secrecy?

Since the young woman had been employed full-time, there had to be a personnel folder on her, probably in Jackson's office. After her Friday-morning appointment, Leanna returned to the estate. No one was likely to be around at that hour. The girls were in school. Betty was off shopping, and Esme had her weekly appointment with her hairdresser.

Tanya had come to live at Bellefontaine shortly
after Jackson had brought his daughter to live there,
not long before the series of events began that put
the plantation in such jeopardy. Harold Broderick
claimed he'd been hired to burn down the house and
steal the harvester, but he was unable to identify
who'd paid him. Denise Rochelle, the woman who'd
attacked Noelani and sabotaged the sugar mill,
blamed Duke for her father's ruin. Did Tanya have
a similar grievance against the family? Could she be
a link in the chain that would lead to the real culprit?

The major suspect in Leanna's mind was still Murray Dewalt. He certainly had reason to hold a grudge
against the family. Jackson's sister Casey had
spurned him as a lover. Duke had bought the family's
refinery at a depressed price, after thwarting their efforts to upgrade it. As for the explosion and fire that
had destroyed the raw sugar, Murray was in the best
position to engineer it, as well as the scaffold col-
lapse that could have cost Jackson his life.

But why would Murray use Tanya? Could they be
lovers? Leanna tried to remember if she'd ever seen
the two together. She hadn't, but that didn't mean
anything. Maybe Tanya was simply a spy in the
house, reporting the family's moves and plans back
to Murray. Did her abrupt departure mean the attacks
were over—or that another one was in the offing?

The house was quiet when Leanna let herself in
the kitchen. Her pulse was racing. She wasn't cut out
for this line of work. Skulking around, spying on
people had never been one of her childhood fanta-
sies, much less an avocation. Worse yet, she was
going behind the back of someone who trusted her.
Jackson and his family had welcomed her into their

home, and they were in danger. She'd promised him she'd help identify their enemies, and she wouldn't go back on her word.

She stepped into the hall and called out. No answer. Her heart was pounding. Her footsteps tapped on the wooden floor, echoed on the walls. If someone appeared, how would she explain her presence?

A light flashed through the back-door window. Her heart stopped. She stood perfectly still. Waiting. Nothing happened, and she realized it was the sun glinting off the windshield of the Kawasaki Mule a grounds man was using to haul fertilizer to the shed beyond the garden. She clutched her throat, sucked in a breath, entered Jackson's office, and went directly to the file cabinet across from his desk. It was locked, but she knew he kept the key in the top drawer of the desk. Not the best security in the world. She paused to listen for anyone approaching the room. All she heard was the distant whine of farm equipment and birds chirping outside the window.

After extracting the key, she returned to the cabinet and popped the lock, again listening, again reassuring herself she was alone, and started rifling through files. Tanya's folder was in the third drawer. It listed her grandmother, Hazel Carson, as her next of kin and gave an address in the city. Once she'd jotted it down on a scrap of paper, Leanna returned the file to its proper place, locked the cabinet and dropped the key back in its hidey-hole. Her chest was still pounding when she strolled out the back door.

She'd picked up her Toyota that morning. Whatever Hal had done to it seemed to have rejuvenated the old bomb. It didn't look any better. The upholstery was still faded and lumpy, but at least Leanna's stomach didn't flutter with fear that the vehicle was going to die every time she stopped for a red light.

The address she was looking for turned out to be a narrow, two-story clapboard building in serious need of maintenance. Its look-alike neighbors weren't much better. Leanna walked up the cracked concrete path, mounted the chipped brick steps of a rail-less stoop and rang the bell. Receiving no immediate response, she was about to leave, when the door cracked open a few inches. A small, white-haired woman gazed up at her.

"Does Tanya Carson live here?" Leanna asked.

"She done something wrong?" The voice sounded frail.

"No, ma'am," Lee said politely. "I just wanted to talk to her."

"She ain't here."

"Can you tell me where I might find her?"

"Probably in Las Vegas by now. Left a couple of weeks ago, real sudden."

"What about school?" Leanna asked.

"She's on semester break."

Of course. Leanna had forgotten how close they were to the holidays. She had a few small presents put away for Elise, but not much. For the moment, though, she buried that particular pang of guilt.

"Had she been planning this trip for long?"

"Who are you?"

"I'm sorry. My name is Leanna Cargill. I know Tanya from Bellefontaine and was surprised when she left so suddenly. I wanted to make sure she was all right. She never said anything about a trip to Las Vegas."

"It came up at the last minute," the woman said,

apparently not pleased with the decision. "She hired on as a nanny because she was broke, then all of a sudden she comes home, packs up her car and high-tails it to that sinful city. I never did understand the girl."

"Do you know when she'll be back?"

"Took most of her clothes with her. Said she's going to get a job in one of them fancy shows. Crazy, if you ask me."

More like very suspicious, Leanna thought. She thanked the woman and returned to her car. Why had Tanya gone to Las Vegas when she was only a se-mester away from getting her degree in music?

The smell of payoff was ripe. But who had bank-rolled it and for what reason?

JACKSON TRADED a few jokes with Stan that after-noon while he sat in the parish clerk's office. The man had just called Richard to say he'd found a dis-crepancy in the paperwork he'd submitted and asked him to drop by as soon as possible to resolve it.

"I'm real sorry, Mr. Cargill, but I'm afraid I can't submit your petition to the court until this matter is corrected," Stan had added contritely.

Jackson could imagine the other man's irritation. But the guy was smooth. When Stan hung up a min-ute later, he seemed almost ashamed. "He thanked me for bringing it to his attention and promised to be here within half an hour."

The time was almost up when Richard walked into the office. He started to say something to Stan, then saw Jackson.

"What are you doing here?"

"I heard you were going to be in the area and figured this would be an opportunity for us to chat."

Richard cast a glance at Stan, who was pretending to shuffle papers. "We have nothing to talk about."

"I think we do." The two men stared at each other across the counter. "Stan, do you mind if we use your private office for a few minutes?"

"Sure thing, Mr. Fontaine. Go right in. If the phone rings just ignore it. I'll pick it up out here."

Warily, Richard went through the swinging gate and into the inner office. "Now, what the hell's so important for you to bribe that genius into being your patsy?" he demanded, when the frosted-glass door was closed behind them.

Jackson raised an eyebrow. His opponent was smart. He'd caught on to the ploy quickly, and he commandeered the chair behind the desk, putting himself in the power position. Not that it would do him any good.

"I understand you're petitioning the court for permanent custody of Elise."

"My daughter's none of your business."

"It is when you identify me as the cause of action, accusing me of being a corrupting influence on the child."

"You're sleeping with her mother in the same room where she sleeps. Sounds morally repugnant to me, and I think it will to the court, as well."

Oh, Jackson mused, *this guy's good with words.* Never mind that he had no proof beyond wet hair and a guilty look on Leanna's face that they had had sex, or the fact that his daughter hadn't been home at the time. Punching him in the mouth would have been very satisfying, but Duke had had a motto—

one he didn't always obey himself—never show anger to an enemy.

"I'm not here to talk about that, anyway," Jackson said with apparent calmness. "I understand you have accumulated a few gambling debts."

"How did you know—" Richard stopped, and for the first time, Jackson saw the breezy facade slip. "Nick Devlin is your brother-in-law."

Jackson rewarded him with the faintest of grins. "My information is that you owe the White Gold Casino $24,658. Is that correct?"

"I'll pay it back. I've just been having a run of bad luck."

"Uh-huh." Jackson watched him, trying to determine if the guy really believed that. He must, otherwise he wouldn't keep playing. "There's just one problem."

"Yeah? What?" Richard asked, regaining his equilibrium, his bravado.

"Nick's cut you off, as of today."

The man's mouth nearly fell open in shock. "He can't do that." He jumped up from the power chair. "He has to give me a chance to recover."

"He already has," Jackson said, "and you flunked the test." His grin was a little wider this time.

Richard took two strides behind the desk, circled around, then seemed to study an award hanging on the wall for outstanding service to the community. He spun to face Jackson, who had his feet up on the corner of the desk.

"What do you want?"

Jackson examined his fingernails. This wasn't taking as long as he'd expected. "I'll make you a deal."

"What kind of deal?" The gambler was worried.

Did he think Nick was going to have his legs broken? Cooking from a wheelchair would be hard.

"I want you to leave Baton Rouge."

"I—"

"I'm not finished yet," Jackson said sharply, though he hadn't raised his voice. "Sit down and hear me out."

Richard sat, albeit grudgingly.

"I'll pay off your gambling debts in full and give you another twenty-five thousand in cash on condition that you agree to leave Louisiana and not return as long as Leanna and Elise live here. In addition, I want your promise not to communicate with Elise before her eighteenth birthday, and after that, only if she initiates the contact. You're not off the hook for child support, and I promise the court here will track you down if you miss a single payment."

That would change if Leanna agreed to marry him and Jackson was able to legally adopt Elise. But he was getting ahead of himself. He'd spent half the night debating the wisdom of what he was doing—coming between father and daughter. Elise loved being with her daddy, but the child deserved to have a caring father in her life, not this opportunist, this user.

Jackson had been mad as hell when Duke had urged him to pay Janis off and abandon his daughter. He didn't know at the time that his father had himself done just that. Jackson had later been even more angered by his parents' selfish decision to keep Noelani out of their lives.

Now he himself was playing God. There was one big difference, though. Richard would do his daughter harm. Leanna knew it; Jackson knew it, and he couldn't let that happen. Richard could always tell him to go to hell, of course—

"You can't make me give up my visitation rights," Richard said, but Jackson could see he was weighing the matter very seriously.

"You're absolutely correct," he replied, unconcerned. "So here's how we're going to handle it."

He picked up the attaché case he'd carried in with him, placed it on the desk and opened it. Out of the corner of his eye he watched the other man's reaction when he saw the stacks of bills neatly aligned there. From the lid pocket, Jackson removed a manila folder and laid its contents on the desk.

"This is an agreement, duly drawn up by my attorney, in which you agree to the terms I just outlined in exchange for a cash payment of twenty-five thousand dollars and the settlement of your gambling debt to the White Gold. You sign it in the presence of witnesses, and I hand over this fine leather case and its contents to you. I expect you to leave town within twenty-four hours."

"This is preposterous and illegal."

"Possibly." Jackson was unfazed by the accusation. Shelburne Prescott had been very leery about drawing up the papers. "But you don't have much choice, do you? It occurs to me that even if you are able to make some sort of arrangement with Nick Devlin to settle your debt to him, you'll never get it paid off, not with the interest he can legally charge you. So for the next six years, at least, until you can file for bankruptcy again, you're going to have very little walking-around money. Bye-bye new car, fancy clothes. Did I mention Nick is also passing the word?

You'll be blackballed from every casino from Atlantic City to Reno. So, no fun, either.''

Richard sank into the chair and rubbed his head. "I need to think about this."

"Seems like a no-brainer to me, but take your time. The courthouse is open for another—" he checked his watch "—hour and twenty minutes. Of course, the bank will be closed by then. I don't think it's wise to leave this kind of money sitting around your hotel room or in your car over the weekend— this is Friday—but it's your call.'' He lowered his legs, shoved one copy of the agreement across the blotter, put his feet back up on the corner of the desk and folded his hands behind his neck.

To Richard's credit, he didn't jump at the deal hastily, though he kept eyeing the contents of the attaché case, which Jackson intentionally left open. A full ten minutes went by, seven more than Jackson had calculated, long enough, in fact, to make him begin to worry.

"Where do I sign?" Richard finally asked in a defeated voice.

By now, Jackson had begun to sweat, but he was careful not to let his manner betray his anxiety—or his relief. Slowly he got up, lowered the lid of the case and opened the door.

"Stan," he called out, "we have a document that needs to be witnessed. Do you happen to have two people available who can accommodate?"

"Sure thing, Mr. Fontaine."

A minute later, a middle-aged woman and a younger man entered the room. They didn't have to read the document they were witnessing and weren't asked to do so. They examined Richard's driver's license to verify his identity, watched him affix his signature, then signed on the lines designated for them. As an added measure, though it was unnecessary, Jackson asked Stan to notarize the papers. With that many signatures, it would be impossible for Richard to deny he had signed it or to claim it was under duress.

Jackson thanked them all and let them go. After the door was closed, he again opened the attaché case and asked Richard if he wanted to count the money. To Jackson's mild surprise, he did. Five minutes later, he snapped the case shut and stepped out from behind the desk.

"Good luck," Jackson said. Neither of them made an offer to shake hands.

"Take care of them," Richard replied, picking up the briefcase full of cash. It was his first and only reference to his ex-wife and daughter.

"Stan," Jackson said to the clerk as Richard traversed the outer office, "I'd like to get this document recorded."

Richard paused at the outer door for just a moment, then, without looking back, stepped out into the corridor.

CHAPTER FOURTEEN

"WHERE IS EVERYONE?" Leanna asked Betty, when she arrived home at lunchtime. Since school was out, the girls could usually be found outside playing on the back porch or in the garden, or if the weather was inclement scurrying through the house.

"Madame Frou-frou took them shopping for a Christmas tree. They all sounded like they were on a sugar high when they left."

Leanna laughed. "Christmas-tree buying is a very important job."

She should be the one taking her daughter to select the perfect tree. Another disappointment. Not that she could afford much this year. She'd planned to wait until late on Christmas Eve, when vendors were abandoning their unsold stock. Her dad said his father used to do that because they couldn't afford to spend money on frivolous luxuries, either.

"Well, you can count on Esme to get something so ridiculously big it'll have to be cut down to fit in the drawing room." Betty was trying to sound critical, but Leanna thought she heard a kind of admiration, maybe even wistful sadness, in the complaint.

"I always liked huge trees when I was a kid. The bigger the better," Leanna commented, and was about to ask Betty what kind she'd had as a child, but something in the woman's demeanor intimated she shouldn't go there.

The sound of a car pulling up in the driveway behind the house distracted them both. A minute later, childish giggles and adult laughter emanated from the hallway. Leanna went out to greet them.

"Mommy," Elise cried out with bubbly enthusiasm, "we bought a tree. Auntie E says it's *magnifique,* but I think it's really, really pretty, and it's really big, too." She held her arms out to their full extent.

Leanna knelt and helped her daughter remove her coat. "I can't wait to see it."

"It'll be delivered this afternoon," Esme announced, as she assisted Megan with her furry jacket. "Is the drawing room prepared?" she asked Betty.

"But of course, *Madame,*" the cook responded sarcastically.

"Oh, put a sock in it," Esme snapped at her. "Crack a smile for the sake of the children, or I'll take away your vitriol shampoo."

For a moment the two women faced each other, eyes locked, then Betty burst into laughter. It was the first time Leanna had heard the usually snide woman genuinely loosen up. "You're on, you old biddy."

Esme gave her a twinkle-eyed sneer, then turned to the children. "Come along, *mes petites,* it's time for lunch. Then, after your naps, we need to start stringing garland on the banister."

They ate in the kitchen. Grilled-cheese sandwiches and tomato soup for the girls, soup and salad for Esme and Leanna, followed by fruit compote for all of them.

"I'll have Jackson get that dress down from the

attic for you later," Esme told Leanna after the girls had gone to the bathroom to wash their hands. "It belonged to my grandmother and will probably need some alterations. We're running out of time."

"You're very kind, but I couldn't possibly allow you to alter a family heirloom just for me," Leanna objected.

Esme reached across the table and patted her hand. "My dear, this will be a very special Christmas party for all of us. The first one without Duke and Angelique." Quickly, she dismissed the note of sadness that crept into her voice. "But more important, I suspect Jackson will propose to you. Under the circumstances, *Grandmère* would want her favorite cotillion ensemble to fit you perfectly."

Leanna's breathing stopped. Jackson propose?

Excitement scrambled inside her, warming, frightening. Panic shimmered just below the surface. She wanted Jackson, and the admission scared her half to death.

Before she had a chance to respond, the girls barged back into the kitchen. Together, Esme and Leanna escorted them up to Megan's room, where Esme tucked her grandniece into her bed and Leanna covered Elise with a colorful afghan in what had been Tanya's bed across the room. When the two children were settled, if not asleep, the women left.

"If you will excuse me, my dear, I have some correspondence to attend to before we attack the decorations."

Leanna went back downstairs and into the kitchen to retrieve her handbag and attaché case. She had two appointments that afternoon and hoped they would be short, so she could join the decorating project.

"You're the first woman he's brought home that old woman has ever approved of," Betty said, her back to Leanna, as she hand washed the wooden salad bowls. "And a Yankee," she added with a snort. "I never would have believed it."

Leanna didn't know what to say.

"She can be a fool sometimes," Betty went on, "but she isn't this time." The aging hippie turned, dish towel in her rough hands, and faced Leanna. "You're good for him. Good for this family. I hope you stick around."

Leanna closed the gap between them and kissed Betty on the cheek.

"Now, get out of here," the older woman insisted. "I have work to do and so do you."

JACKSON DECIDED TO WAIT until after dinner before telling Leanna about his negotiations with Richard. As it turned out, it was much later. The Christmas tree, a huge noble fir, had been delivered that afternoon by two men, who were guided by Esme in setting it up. Jackson arrived just as they were leaving. No doubt they'd grumbled while his aunt considered, then reconsidered precisely how to place it, but they had smiles on their faces as they waved to Jackson on their way past him. Esme was generous with her tips when workmen were duly respectful and cooperative.

The usual cocktail hour had been waived so decorating could continue uninterrupted, though sipping wine or—shudder—beer during the project was permitted. At Esme's direction, Betty prepared a tray of sandwiches for dinner instead of the usual sit-down fare. Nothing was to interfere with stringing lights, hanging ornaments or draping garland.

"This is like a party," Leanna commented, as she and Jackson struggled to unravel Christmas lights. He was on his knees.

"I think there's a law of physics that says these things must tangle," he muttered over a totally uncooperative knot, then looked up. "This is Auntie E's favorite time of the year. Wait till you see her at the ball. You'll swear she's twenty years younger."

"Is that popcorn I smell?" he asked Megan and Elise, who were wheeling two big bowls into the room on Esme's tea cart.

"We're going to string popcorn and cranberries for the Christmas tree," Elise announced.

"Ooh, can I help?"

"Be careful, girls," Leanna said with a laugh. "He'll eat all the popcorn."

"I'll let you untangle the lights," Jackson offered as a trade.

Elise examined the rat's nest of wires. "That's okay, Daddy. We can do it."

Daddy?

"No," Megan yelled. "He's my daddy. You can't have him. You have a mommy—" her lower lip quivered and a tear trickled down her cheek "—and I don't. You can't have my daddy, too."

She ran to Jackson, arms outstretched, as if to protect him from this usurper, but then she clutched his neck, betraying fear that he might disappear. Over the child's head, Jackson and Leanna exchanged anxious expressions.

Elise stood, hands by her side, next to her mother. "I just wish he was my daddy, too," she said, trying to explain to her best friend. "My daddy never stays home with Mommy and me or helps us do things. And he tells lies. He makes promises, but he doesn't keep them. Your daddy doesn't tell lies."

Leanna lowered her head and squeezed her eyes closed for a second. Jackson was right. Elise was smart enough to figure things out. Dammit.

Jackson held his daughter with one arm, extending the other to Elise. With an upward glance at her mother, Elise moved into the shelter of his arm.

"We're all family here," he said, "and I love you both."

They snuggled up to him. He held them tight and planted kisses in their hair.

Leanna's eyes glistened.

"So you're going to make me untangle all these wires myself, huh?" he asked after a long minute of quiet comfort.

"You have to, Daddy," Megan said. "We're not allowed to play with 'tricity."

"You're absolutely right. Safety first." He gave each of them another peck on the foreheads, then released them. "Okay, you work on the cranberries. I'll struggle with the lights."

The girls pushed the cart to the other side of the room, where Esme was waiting to show them how to go about stringing the white and red edibles.

"I'm sorry about that," Leanna said quietly.

"Sorry? For what?"

"Elise calling you Daddy."

"You have nothing to apologize for and neither does she. I took it as a tremendous compliment."

"Thank you for handling it so well."

He wanted to kiss her and was about to lean forward, when Nick passed by carrying several boxes of ornaments. "How'd things go today?" he asked.

Jackson groaned and settled back on his haunches. "Mission accomplished. Thanks for your help."

"My pleasure." Nick winked, and moved on.

"What mission?" Leanna asked.

"I'll tell you about it later." Her frown indicated she didn't like being put off. "Don't fret. It's good news, but I want to tell you about it privately."

"If it's good news, why can't you tell me about it now?"

He snorted. "Because it's personal and private. That's why."

"Then how come Nick knows about it?" She was pouting.

"Lee," he said with a note of amusement, "drop it for a while. Please. I'll tell you later."

But she wouldn't be put off. "I just wonder what it could be if it's personal and private, yet Nick is aware of it. Has anybody else been brought in on this secret I'm being kept in the dark about?"

He studied her. She'd been jittery all evening. He wondered why. "What's gotten into you?"

"Nothing's gotten into me. I just don't like being left out of something that obviously concerns me."

He raised himself up on one knee and kissed her lightly on the lips. "All in due course, *chérie*."

LEANNA COULDN'T BELIEVE she was being such a nag, pestering Jackson like a shrewish wife. But Esme's prediction earlier in the day had been playing in her mind all afternoon. *I suspect Jackson will propose to you.* Suppose he did. Suppose he didn't. One prospect was more frightening than the other.

If he asked her to marry him, would she accept? She'd be a fool even to consider it. They'd known each other less than six weeks. Besides, she'd already had one unfortunate marriage. What made her think her ability to pick men had changed for the better? Richard and Jackson were different in many ways, except in one critical area. They were both manipulative. She hadn't recognized it in Richard before she'd married him. Maybe it was marriage that had brought it out, but more likely, he'd been that way all along; she'd just closed her eyes to it until it was too late.

Jackson was another matter. She'd known from the start that he was manipulative. Didn't he have the reputation of being his father's son. Duke had been an expert at playing with people, and hadn't Jackson used her on their very first meeting when he offered not to cause her trouble if she'd agree to investigate for him?

She'd given in because she'd had no choice, or so she'd convinced herself. Ethically, she should have told him to go to hell, but morally, she had a higher obligation to protect her daughter. After all, she rationalized even now, it wasn't exactly a pact with the devil.

Jackson wasn't a bad man. She'd castigated him for speaking with the judge about transferring her case here from New York, but she had to agree with him in one respect; the transfer was in her and Elise's best interest. He said he hadn't discussed it with her first because he hadn't wanted to raise her hopes unfairly. What he couldn't seem to understand was that she wasn't objecting to what he did; she just wanted to be included in the process. Maybe he'd learned his lesson. She hoped so.

She chuckled. The reason she'd hounded him about his good news was that she thought he and Nick might have conspired over an engagement ring. Was he going to propose tonight? Is that what was so personal and private that he wouldn't discuss it in front of the others.

"What's so funny?" he asked, sounding a little annoyed that he wasn't in on the joke.

"Nothing," she said, laughing this time. "Just get those lights untangled so we can string them on the tree tonight."

THE CHILDREN WERE finally in bed. Elise had begged to sleep in Megan's room, and since it would leave the *garçonnière* free, Jackson had no difficulty agreeing to the idea. Now the two adults entered the guest house alone. The door was hardly closed before Jackson had her in his arms, his mouth plumbing hers. He'd been waiting for this minute all evening—this kiss and what was naturally to follow.

"Aunt Esme brought over some wine this afternoon," Lee murmured an inch from his lips. "You must be thirsty. Tree-decorating—"

"I'm already light-headed from the sight of you," he said, "but not sated. I want more." He caught the sparkle in her eyes.

"No wine, then." She touched her lips to his. "Maybe another time."

"Maybe," he whispered. Bending, he slung his arm behind her knees and picked her up. She held on to his neck, making him aware of the expanding and contracting of his chest as her warm breasts pressed against him. "Right now, I think I better get you to bed."

She cupped his cheek, ran her fingers along the stubble of his beard. "It's been a long day," she agreed. "You must be tired, too."

"Hmm." He struggled to carry her up the narrow, winding stairs. The grand staircase at the mansion would have been much easier. Once at the top, he placed her gently on the double bed, brushed his lips across hers and stretched out beside her. His fingers toyed with the top buttons of her blouse. Her hand skimmed the taut muscles of his belly.

She licked his earlobe, setting a hot spike of pure lust streaking through him. He fought to control his fingers, to release the small buttons of her blouse. With each opening his hand explored more of her. His breathing slowed, deepened, heated.

She groped, pulled at his shirt, his belt buckle, his zipper. He was on fire, ready. Past ready. They fumbled with a condom.

In the next minute, they were both naked, hips to hips, arms and legs entangled. He entered. She received. He stayed. She surrounded him. His hands stroked the sides of her breasts. His mouth found one erect nipple, then the other. A kind of elemental joy cascaded through him when she squirmed in frustrated delight.

The ripples grew into a wave, the wave into a wild, frothing crest. He fought against the undertow as the next surge raised her hard against him. He strained for control when he felt her peak and plummet. She sucked the air out of his lungs. He smiled down at her, pleased with himself, in love with her.

She grinned back. "My turn."

"CAN YOU TELL ME NOW what this big secret is you've been holding back on me?" Leanna asked, her head nestled on his shoulder, her fingers roaming the fine sheen of hair dusting his belly.

"You won't have to worry about Richard anymore," he said, with a touch of pride.

Not the answer she'd expected. Instantly wary, she raised her head. "Why's that?"

"I had a meeting with him today. He agreed to leave town and not come back."

She pressed a hand against his chest and propped herself up on her elbow. Her heartbeat was beginning an uncomfortable tattoo, and not only because of the feel of his flesh under her palm. "What's this all about, Jackson?"

"I received a call from the parish clerk Wednesday. He told me Richard was filing papers requesting full custody of Elise."

"He what?" She dropped onto the pillow and stared up at the ceiling. Her chest ached. "Oh, God. I should have known. This was a mistake. *We* are a mistake. I should never have come here." Tears pooled in her eyes.

Jackson adjusted his posture to face her, then reached out to dry her cheeks with his fingertips. "You didn't hear what I said, Lee. He's gone. He's not coming back. He won't be disrupting Elise's life anymore."

She was about to explode. He was playing with her, tormenting her. She jumped from the bed, grabbed the dressing gown from the upholstered chair by the window, put it on and sat primly, facing him.

"Explain what's going on. All of it. Now." Her

tone was angry and scared. She could see by the expression on his face that he had no idea why.

He pulled himself up, realized he was naked and covered himself to the waist with the sheet.

"As I said, Richard went to the courthouse to file for change of custody. The clerk is an old friend of the family. I'd asked him to let me know if Richard came in for any reason. Stan—he's the clerk—agreed to delay processing the petition on a technicality. I'd already talked to Nick to find out if Richard had been in his casino. Of course he had, and he was a consistent loser, but since he had no credit, he was limited to the cash advances he could get on his bank cards."

"He's at it again. He never learns." This time her anger was directed at the man who'd nearly ruined her life with his gambling.

"I asked Nick to extend Richard a line of credit. He agreed."

"What?" She gaped at him. "That's like giving a drink to an alcoholic."

"He was already gambling, Lee. I didn't start him."

"You accelerated the disease."

"I reject the analogy, but we can talk about that later. Do you want to hear what happened, or do you just want to blame me for his vice?"

She huffed, the weight of powerlessness smothering her.

"If it will make you feel any better, yes, I knew he was going to run up a high-dollar deficit," Jackson continued. "In the meantime, I met with Shelburne Prescott—"

"Another old family friend?"

"Our lawyer."

She raised an eyebrow, repulsed by the cabal of connections and conspiracies, yet equally fascinated by it.

"I had Shel draw up an agreement. This afternoon I asked Stan to call Richard, inform him there was a discrepancy in the paperwork he'd filled out and—"

"Was there?"

"A minor one, but it was sufficient reason for not processing the petition. Richard agreed to come in and correct it."

Leanna crossed one leg over the other. She'd worried about this man being manipulative, and here he was proudly boasting he was that—and more.

"I was there waiting for him. I'd already found out from Nick how deep a hole he'd gotten himself into. About twenty-five thousand dollars' worth."

"My God. That's worse than last time. Of course, he had some help," she added sarcastically.

"I made a deal with him, Lee. I offered to pay his gambling debts and give him another twenty-five grand in cash—I had it there in an attaché case for him to take with him—if he signed the agreement Shel had drawn up, promising to leave Louisiana and not contact you or Elise again."

Lee realized her mouth was open and shut it. "You had absolutely no right—"

"He agreed to the deal," Jackson said, rushing on, "without haggling. He counted the money, signed the paper in front of witnesses, picked up the booty and walked out. I imagine he's already left town. Henri Gaudage, the owner of the Sugar Belle, is probably cursing tonight because his sous-chef hasn't shown up."

Leanna dropped her head in defeat. One part of her was relieved that Richard might actually be gone from their lives, finally. After all, hadn't that been her goal in moving down here? But the end didn't justify the means, and the means Jackson had used were underhanded and dishonest, if not illegal.

"You've overlooked a few details," she said after a long pause.

"Like what?" Jackson was sitting quietly, watching her.

"The agreement was obtained under duress and is the result of bribery. It'll never stand up in court. In fact, what you've just given him is a stronger weapon to use against me."

Jackson pursed his lips. "The provisions of the agreement might not hold up in a court of law," he agreed, "but that's not the point. He accepted them, and I have witnesses that there was no coercion."

"It's bribery. By its very nature it's illegal and will be thrown out in a heartbeat," she insisted.

"I also had it recorded at the courthouse, Lee. It's a matter of public record. That makes it hard to quash as evidence." He stood up and put on his underwear, then sat again on the side of the bed, facing her. "Can you imagine a judge awarding custody of a child to a man who would sell his parental rights to cover his gambling debts? I can't. Not in this jurisdiction."

"Because you control the judges."

"Whoa. Stop right there. I may try to influence judges and municipal bureaucrats, but lobbying isn't against the law. It's what you do every time you write your congressman. But I don't control them, and I've never asked anyone to do anything illegal or against his conscience. Believe me, if I commanded that much power over the local government, this place would be run a whole lot differently." He came over, knelt at her feet and rested his hands prayerfully on her knees. "I thought you'd be pleased, Lee. I thought you wanted him out of your life and Elise's. Was I wrong?"

She studied his hands. The emotions prancing through her had her shaky and uncertain. "I'm glad he's gone," she admitted, head lowered.

"What's the problem then?"

She rose, sidestepped around him and crossed the room before turning back. "You just don't get it, do you?"

"Get what?" he pleaded, still on his knees. "You wanted him gone, and now he is."

Leanna knew at that moment that he'd never understand, but she did owe him an explanation.

"I want control of my destiny, Jackson, not to have it arranged for me. Richard did that. He made decisions, ran up debts and kept me in the dark. I won't be a victim again." She paused to catch her breath. "Why didn't you tell me about this beforehand? And what right do you have to kick Elise's father out of her life?"

Jackson heaved a deep sigh. "I didn't kick him out of her life. He chose to leave, just as you wanted him to. He could have told me to go to hell, Lee. He could have raised a stink and publicly accused me of trying to alienate his daughter's affections. He could have demanded the right to at least communicate with her. But he didn't." Jackson stopped, filled his lungs with air in an attempt to contain his mounting anger. "As for not telling you... Until Richard picked up the briefcase and walked out the door after signing that paper, I wasn't convinced the deal would work.''

''You weren't sure he would take the bait, or you were afraid I might not approve?''

He mulled the question over for a second. ''I know you don't like this sort of thing.''

''But you do.''

''Like it?'' He climbed to his feet. ''Lee, I wish the world were full of only nice people who never did anything bad or mean-spirited, who never hurt anyone else. But it isn't, so I will do whatever I can, whatever I must, to protect the people I love.''

There was that word again. Yet he was twisting this around, making her the ungrateful recipient of his largesse, the way Richard had so many times.

''I believe you're absolutely sincere in what you say, Jackson, and that you honestly think what you've done is in my best interests and Elise's. Maybe it is. Afforded the opportunity to plan this out with you, I might have chosen exactly the same course. But neither of us will ever know now, because you didn't give me or yourself the opportunity to find out.''

She pulled her robe a little tighter. ''You've been very generous to me and Elise, and for that I'll always be grateful.''

''What are you saying?'' Panic raised his voice.

''That there's no future for us, Jackson. I hope you'll let us stay through the holidays. For the girls' sake. But after Christmas, I'll find another place for my daughter and me to live.''

She turned away from him so he wouldn't see the tears that were about to roll down her cheeks.

"Lee…"

"Please go."

CHAPTER FIFTEEN

SATURDAY MORNING Jackson was finishing breakfast in the kitchen when Leanna came in. Betty had invited her over for ham and eggs, and had even offered to fix hash browns instead of grits, but she had declined. Now she stood in the doorway and glared at Jackson. He finished swallowing the coffee he'd just taken a sip of and placed the cup on its saucer.

"Good morning. Sure you won't join me?" He was nearly finished.

"No thanks."

Betty glanced over at her with raised eyebrows, poured a mug of her Cajun mud and handed it to her. Clearly, Leanna wasn't interested, but good manners required her to accept it.

"Thanks." She took a tiny sip and placed it on the far end of the table from Jackson.

"Where did you get the money to bribe Richard?"

Betty sucked in her cheeks, pursed her lips and turned back to the sink.

Jackson could see the suspicion in her eyes that he'd been holding out on her, that he'd lied about being cash broke. He buttered half a biscuit. "I sold the Jag."

"You—" She stared at him, stunned, then softened her tone. "Jackson, you shouldn't have. You could have used that money—"

"For what?" he asked politely.

"You have debts...the refinery."

"Your happiness and Elise's is more important to me than a refinery, Lee. Don't you understand that?"

He thought for a minute she was going to thaw, but the warmth quickly faded in her eyes.

"What I see, Jackson, is that you took control of my life without consulting me. What we talked about earlier apparently didn't register."

"Lee, the car was a done deal at that point."

She slowly shook her head, a look of utter frustration on her face. "I don't know how or when I'll be able to make it up to you, but somehow I'll reimburse you."

"I don't want your money," he nearly shouted.

She turned and walked out of the room. A second later he heard the back door close.

"What is it about that woman," he asked Betty, "that makes it so damn difficult for her to accept help? Or is it just help from me she finds unacceptable?"

Betty awarded him a lethargic shrug and began washing dishes.

The rest of the weekend was equally torturous. All his attempts to reopen his discussion with Leanna were quietly, politely but firmly rebuffed. How was he supposed to resolve the issues between them if she wouldn't even talk to him? For that matter, how was he even supposed to know what the real issues were? Surely, she wasn't upset that Richard had left. She'd made it clear by words and attitude that she wanted him permanently out of her life and Elise's, yet when Jackson accomplished just that, he was made out the bad guy. It didn't make sense.

He could understand her being a little miffed at him for not letting her in on his plan. He probably should have informed her, but he figured he was doing her a favor by not making her a party to tactics she didn't feel comfortable with. Why wouldn't she understand he just wanted to make her happy?

"Is Daddy coming to the ball?" Elise asked her mother Saturday afternoon. She and Megan were helping Esme and Betty arrange the figurines in the crèche on the sideboard in the dining room.

"I don't think so, honey," Leanna responded casually, trying not to put too much emphasis on it or reveal the angry judgment she felt against her former husband. "He had to go out of town on business. I don't know when he'll be back."

Elise went very quiet, very still. "He didn't come to say goodbye." Half question, half statement, both painful hurting.

"It happened very quickly," Jackson told her. "But I did see him in town before he left. Wait right here." He hurried out of the room and returned a minute later.

"He asked me to give you this." Jackson held out a gaily wrapped package.

Elise's watery eyes momentarily lit up. "What is it?"

"I was supposed to put it under the tree for you, but why don't you open it now."

"Can I, Mommy?" She gazed up at her mother with a pleading expression.

Leanna cast Jackson a quizzical look. "I guess that would be all right."

Elise's small hands fiddled with the colorful paper. Once she'd torn a corner the rest came off easily.

The exposed cardboard box was shiny red and green. She fumbled getting the lid off, only to find tissue paper. Parting it, she discovered an elegantly carved horse and a young colt. The polished wood caught the twinkling lights from the nearby window.

"He said he was sorry he couldn't buy you a real horse," Jackson explained, "but he thought you might like these, instead."

Leanna bit her lip.

"They're beautiful." Elise hugged them to her chest. "Can I put them here with the Baby Jesus?" she asked Esme.

The older woman smoothed her hand down the girl's hair. "I think that would be perfect."

Carefully, Elise arranged the two animals on the outside of a half wall, looking into the manger scene.

Betty seemed moved, as well. "I think this calls for a cup of hot cocoa with marshmallows. What do you say?"

"Thank you," Leanna said to Jackson as they trailed out to the kitchen. "That was very considerate of you."

He wanted to tell her he was sorry the girl was hurting but that he wasn't the person doing it. Richard was to blame. Casting aspersions wouldn't accomplish anything, however, and would only make him look guiltier than she already thought he was.

"I'm glad she likes it," he responded.

OVER THE NEXT FEW DAYS, they continued to dance around each other in "friendly" conversation. At dinner, she sat across from him, carrying on lively discussions with everyone else at the table. She tried to avoid eye contact, but it happened anyway, and in those flashes before she averted her gaze he caught something. What troubled him was that he wasn't sure what it was. Displeasure, definitely. Annoyance absolutely. But something else, as well. Was it his own vanity, his own desperation, that made him think it was longing? He wanted her more than he'd ever wanted a woman in his life. He needed her. She'd made it clear she didn't need him. But did she want him? Apparently not.

The bright spot in all of this was the children. Their happy laughter filled the house. Megan had been reserved and reclusive until Elise had come on the scene. The two girls were inseparable now. For the first time since she'd come to Bellefontaine, Megan had showed signs of being a chatterbox, even when Elise wasn't around, asking questions that Jackson sometimes found himself fumbling to answer and making observations that caused him to stop and think.

She cuddled up to him more, too, and that was the most rewarding part. To have her kiss him and call him Daddy was the most precious gift he'd ever received. His own father, he realized, had robbed himself of that priceless joy when he'd had his children address him by his first name. To Jackson, no word had become sweeter than Daddy.

The house smelled perpetually of winter pine and the rich, spicy aromas of holiday cooking. Betty was knocking herself out baking and preparing the huge quantities and varieties of food that would crowd the extended dining-room table. Jackson's mother had always been in control of the household, but at Christmastime, Angelique ceded sovereignty—except for the matter of firing Betty—to her sister-in-law. Esme fluttered around constantly, checking details, giving orders to the extra help she hired for this important event. Every year she shuffled things around, then moved them back to the way they'd always been. Every year she complained that her orders were being ignored or not promptly obeyed. Inevitably, she received compliments on how marvelously perfect everything turned out.

TWO DAYS BEFORE THE BALL, Leanna plugged the telephone jack into her laptop and dialed up the Internet. She'd driven by her old apartment the day before and seen a crew busy at work on the complex. Apparently, Gilbert Alain, the landlord, was taking advantage of the situation to make additional renovations. A good idea, she decided. The place was run-down. A few improvements, like painting the outside, were long overdue. She just hoped he didn't raise the rent on the tenants. Some of the pensioners living there were nearly destitute.

Using her password, she entered the secure network that furnished detailed insurance information. She typed in Alain's name. No action pending. She poked in the address. The Billet Arms was listed as an insured property of the company he'd identified, but there was no annotation to indicate a claim had been filed. She clicked on the history of the rental complex. The last payout had been made four years ago for damage caused by an electrical fire in the laundry room. Leanna remembered noticing the new conduit to the two dryers, so the work had actually been performed.

Why wasn't there any indication of a current claim? It could be a clerical oversight, but the company involved had a good reputation for maintaining their database. She looked at her wristwatch—the replacement she'd bought at a closeout sale in a K-Mart. It was time to pick up the gown Esme had loaned her for the ball. The seamstress's house was only a few blocks from her old apartment. She'd stop by on her way home and see if she could find out what was going on.

TWO DAYS before Christmas, Jackson was in the attic, quietly muttering deprecations as he rearranged the empty ornament boxes he'd brought up to get them out of his office, where Esme had relegated them so they'd be out of the way—her way. He heard his name called.

Peering down the narrow staircase into the alcove at the end of the second-floor hall, he saw the woman he'd hired several days earlier as the new nanny. Delphine was no twenty-something ingenue but a mature woman in her late forties, who'd raised five children of her own and couldn't help bragging about her six grandkids.

"Mr. Fontaine, a man by the name of Murray Dewalt just phoned. He asked you to meet him at the refinery right away. He said it's important."

Jackson checked his watch. It was after five. The crew would already have quit for the day. He'd assumed Murray had left, as well, since he couldn't do anything there on his own.

"Did he say what it was about?"

"No, sir. Only that it was urgent for you to meet him."

What could Murray possibly have found now? Jackson was almost afraid to ask. He locked the attic and descended the stairs. In his room, he grabbed his wallet and keys, and was about to head out the back door, when he decided to try calling, instead. All he got was the answering machine. He left a message that he was on his way.

Since selling his Jaguar to pay off Richard, he'd started using his father's Town Car. The big, black sedan had suited Duke fine, but it didn't match Jackson's tastes. The Jaguar, which his mother had given him last year for his birthday, had definitely been more his style. He missed it, but he didn't for a moment regret giving it up.

The refinery was only three miles away—a trip that took little more than five minutes. With each passing mile, however, Jackson became more concerned. Murray wasn't one to panic. If Delphine had relayed the message correctly, something was very wrong. Why, then, hadn't he been standing by the phone?

LEANNA FELT LIKE A QUEEN as she whirled in front of the full-length mirror at Madame Frobert's Couture. The cobalt-blue, floor-length, washed-silk gown blossomed extravagantly over full crinolines. Delicate ecru lace swept the edges of the round-cut bodice, puff sleeves and a band two inches from the hem.

"*C'est charmante,*" the woman said, as she examined the alterations she'd made. "You are very lovely in it," she continued in French. "Every man in the room will have eyes for only you, and all the women will be jealous. It is as if this gown was made for you and has been waiting all these years, *madame*. Perfect."

It was beautiful, Leanna had to agree, and for a

moment, she felt a flutter as she contemplated what Jackson's reaction to it might be. In her mind, she could imagine his gaze sweeping over her, see his lips part, feel his hands touch hers.

On the drive home, she reminded herself he wasn't a part of her life anymore and never could be. When the ball was over, she would go home alone. The dull edge of sadness settled over her and an ache lodged itself in her heart. So close. She'd come so close to finding the man she could trust and love, a man who would trust her implicitly and love her unconditionally.

She'd nearly turned right onto the street that would take her directly to Bellefontaine, when she remembered she wanted to check out her old address. She continued straight. Several blocks farther she turned left. The Billet Arms stood just ahead.

It was after five. Work had stopped, but the scaffolding around the end of the building testified that improvements were still underway. Leanna stepped out of the car and surveyed the area. Not only was the exterior being painted, but new metal-frame windows with double-glazed, tinted panes had replaced the old wooden sashes. Decorative shutters had also been added.

Mrs. Garnet, Leanna's former next-door neighbor, pulled back a curtain, looked out and a few seconds later opened her door and invited Leanna inside.

''The old skinflint finally replaced our carpet,'' the elderly woman crowed, sweeping her hand to the wall-to-wall commercial-grade Berber. The oatmeal-colored floor covering wasn't top-quality, but it was certainly an improvement over the unraveling brown shag that had been there. ''Finally fixed our garbage disposal, too. We've been after him for over a year to repair it.''

Leanna stayed only a few minutes, long enough to avoid being impolite. She was eager to talk to Alain and find out how he was paying for all this. Renovations went far beyond water damage from a burst pipe.

His apartment was at the end of the building. She knocked on the door.

A wary expression quickly superseded the initial gleam of friendliness at seeing a familiar face. Instead of the customary greeting, he said, ''What are you doing here?''

''It's nice to see you, too, Mr. Alain.''

He frowned. ''Sorry, I didn't expect you around here again. If you're looking for your money—''

''Actually, I wanted to find out when the repair work will be finished so I can move back in.''

''Move back in? But I understood you got yourself a real nice setup at Bellefontaine.''

''Who told you that?'' She'd sent him her bill for clothing expenses and other personal property damage but used her business address. He'd yet to pay up, but she hadn't expected instant reimbursement.

His eyes shifted. ''I guess you did.''

''Not me.''

He shrugged.

She decided to let the matter drop for the moment. ''You're having a lot of work done. Who's paying for all this?''

''Insurance,'' he said quickly.

She shook her head. ''No, they're not.''

He got a startled expression on his face. His eyes

shifted nervously, and he began to close the door. She surprised herself by blocking it with her body.

"What's going on, Mr. Alain?" she demanded. "Even if insurance were paying for the water damage from the leak that destroyed my apartment, it wouldn't cover the cost of all these renovations. I also happen to know you never filed an insurance claim."

"It's none of your business," he muttered, and tried again to close the door.

She not only didn't give way, she pushed the door farther open, making him jump back in alarm. Strong-arming was new territory for her, but now that she had embarked on it, she found it strangely satisfying. This man had something to hide. She wasn't sure why it was so important to her, unless it was his unexpected reference to a *setup* at Bellefontaine, a term her ex-husband would use. Richard had mentioned stopping off here before coming to the plantation. Was there a connection?

"I'm making it my business," she informed the landlord, her voice not nearly as patient as it had been a moment earlier. "Let me lay it out for you, Mr. Alain. My apartment was flooded, forcing me to vacate the premises. Insurance should have paid for the damage, but you didn't report it, and now I see you doing a major overhaul of the entire complex." She narrowed her eyes. "I can draw a couple of conclusions. The most convincing one is that someone paid you to flood my apartment, ruin my belongings and make me leave. That's called conspiracy."

Oh, God. She suddenly realized this wasn't about Richard. He was gone from her life. Besides, he didn't have the kind of money it would take to pull off something like this. He also wasn't this devious. No, this wasn't about her ex-husband. Everything pointed to Jackson. He'd been trying to convince her to move into the *garçonnière*. When she refused, he engineered the overflowing toilet so she'd have nowhere to go but his place. It all fit.

"So I suggest," she said, the anger and threat in her voice real now, "that you tell me who paid you to run me off, or I'll go to the police and have them investigate—"

"No cops." The potbellied landlord's insistence definitely bespoke fear.

"If you tell me who's paying you, things might go a little easier for you. Did you know not reporting an insurance claim is a federal crime? I'll track the money. Even cash can be traced these days. The police will interview all your neighbors, find out who you're associating with. If you think you can keep this secret, Alain, you're very much mistaken."

She was bluffing, mostly. But he didn't know that.

"Who paid you?"

JACKSON DROVE UP THE ROAD leading to the refinery and was surprised to find the gate locked. The compound was empty of cars. Had Murray already left? Why?

Jackson unlocked the gate, parked the Town Car in his usual spot and walked the short distance to the side entrance of the main building. In spite of all the mishaps and delays, considerable progress had been made on the renovation and upgrade. Worn machine components had been replaced, and Noelani was writing a computer program for the operation, which, until now, had been manually controlled. She promised to debug the algorithms after the plant was put into actual operation.

The inside of the cavernous building was dark. Jackson's footsteps ricocheted off the metal walls, lending the place an eerie feeling.

"Murray?" he called out.

No response. No sound, except for his own breathing.

"Murray? Where are you?"

Still no response. The message Delphine had passed on said the matter was urgent. Logic said Murray wasn't here. Yet, a sixth sense told Jackson something was definitely wrong. Perhaps Murray had had to leave abruptly because of an emergency at home. Jackson decided to check the recently reconstructed office to see if he'd left a message there.

He stepped around the side of the first centrifuge. The sun was almost set. The last rays of light slanting through the high windows had no effect on the impenetrable shadows below. He hesitated. Could Murray have turned out all the lights, then come back for something and fallen? Hadn't Delphine said he'd sounded anxious on the phone? If he was injured, why didn't he say so or dial 911?

Jackson called out again. This time he did hear something. A voice? A moan? He took a tentative step forward. The noise was behind him now. He turned and barely saw the upraised arm before the object in the hand slammed down on his head.

LEANNA MADE A DASH to her car, grabbed the cell phone Jackson had insisted she carry—it had been Angelique's—and hit a speed-dial button.

"Merry Christmas. This is Bellefontaine Plantation."

"Delphine—" Leanna recognized the woman's voice "—this is Leanna. I need to talk to Jackson right away."

"I'm sorry, Miss Lee. He's not here. Mr. Dewalt telephoned and requested that he meet him at the refinery."

"Murray?" Another snafu with the reconstruction project? "Are you sure it was him?"

"That's who he said he was."

Leanna felt breathless. "How long ago did he leave?"

"About twenty minutes." Leanna's apprehension seemed to be contagious. "Is something wrong?"

"If he calls, tell him I'll meet him there. Did he take his cell phone with him?"

"I didn't see him leave, miss. I only heard the car pulling out of the driveway."

Leanna clicked off, then hit the button for his number. It rang, but there was no answer. He might have left the instrument in his car when he went inside.

Leanna started the Toyota, distractedly pleased by the competent purr of the engine. The refinery-office. The phone had been connected late last week. Jackson had given her the number. With shaky fingers, she opened her briefcase, flipped to the back of her notebook, found the number and carefully poked it in. As the connection went through, she slipped the car into gear and pulled out of the apartment-complex parking lot.

The phone rang on the other end, but no one answered.

Delphine said Jackson had left twenty minutes

ago. The refinery was only five minutes away. He should be there by now. Leanna let the phone continue to ring as she drove one-handed through downtown traffic. A taxi approaching from the right slammed on its brakes and the cabdriver blasted his horn angrily as she sped through an intersection. Glancing in the rearview mirror, she realized she'd just run a red light. On a shuddering breath, she took her foot off the gas pedal. She wouldn't have had a problem with speeding if Hal hadn't done such a good job tuning this relic. God, she sounded like Richard—blaming other people.

At last, she turned onto the road to the refinery. Her lungs felt deflated and her stomach hollow as she stepped once more on the accelerator. Where was he? Why wasn't he answering? She hit the redial button. This time the call was answered on the second ring.

She took in a fresh breath and exhaled. "Jackson, thank God I got you. I found out something a few minutes ago, something very important. I know who's behind all this."

She waited for a reaction, a response. All she heard was static on the line.

"Jackson, are you there? Jackson?"

The line went dead.

CHAPTER SIXTEEN

JACKSON WAS AWARE of only one thing—pain. Someone had clamped a vise on his temples and was tightening the screw. Pure agony. He couldn't remember ever having a hangover this bad. Even in college he'd never tied one on that hurt this much. He moved his head in a vain attempt to find a position that didn't hurt. The only cure for a hangover, experience told him, was time, and the best way to spend that time was sleeping. Which was exactly what he'd do. Duke didn't raise no fools. But there was something wrong—besides the pain. Something was out of kilter. If only he could figure out what it was. Later. Thinking was too much trouble. Now he had to sleep.

LEANNA GLANCED DOWN and was startled to see the speedometer needle pointing at eighty. It must be wrong. This contraption couldn't go eighty miles an hour. She pulled her foot off the gas pedal nevertheless, because she was coming up on the turnoff to the refinery. Her tires squealed as she went into the turn. The car lurched and skidded onto the gravel surface. Its wheels spun and kicked up a cloud of dust. She rocketed straight ahead.

The Town Car was parked by the side door. So Jackson was here—but apparently alone. She grabbed the car door handle, only then catching the glint of metal in the woods behind the refinery compound. A dark vehicle was parked where it had no reason to be—except to hide.

Should she announce her presence, or should she try to sneak into the building? Rejecting the stealth approach because the people inside must already have heard her, she pressed the palm of her hand on the horn. For so modest a vehicle, it made an amazing amount of noise bouncing off the corrugated siding of the building.

''Here I come, ready or not.'' She climbed out of the vehicle.

The side entrance stood open. Was that a positive sign?

The cavernous hole seemed to breathe, sending an icy shiver up her spine. She inched her way along the wall, her eyes gradually adjusting to the dim light that fanned in through the doorway. She'd been here only once during the day with Jackson and vaguely remembered seeing an electric panel that probably controlled the lights, but she wasn't sure of its exact location. She groped unsuccessfully for a minute and finally gave up. The vast space remained shrouded in inky darkness.

''Jackson?'' she called out, uncertain, afraid.

She stepped closer to the first centrifuge. The office wasn't far, and it had a window. There would be some light.

A groan.

''Jackson?'' she called again, this time more boldly. ''Where are you?''

Another sound, stronger. She was getting nearer.

''Tell me where you are.'' Fear and uncertainty

unsteadied her voice. She took a few more deliberate steps. He was close. She could feel his presence.

She rounded the corner and saw an indistinct shadow on the floor in front of her. A body?

Another moan and she knew instantly who it was.

"Jackson!" She started to bolt toward him, when she felt a presence loom up behind her.

Spinning around, she instinctively put her arm up to protect herself. Too late.

JACKSON STIRRED. A foghorn, or maybe it was an alarm clock, and now Leanna's voice penetrated his mushy head, and for a moment he thought he was hallucinating. Then he decided she was lying beside him in his dark bedroom. The idea banished the sharp drilling in his skull, if only for a moment, but when he reached out, all he felt was rough concrete. It was that, combined with the ache in his joints from lying on the cold hard surface, that finally propelled him through the thick miasma of stupor.

Where the hell was he? Who was here with him? Why did he feel as though someone had used his head for a baseball? And hit a homerun.

"No!" Leanna's voice.

Jackson opened his eyes. He knew where he was now and how he'd gotten here. His vision adjusted to the darkness. He saw Leanna stumble back and practically fall on top of him. He'd gladly catch her—if he could convince his arms to follow orders. Before he had time to act, she recovered her balance and stood off on her own, a dozen yards from him. He wanted to reach out, envelop her in a sheltering embrace.

Should he continue to play dead, or should he

spring and overwhelm their adversary? The macho alternative appealed to his sense of manly honor and protectiveness, but his brain was functioning well enough at this point for him to understand he didn't have the energy or strength to take on anyone. And if he wasn't mistaken, the man standing a few yards away had a gun pointed at her. A clumsy move—all he was capable of at the moment—might kill her. He had to think. He had to marshal his reserves. If only the pounding in his head would stop.

"Get over there by him," the man ordered her, his voice harsh with anger.

Silently, Leanna edged toward Jackson. He managed to pull himself into a sitting position. Raising his head helped marginally. The pain was still there, but not nearly as intense as it had been.

"So you're awake," the voice scoffed.

Jackson said nothing, afraid his words would come out as a croak and reveal how weak he was. *Never show an enemy your fear or your weakness,* his father had preached. Duke had bullied his way through most situations in his life—until his arrogance killed him and Angelique. Jackson understood that now. He wondered if his father ever had. Jackson had loved his father, but he wasn't blind to the man's flaws.

He twisted his stiff body onto all fours, then slowly rose to his feet. He was wobbly, but his strength was building. He could also feel Leanna watching him, sense the concern emanating from her. Still, she kept her distance. Maybe she felt more in control that way. Above all else he wanted her safe. Hadn't he told her he loved her? He should be the one safeguarding *her,* shielding *her* against evildoers.

"Why?" she demanded with the cold determination she'd used with the tow-truck driver. God, he loved this woman. "Why are you doing this?"

Roland Dewalt laughed, his eyes glinting even in the shadows. "Ask Jackson. He knows."

She moved to Jackson's side and extended her hand. Greedily, he took it, entwining her fingers with his. They fit so well he wanted to savor the moment. Her pulse was rapid, and there was a tremor of fear, but what took prominence in her grip was strength and power. She tightened her hold, and a rush of adrenaline slammed through him. It cleared his head, which still ached, but the pain no longer mattered. They were connected.

And facing a gun.

"He hates us," Jackson stated, encouraged when his voice came out sounding normal. "I'm sorry, Lee. I never meant to put you in danger." Her hand squeezed his.

Even in the semidarkness, he could see the vicious sneer curling the old man's lips. "He stole Angelique. He ruined everything."

"Then Duke bought this refinery, your refinery," Jackson said.

"Not bought," Roland shouted, his words bouncing off the ceiling. "Stole." The lament was childish, even in his raised voice. "It was unfair. He had no right."

Jackson had to concede Roland was partially correct. He'd been legally swindled out of this plant. Duke would emphasize the word *legal,* but it didn't change the fact that swindle applied, as well.

"You killed them. How? They were in Europe?"

"Riley," Leanna murmured. "That's what I came to tell you. Riley—"

Roland laughed. "Duke should have remembered money can buy anything, anyone. I got enough cash for this place to do what I had to."

"You hired Riley to sabotage the plane," Jackson said. That explained why the man had turned into such a bitter alcoholic, when previously he'd been a happy drunk.

"I talked to him before he went to Europe with Duke and Angelique," Roland admitted with a chortle. "Offered to compensate him handsomely if he got rid of them. We pretended I was joking, but I saw the way his eyes lit up when I told him how much I'd pay."

Leanna's thumb brushed Jackson's—a silent act of condolence.

"Maybe he wouldn't have done it if Duke hadn't fired him," Roland boasted. "Riley called me from Italy, wanted to know if the offer was still good. I wired half the money to a Swiss account he opened. Two days later, after he'd done what he promised, I transferred the other half."

"But he claims he's broke," Leanna objected.

Roland shrugged unsympathetically. "It was his choice to stop off in Monte Carlo before returning home." Another gambler ruined by his vice.

"And the accidents?" Jackson ventured. "You hired people to do them, too, didn't you?"

The old man chortled. "Broderick screwed up the house fire. Esme should have died."

So could my daughter and her nanny, Jackson thought with a sick heaviness in his chest.

"If your sister had married Murray like I wanted, instead of that gambler, none of this would have been necessary. Our families would have been united."

Jackson couldn't picture Roland retiring to the veranda, quietly sipping good whiskey and patting grandchildren on their heads. The smoldering hatred wouldn't have died out, and Duke certainly wouldn't have ceded any power to a man he considered a bumbling fool. The competition between them would only have intensified.

"What about Denise Rochelle?" Jackson asked. She'd sabotaged the mill and attacked Noelani but vehemently insisted she'd acted alone.

"No need to give her a penny." The old man gave a self-satisfied chuckle. "I just reminded her what Duke did to her father. The girl figured the rest of it out all by herself."

Roland edged over and propped himself on a metal instrument panel that was bolted to the floor.

A car pulled up outside.

"Who's that?" he demanded, his eyes wide, frightened.

Equally curious, Jackson and Leanna said nothing.

A door slammed.

"Keep your mouths shut," Roland hissed. "Don't make a sound."

Footsteps tapped on the concrete floor. Approaching.

"Jackson, Leanna? Where are you?" Murray called out.

The old man muttered an expletive.

They heard switches being popped. Suddenly, the area was flooded with yellow-white light. Jackson rocked back and raised his free arm to shield his eyes from the blinding glare. The sharp, stabbing pain in his head forced out an involuntary groan. Roland had also put up a hand to protect his eyes. Had Jackson been prepared, he told himself, he could have used the distraction to charge the old man, to wrestle the gun from him. Another opportunity missed. Even now, for the agonizing pressure in his eyes to subside and his vision to adjust took a full minute.

Murray Dewalt stood gaping at the corner of the towering centrifuge, equidistant from his father and his father's captives.

"Dad? What…what's going on here?" he asked angrily, the way a parent might speak to a recalcitrant child.

"Get out," the old man yelled. "This has nothing to do with you. It's between him—" he waved the gun toward Jackson "—and me."

Murray blinked hard. For a second he seemed to wilt, then he stiffened with determination. "You've done enough damage, Dad, hurt enough people. Jackson has never harmed you."

"He's a Fontaine. They're all no good, all out to get me."

At that moment, Jackson knew Roland was mad. There was no telling how long he'd been insane, but Jackson understood the seeds of the psychosis went back to a Christmas long ago when a happy bride-to-be brought a classmate home to help plan a wedding and lost her fiancé and her dreams for a future as a wife and mother. Roland had robbed Esme of them all. Perhaps the lingering guilt of that betrayal so many years ago had ultimately driven him over the edge.

Murray looked at Jackson with pleading eyes. "I swear I didn't know—"

"What are you doing here anyway?" Jackson asked.

"Stopped by your place…Delphine told me—"

"Get out," the old man snarled again at his son.

"Put the damn gun down, Dad." Murray stepped forward slowly, cautiously but without flinching.

"I'll kill him first," Roland screamed.

"Dad, this is Jackson, not Duke. Duke is dead."

The statement didn't seem to register on the old man.

"Let Leanna leave," Jackson begged. "She has a child who needs her. Her little girl didn't do anything to you."

Murray took a step closer to his father. "Give me the gun, Dad." He reached out to him.

Roland extended his arm, his hand not quite steady, and pointed the revolver directly at Jackson's head. His finger began to tighten on the trigger. The hammer drew back.

"No-o-o," Leanna screamed, and bolted forward, her hands outstretched to shove the weapon aside. Jackson crouched and rolled on the floor toward his assassin. In the same instant, Murray leaped.

The three ganged up on the senior Dewalt simultaneously. The mad shuffle lasted mere seconds. A gunshot echoed through the tin barn. Everyone froze. With a grunt, Murray collapsed at his father's feet.

MURRAY WAS air-evacuated to the hospital and taken directly into surgery. Jackson was transported by ambulance. Leanna's injuries amounted to no more than a few superficial scrapes, but the paramedics persuaded her to go, as well. In spite of the bump on his head, Jackson passed all the medical tests and, though warned to be on guard for symptoms of concussion, was released.

Murray had lost a good deal of blood, but he was in stable condition by the time they left. The bullet had penetrated his thigh because his father had lowered the gun, trying to shoot Jackson as he rolled toward him. Luckily, it missed the bone.

From the emergency room, Jackson and Leanna were escorted to the police station, where they gave official statements and filled in details of the events of the evening to Remy Bouchard, the detective who'd been working on the Bellefontaine case from the beginning. Remy personally drove them to the plantation a little before midnight.

"Y'all sure gave me job security with everything that's been going on around here," he quipped as he opened the back door for them. "But I'm fully vested, so you can let things calm down now." Turning serious, he said, "I'm real sorry about your parents, Jackson. I wish we could have solved this case sooner. I just never thought that old guy—"

"We all underestimated him. Fortunately, no one else was hurt. The fire came close—" Jackson stopped. He wasn't going to dwell on what might have happened. He offered his hand. "Thanks for sharing what information you could with us."

"It'll all have to be verified, but I figure you have a right to know how things stand. Unless Dewalt turns out to be brilliant instead of crazy, this case will never come to trial."

"Sad," Leanna said.

Bouchard nodded. "Give my best to your family and wish them all Merry Christmas."

In spite of the evening chill, Nick and Adam were waiting in the cushioned, white wrought-iron chairs on the veranda. Betty, who should have gone home hours before, was sitting in the kitchen with the other women in the family. She offered to make tea or a fresh pot of coffee for the new arrivals, but Esme, putting on a front of imperturbability, suggested that a belated cocktail hour might be more appropriate. No one disagreed.

While Leanna checked on the girls—Elise was once again sleeping in Megan's room—Jackson cleaned up and changed clothes. He came down to the drawing room, where Nick had already prepared mint juleps for Esme and Noelani, uncapped bottles of beer for Casey, Betty, Adam and him and poured a glass of chilled white wine for Lee. Since his head still throbbed slightly, Jackson opted for Perrier.

The warm atmosphere of being surrounded by family relaxed and invigorated him at the same time. He and Leanna found themselves finishing each other's sentences, elaborating on each other's comments, reinforcing each other's thoughts. Duke and Angelique used to do that. He missed them tonight more than he had previously, perhaps because for the first time he felt they were really gone. Apparently, he wasn't alone.

His sister Casey's face was dark with pent-up anger. "That miserable old..." She took a breath. "Did he think he'd be able to buy us out?"

"He's crazy, Sis, not stupid," Jackson reminded her with a wry grin. "The Dewalts have never had that kind of money. He just wanted to see us all destroyed and Bellefontaine gone the way of so many other plantations."

"How did he know about the raw sugar in the warehouse?" Nick asked.

"He saw a couple of truckloads going down Refinery Lane. Only one place they would have been headed. I'm willing to bet he still had a key." Jackson scowled. "I should have changed the locks."

"He reckoned your father was holding out—" Adam started.

"It wasn't an unreasonable assumption, given Duke's history."

"Roland called in the tip to the coalition that sugar was being illegally stored," Leanna said. "When nothing seemed to happen, he figured Jackson had quashed the matter, so—"

"He paid Riley to blow the place up," Jackson finished.

"Where's Riley now?" Noelani asked.

"He was picked up at the La Grenouille a couple of hours ago."

"I bet he croaks like a frog," Adam commented, "to save his sorry—"

"He could have blown up the whole plant," Casey interrupted. "Why didn't he?"

"He was supposed to," Jackson explained. "But when Roland drew the floor plan of the place, he forgot about the fire wall Murray had installed."

"Acting on Roland's behalf, Riley also bribed Gilbert Alain to flood my apartment in an attempt to scare me off," Leanna added.

"What? When did you find this out?" Jackson asked.

"Today." Leanna grinned at him, her eyes twinkling. "I'm an investigator, remember? In spite of what you may think, I'm pretty good at my job. When I discovered this afternoon that Alain had never filed an insurance claim, I confronted him, told him he could be charged with insurance fraud for not reporting legitimate damage.''

"That's absurd," Nick remarked. "Isn't it?"

Leanna laughed. "Of course it is, but Alain didn't know that. I could tell he was feeling guilty about what he'd done, so I just took advantage of his paranoia.''

"You manipulated him," Jackson said proudly as he stroked his thumb across the back of her hand. Her skin was soft, alluring.

She nearly giggled. "Desperate people do unexpected things. Anyway, Alain fingered Riley and I went to the refinery to tell Jackson. Actually, I hadn't put all the pieces together yet, but I figured flooding my apartment had to be related in some way to the other things going on here." She didn't mention that, initially, she'd thought Jackson was responsible for her private disaster. "I figured between us, Jackson and I could figure it out. That's why I went looking for him.''

"And walked into a gunfight," Jackson said angrily.

"Did Murray know about his father?" Esme asked. She'd been listening quietly throughout the discussion, her watery-blue eyes shifting from one speaker to another. She looked unbearably weary.

"He knew his dad's mind was slipping," Jackson said, "but he had no idea he'd gone over the edge."

She nodded and sipped her mint julep.

The grandfather clock in the hallway chimed one. Adam yawned and stretched—a signal that it was time to call it quits. Appreciative that the long nightmare was finally over, they bade one another goodnight with hugs and kisses. Betty told them to leave the dirty glasses and dishes of snacks she'd put out where they were. She'd clean up in the morning.

"But if you're here before ten," she added acerbically, "you'll have to get your own breakfast."

"Delphine doesn't come in till eight," Esme noted. "I'll take care of the children's morning cereal."

Betty paused a moment, studied her, then nodded. "Thanks."

Esme smiled ruefully. "You're welcome."

"You can both sleep in," Jackson declared. "I'm taking care of my girls in the morning."

He ignored Leanna's raised brow and kissed his aunt good-night, then watched her climb the stairs. She'd conducted herself stoically throughout the disturbing chronicle of events, as he knew she would. He ushered Leanna to the back door.

"To know the man she'd been betrothed to was responsible for the misery inflicted on the people she loved must be horribly painful for her," she said. "Did she ever wonder, do you think, what might have been had she never brought Angelique home to help with her wedding preparations?"

"Nick would tell her playing *what if* is a sucker's game," Jackson said sadly. "One that can't be won."

The night air was cool, crisp. Leanna pulled her sweater tighter. Jackson put his arm across her shoulders. He had to hold her, feel her body close to his. She didn't melt under his touch, but at least she didn't pull away.

They reached the *garçonnière*.

"We never used to lock anything around here," he said as he took the key from her hand. His fingers made momentary contact with hers. Did he feel as warm to her as she did to him?

She'd been upbeat all evening with the police, with the family, but he'd seen the remnants of terror in her eyes when she thought no one was looking. Their lives had nearly ended this evening at the hands of a madman. Their girls would have been left orphans. He'd sworn to protect them; instead, he'd almost gotten her killed. The idea settled like ice in his belly.

She stood a pace away from him, maintaining her distance as he inserted the key in the lock. It wasn't far enough for him not to feel the tension emanating from her. She could be in the next parish and he'd still be able to feel her presence. She was a part of him. Now he had to convince her to let him be a part of her.

CHAPTER SEVENTEEN

LEANNA WATCHED HIM insert the key in the lock. He had wonderful hands. Large. Strong. Gentle. She melted when he touched her, which meant her only defense was to keep her distance. There had been no time to think tonight, and she desperately needed to think. What had happened at the refinery had changed her life. Up to that point, everything had seemed clear—her goals, her means of achieving them. Then Jackson Fontaine had yanked open her car door at the refinery. She'd looked up into his midnight-blue eyes, and the world had tilted.

He released the latch. She stepped inside. The place where she lived. *His place.*

She flipped on the lights and for an instant was reminded of the scene a few hours earlier when Murray flooded the refinery with blinding clarity. Jackson bruised, unsteady. A gun pointed at him. She shut her eyes, trying to block out the moment of terror. When she opened them, Jackson was standing in front of her. He'd been shaken by this evening, as well. He'd come face-to-face with madness and evil, and he'd triumphed, but she sensed that he'd lost a kind of innocence, too.

"I know it's late," he said, "and you're tired, but we have to talk."

She took a step back. "Maybe tomorrow would be better. After we're rested."

He shook his head. "I won't be able to sleep tonight." He moved forward and clasped her arms just below her shoulders. "Not without you—"

"Jackson." His name was a plea, and as much as she knew she should squirm out of his grasp, she didn't have the energy or the will to resist.

"You saved my life this evening," he said softly.

She wanted to say it was nothing, that she would have done the same for anyone, but of course that wasn't true. If he weren't the man he was, she wouldn't be here or have been in that predicament.

"Do you see where all your wheeling and dealing and manipulation brought you?" she asked.

The stunned expression on his tired face shocked her.

"You blame me for what happened tonight? You think it's my fault Roland Dewalt murdered my parents—"

"No," she objected. He was doing it again. Twisting her words, heaping guilt on her. "I didn't mean that."

A muscle in his jaw flexed. "What did you mean?"

She searched for words, for an explanation. Finding none, she strode to the kitchen and poured herself a drink of water. The single glass of wine she'd nursed in the drawing room had only made her thirsty. Jackson made her mouth go dry. She jumped when he placed a hand on her shoulder. He didn't back off, though. Instead, he turned her around, looked deep into her eyes, smiled faintly and enfolded her in his arms.

There was no resisting him this time. She had no choice but to let him embrace her, to hold on to him. He smelled of manly cologne and felt like a warm summer night. Pressing her head to his chest, she could hear his heart beating, slow, steady, powerful, and she could feel her own heart ache.

"How about telling me what's really bothering you," he murmured in her ear. He arched back, but didn't release her. "I love you, Lee, and I will do anything to make you happy, but I need your help to understand what's keeping us apart."

She bit her lip and lowered her gaze. Gently, he steered her into the living room and sat on the couch beside her, his arm still pinning her securely to his chest. She savored his touch, his hard muscles and firm contours and prayed for the strength to fight the desire welling in her. Her body, her will refused to cooperate. The mind couldn't rule the heart, and her heart wanted to be exactly where it was, pressed against him.

"What have I done that has so upset you?" he asked gently.

"It's not *what* you've done, Jackson. It's that you keep me out. You make decisions that affect my life and Elise's without consulting me." She gazed up at him and saw a man who truly cared. "You don't regard me highly enough to ask for my opinion or trust my judgment enough to let me contribute to the solution of our problems."

"That's not true," he protested.

"Isn't it?"

Thinking clearly was impossible with his arms around her, with his heartbeat in her ear and the feel of his skin against hers. She straightened, then stood. He let her go, but there was a lost look on his face.

She started counting on her fingers. "You decided unilaterally to hire a private investigator to follow Richard and Elise. You talked to Nick about extending gambling credits to Richard without a word to me. You conferred with a judge about my affairs behind my back. You bribed my ex-husband and took Elise's father out of her life without ever discussing the implications with me." She dropped her hand and looked him straight in the eye. "I'd say that's pretty disrespectful, condescending and patronizing."

She could see she'd stung him, that he wanted to dispute her points, but she'd left him little to say.

"You want to protect me and Elise," she went on. "For that I love you. But I'm not a helpless maiden dependent on a knight in shining armor to save me from some fire-eating dragon."

Pacing in the narrow space in front of the couch, she hugged her waist.

"Your father manipulated people, toyed with them, took advantage of them. In the end it destroyed him and your mother and almost the rest of the family."

Jackson threw his arm across the back of the couch, but his intense concentration as he listened to her indictment of the man he'd grown up with and loved belied the casual gesture.

"I don't want to live that way, Jackson," she continued. "I won't subject myself or my daughter to that kind of life, constantly wondering when someone will be seeking vengeance for real or imagined deeds I had no active role in. I did that once. I won't do it again."

He inhaled deeply and climbed to his feet. He circled an armchair and set his hands on its back.

"I won't defend all of Duke's decisions or actions," he said, "because I myself didn't agree with many of them. You're right. He could be conniving and manipulative. Wheeling and dealing was a game for him. I'll say this, though. He didn't play the game any harder or rougher than his opponents. He was just better at it."

"That doesn't make it right." She sat in the chair across from him.

"No, it doesn't," he agreed. "There's one big difference between us that you haven't considered. Duke sometimes engineered the situations he took advantage of—"

"Like getting the bank to disapprove Dewalt's loan request so he could then snatch up his refinery for himself?"

"Yes, although Roland would have lost it eventually anyway."

"Maybe, but you'll never know for sure. Murray might have saved the place, turned it around. You yourself said so. Perhaps that was what your father was really afraid of—fair competition." She took a deep breath. "You realize, don't you, that his power gambit ended up killing him and your mother."

Jackson bristled. "You're ignoring one salient fact. He was dealing with a crazy man, and there's no defense against insanity."

"The question, which you can't answer, is when did Roland Dewalt go mad—before or after Duke took away his options and what might have been his last chance to redeem himself in the eyes of his son, his community and himself.''

She watched Jackson's jaw clamp, but pressed on. ''What about the way he treated Denise Rochelle's father?''

''Check the records, Lee. You'll find Duke had nothing to do with Rochelle giving up his land. Look,'' he said in frustration. ''I've already conceded that my father made mistakes. In my opinion, the biggest was being unfaithful to my mother, then deserting the woman he'd deceived and the child he'd fathered. Sending money to Noelani's mother and sponsoring his daughter's education can never make up for the callous way he dismissed them from his life, from our lives. I lost a great deal of respect for him when he advised me to abandon Megan. I didn't know at the time he'd already done that very thing. I chose not to, so don't paint me with his brush.''

He was hurt and he was angry. Leanna suspected he'd never voiced his outrage at Duke to anyone, even his sister. She also believed every word he said. He loved Megan. He was a devoted father. She wanted to soothe him, but she'd gone this far and couldn't stop now.

''You bribed city officials to give Nick a permit to moor his gambling casino inside city limits.''

He shook his head, the indignation of a moment earlier turned to resignation. ''I didn't bribe them, Lee, and I didn't blackmail them. I convinced them. Sure, I used tried-and-true persuasive techniques, like reminding them what they could gain by approving the application. Tit for tat. That's the nature of politics. But the decision was theirs. They would have lost nothing, not even my support, if they'd said no.''

She snorted, unconvinced, though he was making a certain amount of sense.

"I believe in helping my friends when I can, but that doesn't include breaking the law or compromising my own integrity. The point I was trying to make before you interrupted me is that I don't create the situations I exploit."

"What about Richard? You bribed him and you set him up so you could."

She had him there. He couldn't deny it.

"I didn't make him a gambler. I didn't force chips into his hands. I didn't deny him anything—like Duke did Dewalt a loan. I orchestrated an opportunity—"

"You knew he couldn't resist."

Jackson shrugged. "I took a great deal of satisfaction in getting the better of your ex-husband, Lee, but that wasn't why I did it. I did it for you and Elise, and I'd do it again. Besides, you admitted that given the opportunity, you would have gone along with it."

He thought he'd won by reversing the tables again, but she was ready for him. "You didn't give me a chance, remember?"

He huffed. "You're right, and that was my mistake, one I won't make again. I apologize."

She believed him.

"But Lee," he implored, "I want you to understand something. I'll do anything and everything necessary to protect the people I love."

She held her ground. "So will I."

He studied her, his eyes measuring, calculating. "Yeah, I figured that out," he said, then shocked her by breaking into a smile. "Dad would have been impressed by the way you manipulated Alain into telling you what you needed to know. Then there was the way you browbeat the tow-truck driver into taking less than he wanted and in a form he didn't trust.''

She stared at him under knitted brows. "Are you saying... You think I—"

He laughed. "No, I'm not saying you're as bad as Duke was. Not even close. Or as devious and underhanded as I am.''

She couldn't help it. She smiled.

He took her hands, held them and looked directly into her eyes. "We all strive to get our own way, Lee. What you did in both cases was the right thing. What I did in the case of Elise's father was, by your own admission, the right thing, too.''

He crouched at her feet. "You're wrong when you say I don't respect you. You're right when you say I should have informed you what I was contemplating. I should have asked your advice.'' He curled his fingers around hers. "I respect your intelligence, your devotion to your daughter, your sense of honor and your willingness to accept burdens unfairly placed on you. I was a total fool to think I could shield you from unpleasant decisions—you've had to make so many. I'd give anything to be able to shelter you from the ugliness in the world.''

"I'm not made of glass, Jackson. I don't break easily.''

He smiled, a little sadly. "I know that now.''

They stared at each other for a long minute, then he grinned. "So we're in agreement. There's no problem.''

If there was, she was having a difficult time remembering what it might be. Jackson was right. She'd lied to achieve her own ends, and she'd taken advantage of Jackson's oiling the skids so she could get Elise's custody case moved here to Baton Rouge.

Jackson rose to his feet and pulled her up with him. "I'm not perfect, Lee. I have a lot of flaws, but with you in my life I'm a better man." He encircled her waist. "I can't swear that I won't make mistakes in the future, but I can promise you this. I'll never lie to you. I want you to be part of my life, not outside it. I want to share my joys and tribulations with you."

She averted her eyes, suddenly embarrassed by the raw emotion of his declaration.

"Marry me, Lee."

The moment of truth. Her chest thumped. Esme had predicted this was coming, so it wasn't as if she hadn't been warned, as if she hadn't had time to prepare herself. Yet the shock of the proposal left her speechless. She wanted Jackson in her life. In Elise's. In the lives of the children they could have together. He would always have a place in her heart, but...would she be doing the right thing by marrying him?

"Marry me," he repeated, his hands nestling her hips. "I swear I'll never keep secrets from you or put you at a disadvantage. I'll never manipulate you—" he grinned impishly "—except maybe into bed."

He gave her a lazy smile, filled with hope and promise.

"Sounds like a challenge." Her palms were sweaty. Her insides quaked. The next move was hers.

"I love you, Lee," he said very seriously. "I want to spend the rest of my life proving it."

When she still didn't respond, he wilted. "Except you don't love me. Is that it?"

"I love you," she admitted in a whisper.

JACKSON COULDN'T wait another second without kissing her. He'd promised himself he would go slow, be patient, savor each delicious moment, but as his hands slid behind her back and closed the gap between them, his resolve faltered. Having her in his arms wasn't enough. His breath caught as he found her mouth. She tasted of wine and desire, heat and passion. He was instantly hard and desperate.

To hell with the winding stairs, with the cozy bed and soft pillows. He wanted her right here in the living room, now, this instant. He couldn't wait. He kicked off his boots.

Chuckling, she stepped out of her shoes.

With trembling fingers, he proceeded methodically to get her naked. Blouse. Jeans. Fighting the urge to tear and ravage, he gently unhooked her bra and filled his hands with her warm breasts. With half-closed eyes and labored breathing, he slid down her panties and bit his lip as she stepped out of them. Need, desire, unbearable tension tightened his body. Cursing his own confining clothing, he yanked at his shirt.

"Let me help you." She gently pulled his hands away and undid each button, all the time smiling at him.

He was certain he was going to explode when she tugged on his belt, loosened the buckle, then drew down his zipper. Hungry, ravenous for the taste of her, he leaned forward to capture her mouth, but she avoided him with a vicious giggle and twinkling eyes as she coaxed his briefs over his throbbing bulge.

They stumbled to the couch. She lay down, arms outstretched. He arched over her, one elbow at her side. While his tongue explored her mouth, his other hand roamed her skin, the soft, alluring curves, the delicate silky textures, the warm, wet places.

He moaned in frustration when she bucked out from under him, moaned again in surprise when she reversed their positions and suspended herself above him. She dragged her fingernails lightly down his chest, the sharp points of his nipples, the contracted muscles of his belly. He stiffened when she cupped him and squeezed, sending a shock of high voltage shooting through him. He'd never been more alive, more filled with sensations and needs.

She reached into the drawer of the end table and removed a packet. His eyes grew wide at the sight of it. A broad grin lit his face.

"I didn't know you were a Girl Scout, always prepared."

"There's a lot about me you haven't discovered." She grinned maliciously as she sheathed him.

He fondled her silken breasts, lightly grazing her erect nipples with his thumbs. She straddled him.

"You're in control now," he said, looking up at her intense expression. "Go for it."

EPILOGUE

BONFIRES BLAZED along the shores of the Mississippi in the centuries-old Christmas Eve tradition. Lumenarias dotted the regal main drive approaching Bellefontaine. The house itself was a fairyland of tiny white lights.

Inside, sweet string music charmed guests as they enjoyed a seven-course meal, served by young men and women in domestic attire of the nineteenth century. Everyone, including Megan and Elise, was remarkably quiet, as Jackson recounted the latest and hopefully the last adventures in the long feud between the Fontaines and Dewalts.

"Murray's going to be fine," he informed them. "They've already got him up on crutches."

"And Roland?" asked Ridley Spruance, president of the Sugar Coalition.

"Destined for the booby hatch, where he belongs," Esme declared. "He should have been locked up in an asylum long ago. I've been telling people for years that he's unbalanced."

"I feel sorry for Murray," Casey said. "Roland may be off his rocker, but he's still his father."

"Where is Roland now?" Noelani asked.

"In jail. The D.A. is scheduling a series of psychological evaluations for next week. If he proves mentally incompetent—and there's every likelihood he will—he'll be committed to a state hospital for an indeterminate time.''

''What will Murray do?'' Nick asked.

''He's not sure yet,'' Jackson responded. ''He's considering selling the plantation. I'm trying to talk him out of it, at least until our parents' insurance money comes through, so we can buy it from him.''

''Ironic,'' Adam offered. ''Roland wanted the two estates to be joined. Looks like they might be after all.''

When the sumptuous meal was over, Esme rose from her chair. She was wearing a full-skirted silk gown of purple and burgundy—colors Leanna wouldn't have expected to go together—but the result had an archaic elegance. Puff sleeves fanned down to just past the elbows, below which black undersleeves extended to the wrists, where they were gathered and flared. Her auburn hair was swept up this evening, held in place by a silver tiara of diamonds. Around her neck she hung a matching purple velour choker ribbon with a beautifully carved antique cameo.

''Are we all going to carry our dishes to the kitchen now, Mommy?'' Elise asked. She and Megan were attired in matching pink hoop-skirted dresses that came below their knees. They giggled when they showed people the white cotton pantaloons underneath. Several times Leanna had seen them holding hands as they skipped through the rooms.

Betty chuckled. She was decked out in a floor-length servant's dress of dove-gray linen, with a long, starched, white apron. Her hair this evening was gathered inside a soft cotton bonnet. Her trademark cigarette peeked out incongruously under the cap's frill.

"Not tonight, Missy. Tonight my staff will take care of all. Yvette," she called out to a gangly girl in floor-length calico, "regard the cutlery. Bleed on that lace and I'll have you in stocks."

"What are stocks, Mommy?" Elise asked.

Leanna chortled and shot Betty an inquiring glance.

Esme snorted disdainfully. "Never you mind. It's time now for everyone to dance."

The string quartet just outside the dining room door was still playing Mozart.

"I don't know how to do this kind of dance," Megan said doubtfully.

"We'll have different music in the ballroom," Esme explained. "Megan, my sweet, do you remember Luc Renault from the *cochon de lait?*"

"He played happy music." The girl swayed her blossomy pink dress from side to side. The big-bowed satin ribbon in her dark hair was of the same color.

"And he'll be playing more of that kind of music tonight. Come, *mes petites.*" With the graceful sweep of her hands, she ushered them to the drawing room, which had been cleared of all its furniture, save a few chairs lining the wall.

Jackson watched the girls traipse off with his aunt, then he put his arm around Leanna's narrow waist and escorted her toward the back door.

She had her hair piled high, held in place with tortoise combs. Diamonds cascaded from her ears on silver threads. A folded yellow-and-indigo Japanese paper fan dangled from her wrist by a woven cord.

"You are beautiful beyond words," he said.

Her cobalt gown swirled and rustled around her as she glided across the floor, flowed down the steps and verily hovered above the red bricks as they strolled along Whistle Walk. Lively jazz at the other end of the house wafted toward them—background rather than intrusion.

"You're very kind, sir," she said coquettishly, then chuckled. "How did women in the old days survive in these outlandish clothes," Leanna complained, but not too forcefully. "And I'm not even wearing a corset and bustle."

He laughed. He could see she liked playing dress-up, if only for tonight. "We all have a price to pay. These stiff wing collars are bad enough in winter. I can't imagine how men endured them in the summertime."

His frock coat was maroon velour with black piping; his shirt, snowy white.

She turned and placed her hands on his shoulders, her elbows resting against his chest. "You're very handsome."

He leaned forward and kissed her softly on the lips. Taking her hand, he led her to *their* bench, then waited until she had arranged her voluminous skirt before sitting beside her. "In all the excitement last night—" An understatement if ever there was one. They'd made love till nearly dawn "—you never did answer my question."

She tilted her head, the corner of her mouth turned up in perplexity. "What was it you asked me again?"

He slid off the seat and knelt on one knee in front of her. "Lee, will you marry me?"

Her heart fluttered, raced, refused to settle down.

"I know I've made mistakes—"

She placed a finger on his lips to silence them. "Shh. As much as I love to hear your Southern drawl, Jackson Fontaine, sometimes you talk too much."

Worry clouded his eyes. Did he really think she would let him go?

"I learned something last night," she said. "I already knew I loved you. Last night I realized living without you would be unbearable."

Jackson clutched Leanna's hands between his.

She looked down at their joined hands. The strength and warmth flowing from him promised protection, but she knew she could slip out of their grasp. He wouldn't hold her if she didn't want to stay.

But she did want to stay. She needed this man's love, his generosity. With blurred vision she looked up at his face. Handsome. Intelligent. Full of humor and goodwill.

He released her left hand, and reached into the pocket of his silk-brocade waistcoat.

"Leanna—" he presented her with a ring that had been his grandmother Fontaine's "—will you marry me? Will you be my wife?"

"I love you, Jackson," she said. "I love you with all my heart." Tears pooled in her eyes, threatened to fall. "Yes, I will be your wife."

For a magical instant, he seemed shocked, then relieved and finally ecstatic. "You will?"

She nodded. The tears won and now wetted her cheeks. "Yes, Jackson, I'll marry you."

ESME STOOD in the shadows, a smile curling her lips. Crying would be unseemly and unladylike. Besides, it would ruin her carefully applied makeup. But she did allow herself a nod of approval.

"You were right," she muttered to the woman beside her. "It was worth every cent I paid that twit Tanya to get out of town."

Betty snickered. "It's about time you admitted some Yankee blood into the family."

Esme sighed. "Welcome to Bellefontaine, Leanna Cargill Fontaine."

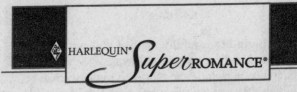

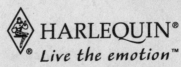

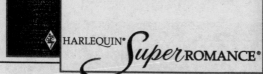

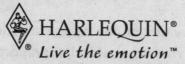

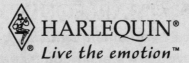

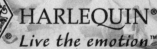

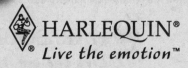

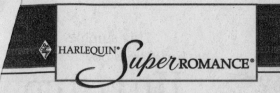

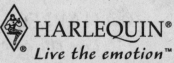